the apocalypse rebellion

NICK VOSSEN

PARLIAMENT HOUSE PRESS

The Apocalypse Rebellion

The Eldritch Twins Book 3

Copyright © 2023 by Nick Vossen

ISBN: 978-1-956136-60-9

All rights reserved.

Edited by: Megan Hultberg and Hayley Frerichs

Cover art by: Shayne Leighton

Parliament House Press

———————————————

Prologue

———————————————

*Eldritch Island, MA, United States – 25-ish years until the
end of the world*

A GUST of cool wind from the Eastern Sea blew through the
dry and dusty room. Behind the desk, a gentleman, looking
distinguished but exhausted, hovered over a pile of old books
and yellowed papers. He buried his nose deep between the
pages of a ragged tome that hadn't seen the light of day for
ages and scrawled page after page of notes into a journal with
his right hand. He looked up slightly when the office door
swung open and a beautiful woman stood in the doorway. She
had light chestnut, softly curled hair and the most deep and
profound blue eyes.

"Tobias, it's almost three in the morning. You really need
to come to bed. You'll catch a cold with these windows open
all night."

The man smiled softly. "Tiny, microscopic critters are
responsible for colds, my dear. Not cool air blowing into the
office."

"I know, my *dear*," the woman retorted with a cheeky
smile. "But nothing stops the wind from blowing those little

things right into your lap. It's going to be a harsh winter this year, I can tell. You'd almost think even the seagulls could start sneezing at any moment. The cold is going around, I tell you."

Tobias looked up and gave his wife the warmest of smiles. He slammed the old book closed. "There's nothing healthier than the sea's fresh, salty air. But I'll make sure to be careful. Please, Emily." He beckoned her over. "Come sit. I have something very exciting to show you."

Emily made her way toward the desk, but instead of sitting down, she closed the creaky wooden windows. Then she plopped on the chair and felt nervous. She didn't know what Tobias wanted to tell her, but she had news of her own that would certainly be as special and life changing as the very day they met and the day they had married.

"Look over here." Tobias pulled up a few pencil-rubbed sheets full of strange symbols and peculiar markings strewn across them. "These supposedly come from the famous Tablet of Mao, the obelisk of Coatzetatl, and the stone circle near the ruined manse of Upper Cloghan. Remember?"

Emily nodded. "Yes, I do," she answered almost absent mindedly. Her mind was busy running through different scenarios of how her husband might react to her news.

"I cross-referenced these strange markings and symbols with others found on ancient artifacts and ruins all over the world, and I've consulted with William. He told me that the museum in Marblehead has procured a similar type of engraved rock that was found in Nova Scotia. There are supposedly never before seen symbols engraved on this piece. The captain and crew of the boat that transported it swear on their lives the thing is cursed. This is so exciting! A chance to experience true paranormal events."

"That… That is amazing and fascinating, Tobias. And, even though I think you should not put your trust into William's peculiar tales as much as you do, I am sure if there is anyone who is able to get to the bottom of this, it's you."

Emily looked down, shifting awkwardly in her chair. There was something she had to tell him.

"Yes, I must arrange a meeting with the museum's curator at once and—" Tobias fell silent when he noticed the pinch of fear behind Emily's eyes of the deepest blue. "Em… Is something wrong? What's going on?"

Emily sighed loudly, and her lip quivered a little. "I'm… Well, I'm scared, Tobias."

"What on earth for?" Tobias, worried and somewhat shaken up, took his wife's hands.

Emily squeezed his firm hands, and his trusting, almost aura-like demeanor made her feel warm inside, just as it always had. "Tobias…" She smiled softly. "I'm pregnant."

PART I

Curse of the Swansongs

Chapter 1

Sussex, England – 5 days, 14 hours, and 23 minutes until the end of the world

QUINCY DASHED down the flight of stairs at such an incredible speed that he had to restrain himself and think rationally before he decided not to jump out of a window for an even faster, and surely more painful, getaway.

"Stop right there, *scum*!" A frail but very agile man dressed in red robes ran after him. He was fast, quick on his feet, and unrelenting, trailing Quincy by mere inches. He grabbed and snatched at his collar with one hand while a book was clutched in his other. "Drop that tome this instant!" the cultist yelled. "You have no idea what powers you are meddling with!"

Quincy, panting and sweating, looked behind him and threw a sly smile at the aged face beneath the robe's bright colored hood. "Trust me, old timer. There's little to nothing that can faze me anymore. I have died and experienced rebirth, both of my frail body and my soul. I have seen the black abyss yawning and churning beneath the wobbling thin thread that separates rational human thought and utter and complete madness." Quincy ran out into the broader, open hallway that overlooked the monastery's inner garden. The weather was typically English—gray and drab. He looked behind him to see the man in the red robe losing distance on him. He smirked. Perhaps the old geezer wasn't as fit as he might have thought.

Or perhaps his words resonated with the guy? He always wondered how it would be to make the most terrible and cursed statements regarding humanity's survival and the existentialism crisis. Quincy *did* think his words had some sort of profound impact on the somewhat frailer members of the Esoteric Order of the Final Dawn, but only for a second or two, right before several more cultists appeared in front of him with shining silver daggers they waved menacingly toward his face.

"Ah shit!" Quincy exclaimed before diving through one of the open arches that lined the right side of the half-open hallway. He landed painfully on his shoulder, but managed to roll through most of the impact, a maneuver Lilly once taught him to, in her words, *"You know, not die so quickly."* Quincy was back on his feet, adrenaline pumping through his veins. He diagonally crossed the courtyard and was on the other side in a matter of seconds. The bright mass of orange and red-cloaked individuals scampered over the little highway, but with a lot more trouble than Quincy had anticipated. *Good*, he thought, right before instinctively ducking upon seeing the glimmer of a mace swinging toward his face. Quincy pushed the somewhat clumsy mace-wielding cultist back with all of his weight, knocking him on his butt. The heavy mace landed right on the guy's chest and a gust of strained breath released from his mouth as he blacked out. Quincy waited a couple of seconds to see if the guy would wake back up. His eyes darted from left to right. Nothing.

Good, he thought again, and brought the walkie-talkie to his lips. "Okay, so I met with way more resistance than we thought," he panted, still dashing toward any possible exit. "How are things on your end?"

"Sean ran into some red-hoods when getting the cross relic, but nothing too bad. We're ready to pick you up at the parallel road next to the Woodland Inn, right on cue." Moira's familiar voice came through the walkie-talkie. "That all right with you, Quince?"

"Sure, I…"

Quincy sped through an apparent servants' corridor and emerged on the north-facing side of the old structure. There he found a quiet graveyard full of weathered and overgrown graves and headstones, surrounded by a rusty iron fence and thick oak trees. This was not the most peculiar thing because there was something that instantly shut Quincy up. In the middle of the old graveyard stood a strange man. He was of average height, sported an impressive but finely kempt beard, wore peculiar seventeenth century nobleman's clothing and, this was the big one, was literally ripping Final Dawn cultists in half and spreading their viscera all across the yard.

"Come out and fight! Do not stand on ceremony in front of *me*, evildoers. You slick orange lapdogs of Satan, you swine of Beelzebub, come forth and face the wrath of your Maker!"

The man's face contorted for a moment before he spoke again. "BLOOD FOR THE GOD OF DEATH, FACE ME MORTALS AND TREMBLE IN FEAR, YOU KNOW NOTHING!" he yelled, shaking his head in confusion and closing his eyes for a bit.

"You cannot control me, demon! For the righteous will always prevail."

Quincy looked behind him. There was a distinct lack of any pursuers. In fact, he saw one of the windows above him slam to a close and heard what sounded like boards being nailed over it from the other side.

"Quince? Are you still there?" the voice coming through the walkie-talkie crackled.

The crazy man's eyes flashed toward Quincy and he started sweating profusely under his gaze.

"Who stands before me now? Another pawn of the Antichrist? Perhaps another shadowy denizen of Carcosa in disguise, flaunting itself like a scholarly individual, hmm?" His eyes grew wide. "GO ON, GASH OUT HIS EYES AND HIS TEETH AND HIS… MASTER SWANSONG?"

Quincy's jaw dropped to the floor. If this was who he thought it was, the world had officially started to end, for pigs flying was definitely a sign of Final Dawn's Apocalypse. "Tim?" Quincy asked carefully. "Tim, is that you? W-what are you doing here?"

"RIDING THE COATTAILS OF THIS ONE, A MOST PECULIAR ONE I'D S—" The man stuck out his tongue, started blowing raspberries while looking crooked eyed. He spoke again, using the other voice now. "Do not listen to that devil that has attached itself to me and is trying to trick me into using my glory for nothing else but its own nefarious ways. I have returned from very far away, for evil once again walks the land of old Europa, and it is up to me to cleanse it. In the name of our Lord, I am a warrior of God Almighty and nothing will stand in my way. Jolly good times, old chap, I'd say!"

Quincy stared at the man, not quite knowing what to say or think. He looked hard at the pale, somewhat flaky skin. He stared deep into the cold lifeless pupils that bore into his soul. This man was dead. Or at least he had been. Quincy cleared his throat. "And who…*are* you, exactly?" He asked the question as lightly as possible.

"FEEBLE M– Frail youth, how can anyone not recognize the master in front of them, *pip pip*. My name is Matthew Hopkins, Witchfynder General and– HE IS WEAK FLESH AND BONE, MOTTLED I am pleased to make your acquaintance. Will you ride with me, youth AND ONCE AGAIN BASK IN THE GLORY OF TIMAXOATI-LACILUZIPTA BANE OF THE ANCIENT COSMOS and become my apprentice in banishing evil from this land? AND KILL EVERYONE THAT STANDS IN OUR WAY."

Quincy had no words. He dropped the walkie-talkie and scratched the back of his head.

"Quincy? Are you okay?" Sean yelled through the speaker. "Do you need a pick up? Quince?"

SOMEWHERE IN ENGLAND – *14 days, 15 hours, and 5 minutes until the end of the world*

"QUINCY!"

A huge bucket of water splashed across Quincy's face. He bolted out of the bed and screamed bloody murder as he grabbed Sean's arm. But Sean wasn't standing in the desolate little churchyard, nor was he standing in a parking lot outside of an old inn in Sussex speaking into a walkie-talkie. He stood next to Quincy's bed. Moira ran a handkerchief over Quincy's forehead. She looked worried. Quincy's skin was a sickly yellow and his eyes were bloodshot. He was visibly shaking and sweating profusely. The small bedroom, cramped and hot, had the windows barred and only a few snippets of daylight seeped through a few cracks and holes in the wooden planks. With the exception of the bed, the room was nearly empty, save for a nightstand with a single half-filled glass of water and Quincy's journal on top.

"Did I do the screaming again?" Quincy asked weakly.

Moira nodded. "Screaming, kicking, yelling the name Tim over and over. The whole bloody affair."

Quincy swallowed hard. "The cathedral, or monastery or whatever it was. Again. The crimson-red robes. The church-yard…" Quincy halted for a second to catch his breath. "It was about five days until the end this time. Somehow I always know. I remember…a calendar. It said the sixteenth… Wha-what date is today?"

Sean laughed. "Well then, Mr. Prophetic Dreams, it's the seventh. So what does that give us? A good two weeks? If things go our way, we'll be home before Midsummer, very appropriate. If they don't…well… No crying over spilled milk, I suppose."

Quincy looked grim. "Laugh all you want. If these dreams really are prophesizing the end, an Apocalypse to finally finish what started years ago, then it means I really did inherit that dreadful curse that supposedly plagued my great uncle."

Moira scoffed. "If all of that is true, and it means the end will come for all of us, then why worry about some supposed curse? I don't mean to downplay your predicament, Quincy, but I think there's more at stake here."

Quincy sighed. "I know, I know. Still, if we do somehow manage to save, well, everything and everyone, it doesn't mean I can kick back and lead a normal life ever again."

"As if you ever had the chance," Sean said with a grin.

"That's not funny." Quincy's sleepy, bloodshot eyes turned to Moira. "Do you think this is funny?"

"I don't think it's funny." Moira suppressed a smile while she shook her head.

Quincy sat up against the bed's headboard. "We've got to find out where this place is. Somehow I know whatever I take from there is very important. It feels important too when it's in my hands…" Quincy looked down at his fingers. They were all bloodied up and scraped from clawing against the side of the bed during his restless sleep. "It's hard to describe. We've got to find it, and we've got to find it before we're too late."

Moira laid a hand on Quincy's shoulder. "We will, Quince. We will find it."

"Okay, let's go, man." Sean gripped his friend's wrist tight and helped him out of bed. "Once this is all over, I'm going to want you to dream me up some lottery numbers, okay?"

SOMEWHERE IN THE *continental United States — 14 days, 11 hours, and 57 minutes until the end of the world*

• • •

LILLY HELD the whirring vacuum cleaner hose up in the air and bounced her head to the beat of the music seeping through her headset. "Eighty twoooo!" The vacuum brush end plopped down on the floor. "Dooooo!" The cozy living room was filled to the brim with wooden furniture, little tables topped with dozens of flowerpots and cacti, several small decorative rugs, and a bigger rug with an Aztec-like print underneath a wooden coffee table with a glass top. In the corner, a beautiful marble chess set sat on a decorative table edged with images of tree leaves. It appeared to be mid-game, although the dust gathered on top betrayed that it hadn't been touched for a while. Lilly pulled the vacuum back and forth over the rug and danced. She had a huge smile on her face. "Heeeeeaaaat of the…"

Liz appeared in the room behind Lilly, sporting a huge grin. She stood there for a few moments until she went ahead with her surprise plan. She poked her girlfriend in the side and pulled off her headphones. "Attack! Attack!" Liz yelled while tickling Lilly beneath the armpits.

"Yikes! Stop!" Lilly responded, jumping nearly three feet up into the air and holding the end of the vacuum like a quarter staff, ready to strike her enemies. She immediately knew it was Liz, which somehow made her feel kind of riled up, albeit in a playful way. She pressed down on the power button and dropped on the couch, where Liz had already nestled into the back corner. Once she calmed down a bit, she couldn't help but laugh as well. "You really shouldn't do that, you know. For all I know you could've been a Haven agent, some kind of angry spirit, a monster, an R.O.U.S.s…"

"Arr Ooh Yoo Esses?" Liz looked confused.

"R-O-U-Ss. Rodents of Unusual Sizes," Lilly responded.

"Ah, of course."

Lilly read Liz's expression like an open book. "You can laugh all you want but trust me when I say you do not want to run into any of them."

"I didn't want to scare you, obviously," Liz admitted.

"Although, I feel like we've hit a new chapter in *The Mysterious and Exciting Life of Lilly Swansong?*"

"I sincerely doubt you'd want to hear me blather on about hosing down swarms of mutant rats before breakfast every day for two weeks while I was on duty."

Liz appeared disappointed. "But it sounds exciting!" Seeing Lilly's expression of total indifference when it came to telling the story calmed Liz down.

"It's annoying and gross. But that's pretty much everything there is to tell," Lilly said. "Let's change the subject." She stood up and started going over to the kitchen.

Liz glanced sideways. "Okay, but you're really not going to like this."

Lilly's head popped out of the kitchen. "Hold that thought, be right there." A few moments later, Lilly returned with two fresh cups of coffee in her hands and two muffins squished between her arms and breasts. She handed Liz her cup and let a muffin roll into Liz's lap, perfectly executed. Then she sat back down. "Okay. Shoot."

Liz took a sip. "Well, I've been noticing some strange things happening in town over the past couple of days. And I think we might need to discuss them."

Lilly laughed, then looked a bit confused. "Tenebrae is a pretty weird town, I admit. There's no doubt in my mind there's at least a few Vampires, Doppelgängers, and/or, Snatchers making their rounds downtown. But that's par for the course anywhere. Why the concern?"

Liz sighed and looked down at the steaming black liquid. She let the steam reach her nostrils and took in the glorious aroma of a perfect cup of freshly brewed coffee. "It's like… It's like *Twin Peaks*."

"Like…a TV show? Or something more specific?"

Liz pondered this for a while. Lilly nearly heard the gears in Liz's head creak before coming to a somewhat well-rounded and logical answer. "It's…both?" Liz answered as if questioning herself. Maybe it wasn't as well rounded as Lilly might've hoped. "Imagine going on your bike for a nice ride in the fresh air—"

"Okay."

"You hop off and sniff the fresh mountain air. You can smell the strong scent of the pines rising up from the damp earth. The fresh spring rain has brought life and water to all the denizens and plant life just beyond the broken fence in the backyard, leading up a slope into the mossy wilderness beyond."

"Okay. You're killing this, by the way. Totally invested."

Liz placed a finger on Lilly's lips. "Hush." She closed her eyes. "Now imagine taking that bike and riding from the porch toward the marketplace. You pass The Junction on the right and the old gas station on your left. The old man, Withers I believe he is called, is there. He's always there. Just like the woman with the super thick glasses standing outside the grocery store with her two brown bags, one of them with the…"

"…the bananas sticking out of the top," Lilly whispered, Liz's finger still lingering over her lips.

"And then you suddenly remember that even though you have a vivid image of your neighbors in your mind, you always seem to come across them at the same times, doing the exact same things. Like cutting their hedges, chopping wood, or walking their dog. Always with the dog, always near the dirt path that leads up to the lumber mill. Never somewhere else."

Lilly swallowed hard. "I think I know what you mean. Like it all seems very mundane on the surface but there's something underneath that's just so…strange and unusual you can't put your finger on it. It *is* like *Twin Peaks*."

"Exactly." Liz nodded. "It's even more strange than what we can expect from this day and age. Although, I'm not really sure what to do with this information. It could be anything. Even our imaginations. I mean, Tenebrae is pretty isolated. Could be some kind of cabin fever?"

"Or maybe something else is messing with our brains or

thoughts." Lilly took a big bite out of the muffin but kept talking. "It happened before, remember," she said, barely articulate through her chewing. "This could be the same thing, only more subtle and maybe more sinister. I hate to say it, but in all fairness, it could be another one of those Gibbous Horde things."

Liz shook her head. She tried not to think about the race of evil eldritch space gods that slumbered beneath the earth's very surface. "Lilly, we can't jump to conclusions. Let's just bide our time. If things start going in the wrong direction or, dare I say it, start going really, really badly, we'll just pack up and go somewhere else."

Lilly balled her hand into a fist. "Run away again? It's like a joke, a *running* joke, in my life. Whenever I start to become happy again after…after who knows how long, there's always something ready to swoop in and take it away."

"Lilly…"

"I was a fool thinking I could spend the last few *whatevers* our world still has in peace, quiet, and tranquility. With someone I care a… With someone I love." Lilly grabbed Liz's hand. "Did I do the wrong thing? Did I choose wrong?"

Liz squeezed Lilly's fingers gently. "There wasn't a wrong choice to make. The choice you had was *your* road to choose and *yours* only. Quincy doesn't hold resentment toward you for doing what you felt you had to do, no matter how much you think he does. Likewise, I wouldn't hold it against you if you *did* go with him to Europe and sort all of this out. I would be right here waiting for you either way."

"Aren't you tired of me broaching this same subject nearly every day now for the past…how long have we been here?" Lilly started to drift away in thought.

"No, I'm not," Liz said quietly. She saw Lilly closing her eyes and let her gently slump down the couch, resting her head on the cushion and falling asleep. Whenever Lilly got into these huge fits of worry, it wore her out completely in a matter of minutes. "Whatever we encounter, whatever crosses our path, we'll deal with it," Liz whispered. She pulled a cozy dark green blanket over Lilly, kissed her gently, and rose from the couch. Her eyes fell on the dining table at the back of the room near the kitchen. Today's newspaper laid on top, headline reading: *Final Dawn rising up in the polls across several voting EU countries. Order states it's making 'proper preparations.'* Liz sighed and looked down at her phone. *Four days since the last message,* Liz thought. *I hope you three are doing okay.*

Chapter 2

IT HAS BEEN a long road for the Swansong twins to end up where they are today. And what an actual joy it has been to watch them grow. Even though my whiskers stood on edge just thinking about all of the chaos that ensued, I know in my immortal furry heart that they will succeed. Just like they did before at the brink of annihilation. They uncovered an ancient secret and by sheer force of will, with supernatural intervention and some good friends (and a bit of luck), they managed to save the entire world. However monster-filled and supernaturally hazardous it may still be. Further down the line, the Swansong twins would meet their demise at the hands of a particularly vicious Haven agent by the name of Dutch, no relation to the country or its people. But Death proved to be only a temporary setback for these two gifted individuals as they managed to transcend the barrier of life and death and, with help from their closest friends, returned to life. Besides all that, they have had numerous encounters with strange, eerie, and downright horrific things, all of which they managed to survive and overcome. But something bigger and worse is brewing beneath the surface. So when they came back to life, they did so right when the world needed them the most. At least, that's what Quincy Swansong thought.

The twins' path seemed to always get darker. Deep into a black hole of uncertainty and fear. Their adventures often found them crawling into basements and old ruins, always heading toward an uncertain goal. But metaphorically speaking, these pits went even deeper than the dusty catacombs they traveled. For Lilly Swansong, they went down to the soul. All these revelations scratched up the very essence of her being, up to the point where she feared she would lose herself in its uncertain murkiness. So when Quincy Swansong, newly revived from the dead and having inherited his mother's sense of righteousness and justice, got ready to battle evil and destroy it once and for all in Europe, Lilly stayed behind. It broke Quincy's heart, but he was the only person in the world who could understand why. He was, after all, the only other person who went through everything she had. It is said that being twins gives you some sort of uncanny connection with each other. For the Swansongs, that connection was *everything* and it could never truly go away. But Quincy realized once he put an ocean between him and his sister, that connection turned into a painful, lonely longing.

In the aftermath of what was now called the Night of Deadly Silence, when many rebellious monster hunters, GDF veterans, and other individuals opposing Haven were either brainwashed or 'silenced' in other ways, the group consisting of Quincy and Lilly Swansong, Lizbeth Borden, Moira LaGrande, and Sean Cooper went their separate ways.

The influence Haven, with the help of the Gibbous Horde beings, had on the supernatural world seemed to be stronger than ever. As strong as it was a couple of months ago during the winter of Swansongs' untimely death and resurrection. There were less reports of strange or paranormal occurrences and the general public seemed to be far less in tune than ever before. What little the two groups saw with their own eyes was perhaps only noticeable because they were actively looking for, and expecting, some kind of trouble. These few new happenings seemed a lot more deliberate, as if things were actively being 'tested' somehow by Haven. Neither Lilly and Liz nor Quincy, Moira, and Sean were eager to dive headfirst into trouble. So, they stayed clear of most of it and in turn, most of it left them alone during their journeys. Haven was, however, still crawling around everywhere, much to the dismay of everyone involved in trying to stop them. Haven was a plague upon the world. Sean for one, couldn't wait to see them depart—violently.

Lilly and Liz took the twins' gray Ford Fiesta and drove it all the way to the northwestern part of the United States. They did their best to keep away from Haven's prying eyes which, to be fair, was made easier since many of the organization's grunt soldiers and petty lower leadership thought the twins had been disposed of. Neither Lilly, Quincy, nor any of their allies had any clue if it was widely known that the twins were back. It felt like a lucky break, and one they had to take advantage of. Lilly and Liz eventually rendezvoused with a few members of the Night Lights, Liz's witch coven, near Minneapolis at the northern U.S. border. The grand warlock of this local branch, Anatole, took them in for a few days but the women had no intention of staying for long.

The safety of the coven was pleasant, but Liz and Lilly's end goal was to be alone and out of the limelight. When asked if they wanted to join the Night Lights in investigating reports of Black-Eyed Children on the town's outskirts, Lilly and Liz politely declined. They took this as a sign it was time to move on and their journey led them further west to a town called Tenebrae.

You could say Tenebrae was one of those true to life *middle of nowhere* towns. It was in the middle of the woods, the nearest interstate was miles and miles away in every direction, and the local population barely exceeded a couple hundred people. The pair lucked out when they managed to find a cheap little rental house, the space not much bigger than a large cottage. Living in a small town gave them the advantage of not having many financial worries. Anatole had been quite generous and the rest of the expenses they would bridge by selling flowers, herbs, and vegetables they grew in the backyard. For a few months, life was quiet and uneventful.

For Lilly it was bliss, but she noticed how sincerely she missed her brother. She was lucky to have Liz for comfort whenever she thought too much about whatever bad things might befall their friends.

All good things must come to an end. When Lilly and Liz learned that a crazed cult called the Esoteric Order of the Final Dawn was gathering followers all over the country, they knew it was only a matter of time before their peaceful life would end, perhaps for good.

Let's go back to right after the Night of Deadly Silence. Quincy, Sean, and Moira were determined to end the looming end times caused by the Gibbous Horde once and for all. In the days following the Silence, after they had said their goodbyes to Lilly and Liz, it became clear that Haven had been sloppy with mopping up their opposition. There were still stragglers all across the country. The trio eventually made their way to Marblehead, Massachusetts, right at the edge of where, only a year ago, the Daemonic Depths swallowed most of the northeastern continental U.S. landmass and just about the entirety of Canada. Sean, Moira, and Quincy caught up with another group of rebels holding out beneath the local museum. Quincy, who noticed a distinct lack of being *wanted dead or alive* for once just like Lilly had, kept his identity to himself. He was happy to know that both Sean and Moira understood why it was better for him to be a 'faceless rebel nobody' rather than one of the key figures pissing Haven off as Haven committed near genocide.

Holding out in Marblehead for a few days, Quincy first experienced his strange prophetic dreams and realized he could not stay for very long. Soon after, he, Sean, and Moira started to pack up. Sean left the survivors with instructions on how to set up new radio communication with other struggling Haven opposition across the country. More importantly, he shared some good tips with them on establishing and *keeping* communication through a code language he invented. Sean realized that, if they ever wanted to win this war completely, they needed all of the help and allies they could get. Even if those allies would have to fend for themselves for a while at first.

Quincy was having some trouble with their plan's slow advancements. Having no other clue to go by except for his father's old journals, he told his friends that England was their first destination. It was a small miracle that Sean managed to rig a small prop plane at a private airfield in Marblehead and, apparently being quite the talented pilot, flew it all the way to England's western shores. It was another miracle that they managed to make the flight with only one filled tank and an even bigger miracle that they did so without some kind of horrific Thunderbird, Roc or Pterodactyl Mutation snapping them out of the sky. Then again, there was that thing about monsters and peculiars showing up in controlled outbursts rather than at random. They hoped it meant Haven wasn't tracking them.

They ended up staying a while in Cornhop, a remote coastal village. The inhabitants weren't too bothered by their local spirits and ghost ships. There were a pair of somewhat menacing scarecrows that liked to spook the children at night, but that too became a commonality after a while. From Cornhop, the trio slowly but surely tried piecing together where to go next. Unfortunately for Quincy, but fortunately for their plans, his anguishing fever dreams ultimately provided them with enough hints to find their next destination. Assuming the dreams had any meaning at all…

CORNHOP, *England — 14 days, 11 hours, and 33 minutes until the end of the world*

An early morning fogbank rolled effortlessly through Cornhop's narrow and cobbled streets. There wasn't a soul outside or awake, Quincy noticed as he looked out the window. An ancient and rusted weathervane on a nearby rooftop creaked as a light breeze passed by. Across the dirt path at the back of the little house and over in the fields beyond, something special was about to happen. Quincy saw translucent pink, purple, and turquoise jellyfish-like things rise from the ground and push, flutter, and then float their way up into the sky. The creatures gave off a faint light and whenever their tentacle-like appendages touched the edges of the mist swerving across the farm, there came a tiny electrical discharge. He looked up in wonder as the creatures disappeared into the sky. Quincy watched the last little straggler at the end of the convoy as it too made its way up into the clouds above.

"Wow. I've never seen something like that before," Moira said. She had quietly crept up to the window while Quincy was distracted. "Oh, I'm sorry," she said, realizing she had startled him. "I didn't mean to scare you." She pressed her face close to the window. "What were those things just now? The sky jellyfish, I mean. They were beautiful. I'm awestruck, really."

Quincy smiled. "Yeah, they're cool, right? I never thought I'd see them again. We used to see them now and again whenever Lilly and I went for morning walks back in New Orleans before Lilly was drafted. We used to call them the Migrators because they always seem to come from the earth below and float up to the clouds, as if they are leaving the planet to find some better place." Quincy chuckled. "It's strange but whenever we saw them, it was usually near one of the cemeteries or some of the boglands at the outskirts. Somehow we knew it was never the same group of them, if that makes sense."

"You could feel they weren't the same?" Moira asked.

"Well, maybe not feel. We *knew* somehow. It doesn't make much sense, but hey, what does, right?"

Moira shook her head and laughed. "Ha, nothing much, Quincy. Nothing much. But you said you *used* to see them. Any idea what happened?"

Quincy swallowed and looked grim. "Well, we would get this idea that whenever the Migrators showed up something really, really bad was going to happen. Lilly and I joked that they were the harbingers of the end times, and they were the only creatures smart enough to evacuate our planet before it was totally destroyed. Sure enough, every time the Migrators showed up something bad usually followed. It wasn't always something earthshattering, literally or figuratively, but it usually was…bad. The last time we saw them was right when Lilly was about to be drafted for her first stint in Eastern Europe. She was never the same when she got back. A darkness had taken hold in her heart, even though she'd be the first one to deny it. But I could see it, all the way back then."

Moira folded her arms and looked up to the now slightly hyacinth-colored clouds. "I didn't have the chance to talk to Lilly a lot before we split up, but I think I know what you mean. There is a cheerful façade over her even though she has been broken in two more times than she is willing to count. There is no shame in admitting you have had enough. As she has."

"I know," Quincy answered, a little bit annoyed. "Sorry, I don't need you to constantly remind me of what I already know and have made peace with."

"I'm sorry, I—"

"No, it's okay," he sighed. "Sorry, I'm still tired and overwhelmed. Anyway. The Migrators, what was I saying about them?"

"You said they could be harbingers of bad times." Moira looked grim. "How sure of that are you?"

Quincy rapped his fingers on the windowsill. "I never told Lilly this, nor anyone else until now because I didn't really think it had any relevance, but I did see them one more time. In New Orleans, actually."

"Oh, when was that?"

"About ten minutes before that Haven agent showed up who wanted to snatch our inheritance and get rid of us in the process. Right before a gigantic thunderstorm broke out and facilitated our escape."

"Damn. Yeah, from what you told me about all that happened once you got your hands on that key... These things must never be a good sign. No matter how cool or cute they might look."

"Cute?" Quincy looked confused.

Moira chuckled. "C'mon, *pink* jellyfish that are see-through? What's not to love?"

"Everything else about them." Quincy could barely conjure a smile. "Seriously though, I've never seen so many of them at once. And so frequently. I've seen them every rainy or misty morning or evening ever since... Ever since the Deadly Silence."

Moira sucked in her breath. "That's troubling. So when the Migrators start leaving the planet in droves..."

"Earth is doomed."

"What are you two mumbling about over there?" Sean appeared in the doorframe. He was carrying two big bags filled with supplies. It was still cold for this time of year, but bullets of sweat were dripping off his forehead. "I managed to pawn the prop plane and got a pretty dang good deal on an old Volkswagen, plus two military grade duffel bags with complementary foodstuffs." Sean threw a can at Quincy, who caught it in the nick of time. "Expiration date is still six days away. That means it's still good for another twelve years or so. After that, the rot-taste really starts settling in. Anyway." Sean finally stopped talking and took a good look at his companions' faces. "You two look as if you've seen the white lady ghost of the Cornhop churchyard just now, but only if she had a dog's face and started speaking in tongues. And I mean *literally* spitting tongues. What's going on?"

Moira shook her head. "It's nothing. Just…some doom thinking, which, I know, we agreed to stop doing."

"Damn right." Sean nodded. "Because we're going to nip this thing in the ass before it even starts, right, Quince?"

The corners of Quincy's mouth curved slightly upward. He wanted nothing more than to agree. "Well, we'll certainly give it all we've got," was all he could say. The situation looked grim, and everyone knew it. Still, Quincy agreed that fear-mongering was good for absolutely no one. It was best not to dwell on the inevitable horrible and possibly fiery death they would all face sooner or later. Probably sooner.

Sean laughed. "Alright, alright, alright. Quincy, are you one-hundred percent sure about our next location?"

"I vividly recall a wooden sign saying it was about eight kilometers west to see Lewes Castle. So, it should be Sussex. Even better, if I'm correct, it would mean we're getting this cross and book in our hands a lot earlier than we *would* have."

"Yes, the holy relics that we still have no idea what to do with, but we are perfectly willing to grab out of a dangerous cult's possession because it might mean something down the line." Moira sighed. She had been fearful and skeptical of Quincy's dreams. She believed he saw what he said he did, but she doubted everything else surrounding these *lucky breaks*.

"We have no other plan," said Quincy. "It is what it is for now. My father's notes at least mention a cross relic. It's the best lead we've got."

"I know," Moira acknowledged. "It doesn't mean I think it's a good idea."

"At least we've got an idea!" Sean interjected and slung one of the duffel bags back over his shoulder. "Let's go now, friends. We're going to have to go through the Brighton & Hove Quarantine Zone for a while which is going to suck, but not as much once you figure out how hard the seats are in this Volkswagen I got. Let's go!"

. . .

TENEBRAE, *WA, United States — 14 days, 6 hours, and 4 minutes until the end of the world*

A shambling pile of bones was crossing the road. A shambling pile of disgusting, dirty, bleached bones with rotten meat flapping off the side. It had no distinct shape to it. It was just that—a pile. Its only distinguishing feature were two glowing yellow eyes and something that could be a mouth if you squinted really hard and had a vivid imagination.

Lilly followed the spectacle as it slowly made its way to the other side of the street toward its home, presumably, between the dumpsters in the alley behind the Sea of Pines burger restaurant. "There are some things we never really get used to, right, Mrs. Norwich?" Lilly gave a friendly nod to the old lady waiting with her for the traffic light to turn green. They were on the curb parallel to the street the thing was crawling across.

"What's that, dearie? What do you mean?"

"The Jittering Horror crossing the street just now," Lilly answered. "It looks very frightening, but luckily they only eat garbage, right?" She looked a bit more apprehensively toward the tiny old lady.

Mrs. Norwich's ears pricked up when the light turned green, and she began to walk. "I have no idea what you are talking about, dear. Maybe it's time to stop filling your head with all that comic book nonsense and read something more productive."

Lilly watched the little lady scoot away. "I don't read comics..." Her voice trailed off into a whisper. *Why couldn't she see it? It was there, clear as day.*

Inside the Sea of Pines, Lilly sat down at the diner's counter. Within a few seconds, the cheerful blonde waitress came prancing over. Lilly had seen her a few times before, even though she didn't frequent the diner often. The waitress, Annie according to her nametag, smelled of stale discount perfume and cigarettes. She smiled at Lilly, but her hazel eyes did not shine with the light of a truly happy individual. The cheerful persona was all make-believe. *Nobody would be happy in this dead-end job*, those eyes seemed to exclaim.

"What will it be for you today, hun?" The woman smiled through gritted teeth. *God, kill me if I need to utter one more* hun *today*, the eyes betrayed.

Lilly twisted one of her curly locks around her finger. "Uhm, just black coffee I guess," she said, feeling dead tired.

Annie wrote something on her notepad, which didn't look like anything that came close to 'coffee,' stuck the pencil back in her huge bun towering on top of her head, and glided back toward the other end of the counter where a stained coffee pot appeared to have been brewing for the last ten years. She returned just as swiftly with a yellowed cup, a piece of lint covering the handle. She poured the coffee, which was like black tar, into the cup. With a painful strain, she lifted the corners of her mouth back up and giggled uncomfortably.

"You let me know if there's something else you need, okay, *hun*?" The woman looked absolutely dead inside.

Lilly glanced at the other end of the diner where a moldy skeleton sat slumped over in the corner booth. The almost entirely decomposed body was wearing a tattered dark blue suit and burgundy tie that was halfway eaten away, presumably by moths and other critters that like to feed off things the dead have no need for. A button that read *Ask me about the Reagan Administration* was pinned to the remains of the dress shirt beneath the suit. "Well, there is one thing…" Lilly raised an eyebrow. "I'd very much like to know why there is a dead person in the corner booth over there. Seems a bit unappetizing, wouldn't you agree?"

"Dead?" The waitress scoffed and looked even less interested in actual human interaction than she had before. "No, that's just Mister Goodsprings. He's here every day. He just doesn't say all that much."

Lilly shook her head. Outwardly this didn't appear to phase her, but inside she was confused and concerned about this absolute lack of observation. "No, I am pretty sure that

Mister Goodsprings isn't the strong silent type because, for one thing, there appears to be a family of maggots living in his right eye socket and…oh wait…yup, his left eye socket as well. I'll be, isn't that peculiar?" she responded. *If something as simple as dead bodies are looked over, what other things could have been looked over in this town?* Lilly thought with a shudder.

The waitress yawned and scribbled something else on her notepad. "I don't think it's very nice of you to talk about Mister Goodsprings, one of our best customers, like he is some common ghoul or…" It was as if something had short-circuited in her brain. The woman's eyes twitched once or twice and a loud crunching sound came from inside her mouth, as if one of her teeth had just been ground into pulp. "I mean…don't say bad things about Mister Good-springs. He is one of our best customers, and he can't help suffering from acute narcolepsy. He is trying really hard, okay?"

Lilly's head fell into her hands. "Are you freaking serious?" She hid her panic. Something strange was happening. But what else was new? Her eyes drifted back to the body with its nasty molding clothes and the big button stuck to its shirt. *Reagan administration? Wait…* Lilly thought suddenly.

"Miss!" she called the waitress back.

The woman flew back from the other side of the counter. She appeared to be busy even though Lilly was the only (living) person in the diner. She was constantly brewing new pots of coffee, none that seemed any less disgusting than the boiling jar of black slime that stood in front of Lilly. "Yeah, whaddayawant now?" The waitress sighed.

Lilly swallowed. "Uhm, how long has…Mister Good-springs been coming here? You said he's a regular?"

"Why don't you ask him yourself?" the waitress answered, annoyed. The more questions Lilly posed about this 'man,' the more defensive the woman became.

Lilly decided she'd play along. "Well, of course, I would, miss. But he appears to have fallen asleep again, see?" Lilly pointed to the skeleton. One of its ribs fell off with a crack as it landed on the black and red checkered floor.

"Oh, I see." The woman seemed confused at first, but then a smile crept up. A genuine smile this time. A smile that said *I am glad you finally understand.* "Of course. I myself have only been working here since about '98," she said, "but I'm sure my mother once told me Mister Goodsprings has been coming here ever since the '80s." She looked at the skeletal corpse. "Isn't he sweet, sleeping in his favorite booth so peacefully?" A three-headed Lightning Rat crawled out from the empty spot created by the broken-off rib.

Lilly winced. "Yeah…cute…" Different scenarios raced through her head. *This thing's been here since the '80s? That doesn't even make sense in the context of when the Awakening happened. Is she lying? Or am I remembering my facts wrong? No, she must be lying.* Lilly glanced over the little notepad in the woman's hand. Lilly swore she read the words 'non-compliant?' at the top and 'call overseer' near the bottom. She swallowed hard. "Hey, would you look at the time." She chuckled nervously. "I've got things to do and places to be." She plopped two crumbled up dollar bills on the counter and gave a big fake smile as she bolted through the door, emerging on their peculiar little town's rain swept, quiet main street. She pulled her ancient flip phone out and started hammering out a text to Liz. *The owls are **indeed** not what they seem D,* it said. Lilly's pace quickened as she headed in the direction of home. She had the feeling that Tenebrae was no longer the safe place that they had imagined.

ELDRITCH ISLAND, *MA, United States — 25-ish years until the end of the world*

The old house, newly renovated just the year before, creaked and groaned with each gust of wind the Eastern Sea blew against its sodden walls. Tobias Swansong hung his drenched coat on the hanger. Years of dripping raindrops had softened and molded the wood below into a dark, smelly stain. *I'll need to look at that soon*, he thought to himself. Tobias gazed into the mirror hanging in the gallery. He noticed the dark circles around his eyes, the wrinkles on his forehead, and his increasingly graying beard. He smiled weakly at the visage that stared back at him. *When did I start looking so old so quick*, he wondered. Only in his thirties, he could theorize what things had had such an impact on him that he started looking *wise* beyond his years, or perhaps it was merely *beyond his years*, no wisdom in play.

He opened the door at the end of the hallway and stepped into the living room area. A fire burned brightly in the hearth and several candles were lit on the mantelpiece, the windowsills, and the reading table. Tobias's cold and shivering bones were warmed by the roaring fire, the room's cozy atmosphere, and the beautiful image of his wife sitting in the rocking chair reading softly to their unborn child. He or she had yet to be welcomed into the world, but they were already the most important thing in their lives.

"'Ah,'" she quoted, "'to come is easy and takes hours; to go is different—and may take centuries,'" Emily whispered, flipping the page of the old leather-bound tome.

Tobias rubbed his hands in front of the fire. He slyly smiled at Emily. Her unkempt hair was tied up in a big bun, and she still wore her pajamas. She would say she'd never looked worse, but to Tobias she could never not look gorgeous. "Isn't *The King in Yellow* too…*strong* for a bit of light reading aloud?" he said with a laugh.

Emily shot a smile back. "Growing up in this house, with a father as eccentric as you, our child best be well prepared. And what's better to read and wonder about than these antique ghost stories, fairytales, and classic works of speculative fiction?"

Tobias raised an eyebrow. "I am trying to figure out if that's meant as a compliment or not."

"Well, what do *you* make of it?" Emily grinned.

"I think I—" Tobias noticed the wine glass sitting on the table. "Wait, are you drinking?"

Emily laughed and pulled the wineglass to her face so it also basked in the light of the fire. "Apple juice, love." She moved her glass from her mouth to the table and then back to her mouth. "It's the act, the movement, the mimicry. I'm starting to think I might not even like wine so much." She smiled. "Wait, did you really think I'd keep drinking as if there isn't life growing *inside* of me?"

"Of course not!" Tobias exclaimed, but his eyes confessed his relief.

"Liar," Emily playfully retorted.

Tobias took off his glasses and cleaned the lenses with his sweater. "Leave it to you to find a smart and safe solution for such a thing."

"I learned from the best. But now, honey, come sit down and warm those weary old bones, you're soaked!" She patted the seat next to her chair and took note of the raindrops clattering against the windowpane. "Do you think it will ever stop raining?" Emily paused and waited for an answer. When none came, she closed the book, laid it on the table, and scooted the rocking chair forward. "Toby, are you there?"

"Hmpf?" Tobias groaned. "Sorry, I was lost in thought for a moment."

Emily sighed. "I know your research is important, but you've got to start thinking about yourself. Your little experiments will still be under the gazebo tomorrow."

Tobias shook his head. "No, it's not that, it's... Uh, William contacted me. Something happened to the stone tablets uncovered from Canada. I've been wracking my brain for the past day or two."

"Were they stolen?"

"No, they...they...transformed." Tobias turned to his wife and grabbed her with quivering hands. "This could be huge."

.   .   .

SOMEWHERE IN THE SOUTH DOWNS, *England — 14 days, 5 hours, and 1 minute until the end of the world*

"One... two... three-four... Oh my... five, s-sev-eight... Wow!"

Quincy looked in the rearview mirror, slightly annoyed. His eyes were bloodshot and dark, indicating a severe lack of sleep. "Moira, I know you learned to count a long time ago, so please tell me. What the hell are you doing?"

Moira opened her mouth to ask Quincy if he got up on the wrong side of the bed this morning but closed it because she knew very well that Quincy did not *get* up so much as he *bolted* up. To ask if he didn't have a good night's sleep would just be insulting. She cleared her throat, apologized, and went back to staring out of the window, observing the immense volume of fairy buildings and gnome hovels passing by along with the countryside. Everything else looked fairly normal, but distinctly British, if that was even a thing. Rolling hills, copses of trees like oaks and willows, tiny rivers flowing through them, and endless patches of dry vegetation and dirt. The wild Downs, as they were described and portrayed in so many of the old world's gothic stories, were mishmashed together with peaceful woodlands. That *was* as British as things could be, she thought.

Moira once had a chat with Liz about how everything supernatural seemed to be three or four times as frequent and intense in Europe. Many of the myths and legends we still know about and read today find their roots in old Europa. Moira always saw the Americas as being the more dangerous of the two countries, with its paranormal phenomena having a knack for taking on horrifying and visceral tastes for violence. But Europe? It seemed like a deeper and darker rabbit hole. Maybe a tad less malevolent, but at least six times weirder and ten times as phantasmagorical.

Moira cleared her throat. "Beyond all the hills, plains, and little copses of trees, what's really out there? You said something about a quarantine zone?"

Sean tightened his grip on the steering wheel and sighed loudly. "Yeah, the Brighton & Hove Quarantine Zone. It was one of the first major metropolitan areas struck way back when shit hit the fan. Turns out when the sort-of apocalypse hits, the last place you want to be is near an ocean. Or any body of water for that matter. I mean, look what happened to half of the Eastern U.S. coast, look what happened to Bywater in New Orleans. Zeeland in the Netherlands is now a giant cyclopean city, Sicily a gaping maw into the abyss, Greece is basically gone and…" Sean peered at Moira through the rearview mirror. She looked a bit flustered, or maybe overwhelmed. "Sorry," he said after a pause. "I got a bit carried away there. It's kind of personal."

"Go ahead, if you want." Quincy nodded. He seemed far away at first, too tired to actively engage in conversation, perhaps battling his nightmare's demons in his mind. Still, it appeared he was at least listening.

Sean shrugged. "Not *that* big a deal. When I was a kid, I always wanted to be in the U.S. Navy. My grandfather was a Navy officer and I really looked up to him. Combine that with a love of the sea that I've had since I could remember and yeah, you get an ambitious little dude. Fast forward a whole lotta years and I got drafted. Ready to get my hands wet. Egypt happened just two weeks later, and we're all thrown into this pressure cooker of a combat readiness regime to get us up and running and fighting all these horrible things as soon as possible."

Moira held her breath. "Damn," she finally whispered. "They were leading y'all to a slaughterhouse."

"In droves." Quincy added. His eyes were closed but his ears pricked up every time Sean talked.

Sean nodded. "Exactly. The east Sussex coast in England, with Brighton arguably being its largest city, was the first seaside area to get hit by a Type 1 event. And guess who was a part of the newest and freshest Navy corps to be first responders and head over there?"

"Shit," was all that escaped Moira's mouth.

"Shit indeed," Sean repeated. He pulled the steering wheel sharply to the right and the car exited the small country road and veered onto a larger highway. "So there were these fucking disgusting and merciless amphibious type creatures that just up and walked straight out of the ocean and onto the beach at one of the most popular seaside resorts in the world. You might remember news reports on the Brighton Pier Massacre? That happened two hours before we got there. Never thought I'd see the day the ocean turned red. What made it even worst, it attracted sharks and... Sorry, there I went again."

"It's okay. So why did it become a quarantine zone?" Moira asked.

Quincy scoffed, "Because hell frogs from the deepest oceans apparently aren't enough of a drag."

Sean swallowed hard. "These things carried some kind of venom that instantly reacted when it came into contact with human skin. It was thin enough to seep into pores and start doing...horrible things. We figured out pretty soon that it wasn't just venom but also some kind of sentient alien goo which could self-replicate in a host and...take them over."

Quincy opened his eyes and leaned over to look at Moira. "It's been theorized that they were the same kinds of things that came swimming into Bywater when the floods hit. Who knows what would've happened to New Orleans if they hadn't immediately walled the place off."

"And left the people inside for dead," Moira said angrily. "They could've evacuated them first, they..."

Sean shook his head. He looked grim, but also sad. "If they did then New Orleans would've shared the same fate as the entire southeastern U.K. coast. When we figured out how the slime worked it was too late. We had to get out and leave them to... More than half the armed forces had either died or turned into these...living sacks of— Fuck!" He slammed his hands on the wheel and dashboard.

Moira looked concerned. "Are you okay? I mean, this all sounds horrible…you don't need to continue."

Sean took a few minutes to regain his composure and continued. "I'm fine. I'm done anyway. So much has happened, and I just turned numb to most of it. Again, I'm fine. Nothing more to say," he sighed. "Look, I'm pretty sure there's nothing but death out there, but…" Sean took his cellphone out of his pocket and fiddled around with it a little bit. He threw it to Quincy. "Where did you say we needed to go? Check the nav app real quick."

"Lewes." Quincy yawned loudly. He didn't want to appear disinterested because he actually wasn't, and luckily Sean knew this. Still, he found himself acting quite rudely, the sleep deprivation was not an excuse.

Sean glanced over. "Is that in the red zone still?"

"Smack dab in the middle of it," Quincy confirmed.

"Shit. What now?"

Moira dove toward the window. "Hey, did you guys see that just now?"

Sean perked up and looked back. "No, why? What did you see?"

"We just passed a sign saying there will be a mandatory inspection for all vehicles entering *The Gray Zone*, whatever that is. It's in about four kilometers. All inspections will be handled by authorized, ergh, authorized *Haven* personnel."

"Again, shit!" Sean exclaimed. "The Gray Zone is basically the outskirts of the quarantine zone. If Haven is somehow controlling the quarantine…"

Quincy was wide awake now. The look on his face was a mixture of concern and anger. "If Haven is controlling the quarantine, then I don't want to know what they're doing in there. If the mind controlling they and the Final Dawn are doing everywhere holds up here, then what are they telling the populace? What are they *doing* with the populace?"

"I'm more worried about how we'll even get *in* there with all the Haven men in black lurking around. I'm pretty sure everyone in that organization knows who you are, Quincy. Hell, they'll probably recognize me and Moira now as well. We're seen as rebels and…"

"Oh my god!" Moira exclaimed.

"What?" Sean and Quincy said in unison.

Moira pointed at the billboard along the road. Where a lot of other structures and things seemed worn down in this general area, due to the lack of travelers here, this thing was brand new. And it had a message. And it wasn't pretty. *"Come on over and live in our beautiful East Sussex gated community* Ever After! *Once you arrive, you'll never want to leave! Ever."*

<hr>

Chapter 3

<hr>

LET'S cut the quirkiness for a moment and observe how the world was very much in shambles. Oh, not just the usual shambles of being at the constant brink of extinction caused by supernatural hazards from on, under, around, in, and above the Earth (the around and above part was sort of taken care of during the twins' first adventure). Shortly after their brief flirtation with the afterlife, Quincy and Lilly found out how doomed humanity really was as a species, and the scariest part was that most humans were brainwashed into thinking the exact opposite. The grim reality was that thirteen beings, wretched god-like entities known collectively as the Gibbous Horde, lay dormant and scattered across the globe in the world's darkest places. Five of them, including the Mother entity the twins had encountered, had already awakened. They had started their scheming together with the increasingly madness-filled Haven organization whose true end goal remains as unclear as always but surely just as malevolent. Soon after the Night of Deadly Silence, when a lot of ambitious monster hunters and status quo rebels met their end quickly and gruesomely, the cult-like offshoot of Haven, known as the Order of the Final Dawn, started planting their nefarious seed everywhere they could. With the help of the brainwashing Gibbous Horde, they easily worked their way up huge multinational organizations. They became the leaders for a new world order as they took their places in the upper echelons of national and international politics. They became the figureheads of their so-called one true religion as they wielded the power to make people see what they wanted them to see.

Within weeks, Haven, Final Dawn, and the Gibbous Horde were working together to plunge the world into darkness and bring about the end times. Worst of all was the general public's total negligence toward what was happening around them. The dead rising in the streets. People being plucked off or ripped apart by living gargoyles. Strange visitors from other dimensions opening portals to our world and abducting people who are never to be seen again. It was a daily occurrence, and the only thing the normal population had eyes for was the salvation the Final Dawn would supposedly bring them, even when they were blind to everything they would need salvation from.

This is what frightened Sean so much, just as it frightened the others. What had once been a quarantine zone to keep out a deadly affliction from unknown aquatic dwellers had, in the public eye, now been transformed into a walled off utopia of perfect suburban living. The people simply forgot their history and flocked in droves to whatever madness was going on behind those walls.

Haven was the new police force. Their top agents became the overseers for the general public who were the cattle. Final Dawn were the prophets and holy men. But it was the Gibbous Horde who were the puppet masters.

The Swansong twins and their few close friends would do anything in their power to stop this upcoming end of days, but the chances of success seemed slim. Wouldn't you agree, dear reader? What has been foreseen long ago, and what was written in some dusty old tome or waterlogged scroll, is exactly what was happening on Earth. Quincy, Lilly, Sean Cooper, Moira LaGrande, and Elizabeth Borden... They could not possibly pull it off on their own. Other likeminded individuals were few and far between, and so... And so...it was time. The beginning of the end, an exciting last chapter for the Swansong twins. The time had come to stall what may have been inevitable. To stall long enough to give them time— time to find their fate. The time had come for the four to arise. The time had come, for rebellion. How exciting.

THE GRAY ZONE, *England — 14 days, 3 hours, and 33 minutes until the end of the world*

Quincy looked at the huge concrete wall looming in the distance and shuddered. Whatever was behind it, probably meant certain death for everyone involved. Whatever his supposed prophetic dreams had shown him, it was never quite clear what was beyond the quarantine zone's borders. Well, except for a sign that said Lewes was just a few kilometers away. And trees, there were most definitely trees and fields just like outside the walls.

"I don't think we can simply drive up to the first border guard and expect to be let through. Sounds like wishful thinking to me," he said while staring off into the light fog rolling down from the eastern hillside.

Sean shook his head. "Unfortunately, I'd have to agree with you on that. Seems like we might have to leave the ol' Volkswagen behind. Which totally sucks because I was kind of getting attached to the rusty hunk of junk," he said with a snicker. "All things considered, our best bets is to leave the car behind and hoof it into the Gray Zone. I don't think that will be hardest thing to do, considering anyone with the know-how about this place would probably want to steer clear of it."

Moira sighed. "Be that as it may, I doubt any agent will hesitate to gun someone down on the spot if they see some-thing out of place. They've done so for less. Believe me, I know." She started eying the fog. "Listen, I may have an idea, but I don't know if you'll like it…"

"Hey, if it helps us get in there, go for it," Sean said.

"I'll need to step out and look for some reagents, and a preferably already deceased small animal," Moira continued.

Sean turned his head. "Wait…"

"With a bit of luck, the fog will hang around long enough to pull this off, but I also need several containers and a heat source."

"Are we…" Sean stuttered.

"It's called the Transylvanian Trick. I've performed it once before. It's quick, relatively painless, and has about a seventy-seven percent success rate of turning everything back the way it was."

Quincy's ears pricked up. "Okay, I was already worried when you mentioned the dead animal, but what exactly *is* the Transylvanian Trick, Moira?"

Moira smiled in a cunning fashion. "We'll be turning into a light white vapor and floating across the wind to a destination where we can, preferably, plant our feet back on the ground before the spell ends. It's going to be sweet. Y'all are going to love it."

"What?!" Sean gasped. "I'm not sure about this… You know, I'm kind of afraid of heights and—"

Quincy laughed. "You're a pilot, dude. That excuse isn't going to work."

Moira grinned. "It's the best chance we've got. Besides, we'll be completely invulnerable during the entire ordeal. Even if there was any chance they'd spot us, which there's not, their bullets would just—*poof*—pass through us. How's that for a small time Voodoo apprentice from the south, eh?"

"What about *other* things? Can some kinds of monsters or interdimensional travelers see us? Perhaps flying sub-humanoids? Xenoseckts?" Sean shuddered. "Winged Yuggoth Fungi?"

"It's never been proven," she responded.

"What does that mean?"

"It means I don't know."

"Don't know if they can or don't know what you're talking about."

"I. Don't. Know."

Sean grunted. "Can you at least tell me if we can take non-corporeal stuff with us? We'll be needing the one duffel bag for sure."

"In theory it should be no problem, but are you willing to find out? Do we really need it?" Moira answered.

Sean patted the side of the duffel bag and smiled. "If you want to eat actual almost-food instead of whatever we can scrounge up in there, then yes." He nodded towards something up ahead and swerved the car into a narrow dirt road about a kilometer from the checkpoint and turned the engine off. "The ride was short but sweet, girl. You're an awesome little car."

Quincy was quick to be outside and slammed the door shut. "Pretty sure Volkswagens only speak German," he said, staring off into the distance. "If we're going to get to the cosmic space dust part—"

"Vampiric vapor," Moira corrected him. "Let's not confuse this with Fire Vampires."

"That part," he continued. "Then let's get on with the show. I see three black, unmarked cars heading toward us."

BRIGHTON *& Hove Quarantine Zone – Foxtrot Contagion Area aka the Marina, England – 13 days, 23 hours, and 51 minutes until the end of the world*

"Come, come! Come one and all, do not be afraid. Salvation lies beyond these iron gates!" The black-bearded man with the pointy nose, dressed in a bright orange robe, waved to the crowd. "Witness the majesty of what we are trying to accomplish, my friends. You are the first to partake in the

Alpha, ahem, initial testing phase of our luxurious undersea living space here in the famous Brighton Marina."

The group of candidates huddled together near a dry dock. They looked excited and happy, unaware of their surroundings' actual appearance. The famous Brighton Marina, once glorious and beautiful and filled with a thousand masts of boats large and small, was now a barren scrapyard. Hundreds of rusted hulls floated and bobbed in the dirty green water. The sea was filled with sticky goo, broken pieces of wood, and a mysterious violet slime-like substance. The entire harbor smelled as if a million rotten eggs were piled up in the middle of the boulevard. All the surrounding buildings were dilapidated and looked as if they were about to fall to pieces. Eerie blotches of dried crimson liquid stained many of the waterlogged docks. In front of the group of living space candidates, a brown rusted hatch led down into a tube-like structure that descended down into the sodden marina's murky waters.

"W-what can we be expect to find in there?" a young man standing in the middle of the crowd asked. There was a certain doubt hanging on his lips. The crowd around him turned around, astonished. They could not believe for a second that there was a shred of doubt creeping into this non-believer's mind. It was unheard of.

"He is unworthy, Father Sebastien!" one of the older women from the crowd yelled.

The man who expressed his doubt buried his face in his hands. "Please forgive me, Father. I have no idea what came over me. Once more, I ask you for your forgiveness."

The man in the bright orange robes shook his head at the other man. "There is no need to ask forgiveness, my boy. We cannot and may not be the judge of your worthiness. Still, we know you have a lot of questions. Yet we here at the Final Dawn are certain that the key to a brighter future and a better mind space go hand in hand with comfortable living conditions." He smirked; it seemed wrong, sinister somehow.

"Therefore, I see no reason why you, young man, should not be the *first* to witness the glory of our fantastic undersea Marina apartment complex. But before that, ahem, what is your name?"

"Jonathan."

"Jonathan, you shall be judged by our extremely high tech and sophisticated new artificial intelligence to see if you are a good fit for our fantastic new community we're building here. Not a test of income or heritage, but a test of personality!" Father Sebastien pointed to the hatch. "Enter!" he yelled.

Two men with black sunglasses and clad in black suits bent down and lifted the hatch's handles. Jonathan carefully descended the staircase. When he was about halfway through, the two suited men slammed the lid shut. Father Sebastien eyed his watch for a few minutes. Then, there was a sudden burst of machinery coming to life. The deafening sounds of grinding and scraping filled the entire dockside for a couple of seconds. The noise was unbearable for everyone except for Father Sebastien. But just as the sudden violence started, it went away. The crowd standing around the sinister robed figure and his two lackeys turned back to light conversation as if nothing had happened. The water around the tube was now turning red and there were bits and pieces of what looked like human flesh bobbing on the surface. A finger floated toward the dock before being snatched up by one of the Killer Seagulls that inhabited the coast. The seagulls usually left (whole) humans alone, but a general warning was to keep an eye on your kids when going to the beach, *because the gulls certainly would*.

Father Sebastien smirked at the sight and turned toward the crowd. "*Unworthy!*" he yelled. "*Next!*"

"Unworthy!" the crowd repeated. The next willing candidate, smiling broadly, had already lined up at the hatch.

· · ·

BRIGHTON *& Hove Quarantine Zone, England – 5 days, 20 hours, and 8 minutes until the end of the world*

It had not taken long for Moira to gather the necessary ingredients for the Vampiric Vapor ritual. She had to make do with a couple of on-the-fly solutions, but nothing that should be problematic. A matchstick would certainly work as an alternative to a 'Pinch of Sulfur from the Fifth Layer of Purgatory,' and she was sure that a handful of pine needles would work just as well as the 'Lower-back spines of a miniature were-hedgehog.' The aforementioned animal carcass was a concern at first, but sooner rather than later they had come across the half-eaten remains of a poor jackrabbit. It appeared to have been a victim of a Snaptrap Turtle, which rabbits think they can outrun. They cannot.

And so, without too much hassle, the ritual for the vapor spell was completed and cast. The three brave individuals, already like fish out of water here in Europe, were but a whisper on the wind. Like a gentle breeze, they floated across the entirety of the Gray Zone and crossed the big stone wall that encircled the entire quarantine zone, which stretched for miles and miles in every direction. They had floated on for a while, passing the seaside resort of Hove, which was once a tiny and ancient fishing village, and into the large city of Brighton, laying eerily quiet along the waterside. Where there used to be the sounds of laughter and joy, seaside fun and pleasure, and seagulls calls and roaring waves, there was the distinct lack of any such sounds. There was only the ever-present bubbling of the North Sea, turned back into some sort of primordial state beyond the ken of man, and the soft creaking of rotten planks that formed the world-famous Brighton Pier. The old pier was a sunken, burnt-out husk even before the entire world went to hell.

Feeling the spell's effects slowly wearing off, the three puffs of smoke floated down into a small park in between a block of buildings. Pleasantly surprised that a bit of natural green had survived in the dreary, post-apocalyptic looking city, it was as good place as any to touch down and continue on foot to Lewes County Taking a rest on a dilapidated bench and trying not to get cut up by random rusty scrap sticking out from it, the group literally and figuratively regained their composure. Here at Regency Square, they quickly checked that every limb was still attached and that they were attached in an anatomically correct fashion. Afterward, believing there was no time to waste with the strangely early setting sun on their right, the three followed the quiet boulevard as far east as it could take them.

The seaside city was abandoned but there were signs of struggles everywhere. An old bloodstain decorated the side of a beach chair. A plastic plate, with something indiscernible on top, was held by the remains of a human hand and underarm. Tattered beach towels and numerous bullet shells littered the ground. There were also gooey blackened husks of some form of ocean parasite that had attached themselves above every doorframe and in every darkened corner of the ceilings above the boulevard shops. When the fishlike things first rose out of the sea, no one knew what they were, let alone what other ghastly things were lurking down there. Whatever these things that had nestled here were, they were probably just the next in line on the list of many, many things that could end the friends' lives in a snap. Especially now that humanity wasn't even breaking the top one hundred on the food chain, let alone rising above it.

Within an hour or two of walking and, as luck may have it, coming across absolutely no one, the three made their way past the pier and were close to the marina's enclosed docks. Quincy was the first to notice, but he was followed in a mere millisecond by Sean and Moira, that the waters surrounding the marina had been turned into total carnage. Even the heavy green and thick oozing sea that crashed onto the shore could not hold a candle to this droopy burgundy mess of body parts and blood that drifted across the marina. Quincy quickly dove toward Moira and held his hands over her mouth as she started to retch loudly. He saw the patrol coming, and he dropped down behind a short stone wall with Moira and Sean in tow. He looked into Moira's eyes apologetically. After a moment, she understood the dilemma, and he carefully removed his hand. *I'm sorry,* he mouthed to her. She shrugged it off, but the hairs on the back of her neck stood upright from the horrifying scene that lay in front of them.

"I count two marine operatives, three special agents, a commander and two—no, three orange cloaked motherfuckers," Sean whispered as softly as he could. He turned to Quincy. "I don't know what they're doing over there but I'm guessing we're way out of our league here. I have an emergency failsafe in place but… Hey Quincy, are you there?"

Quincy stared down at his phone. A strange premonition, a flash of a thought that ran through his head, had urged him to log onto the mobile network, if any existed here, and check the internet. "Oh no…" he whispered.

"What's going on?" Moira quietly dragged herself over to Quincy "Did you get a message? Is it from Liz?"

Quincy stared at his phone in disbelief. "Sean… Moira… Check your phones please and tell me the date."

Sean pulled a primitive phone out of his pocket and snapped the lid open. He tapped the buttons for a minute. Moira did the same with hers.

The only thing that escaped Sean's mouth was, "What the fuck's the meaning of this…? Is this real?"

"Time loss…" Moira whispered. "We lost more than a week… How did we lose more than a week? What—"

The three gasped as they looked up to the sky which suddenly turned bright red, a storm forming over the city. It was like a dense snowstorm, only it wasn't snow that was quietly covering everything with small flaky particles. It was ash.

"We've lost ten days, I… The dreams are always correct…" Quincy whispered, trying to keep his anger contained. "Can't screw with a prophecy, right?" He turned to

Moira and Sean before looking up and catching one of the ashen flakes in his hand. He rubbed the black soot between his fingers. "The end is approaching. Looks like we've got less than a week."

"You've got to be kidding," Sean retorted.

Quincy chuckled in sorrowful disbelief. "I'm afraid so. It's always something… It really does feel like… It really *is* a curse."

Chapter 4

Tenebrae, WA, United States - 5 days, 19 hours, and 47 minutes until the end of the world

"IT'S A *FUCKING* CURSE, I tell you," Lilly removed her hands from the blinds to let them snap back into place.

The women had been keeping their heads low and their presence in Tenebrae as covert as possible over the past week and a half. Ever since Lilly's encounter with Annie from the diner and the waitress' favorite dead body slumped in the corner, both women felt a sense of unease that was now amplified by a thousand. The strange townsfolk repeated their same business day after day, like complacent little workers building toward an uncertain future at their same stations who continued to hose those lawns and clip those hedges. Mr. Woodtick always needed another fresh can of paint for his home improvement project, and Mrs. Horne was in the park every day showing pictures of a dog to the same people. She acted as if it was the same dog, but the breed always seemed to change in the photos, which was unnerving on its own. But the people Liz and Lilly had noticed were more *normal*, those who had lives to live and different errands to run day to day, always wound up missing. Even though they only consisted of a fraction of Tenebrae's populace, the town and community were small enough that such things tended to be noticed right away. At least if one had the mental capacity to actually notice these kinds of strange things.

Even worse were the Haven agents and the peculiar and creepy robed cultists of the Final Dawn that were garnering an ever-increasing interest in the small community. On more than one occasion, Lilly and Liz had to scramble away from wherever they were at that moment—a parking lot, main street, the dairy aisle—and try to get the hell out of the way before they were spotted. Once again, Lilly thought about how she might not even be that interesting to Haven if they still thought the Swansong twins had perished, but she wasn't keen on finding that out for herself.

They had even seen the sinister red bulbous eyes of Mothmen floating in the sky above Tenebrae on more than one occasion. Sometime after the Antarctica incident when Lilly and Quincy, by no real fault of their own, sent a Haven base and all of its personnel up in flames and kind of saved the world, Haven had started training these horrifying flying beasts. With an average wingspan of thirty-two feet, these silver and white-haired abominations were first seen flying over the night sky of Yellowstone National Park. They were supposedly the offspring of a cloning experiment Haven scientists conducted after finding the *real* Mothman and shooting it out of the sky ages ago. Whatever the case, the two young women weren't eager to get up close with one of those monsters.

Lilly blamed herself for the transgression in the diner, which she theorized led to the many disappearances. Liz had reassured her that Lilly played absolutely no part in any of the disappearances, and their main goal over the past week had been to quietly prepare, pack, and get out of town as quickly as possible. Liz even rehearsed a few simple spells she had taught Lilly during their brief stay with the Night Lights coven. To be fair, the 'create elements' four pack of spells were as basic as a young nature witch could get, but hey, it was something. Now neither of them would have to worry about keeping warm or creating a flame, keeping cool or creating a breeze, being hydrated or dousing those flames that were now out of control, there's a lot of uses for earth and dirt.

"They're out there right now," Lilly said and panted as she lifted the heavy backpack from the couch onto her shoulders. "Going from house to house, invading the home of anyone who had the gall to so much as look at an agent funny in the past two weeks. If they get here and find me, *oh unfortunate bearer of the likeness of Lilith Swansong, most wanted woman of the world*, I'm dead meat. *We're* dead meat," she said with a scowl. "Man, seriously. Screw my bloodline."

"This isn't some kind of curse meant to screw you and Quincy over, Lilly." Liz held Lilly by the shoulders before letting her hands slip down to hold hers. "This is just a fucked situation because some assholes took over the reins controlling the world. It's because you and Quincy screwed up *their* plans on more than one occasion and gave you a target on your head, not because of your heritage."

"Yeah man, fight the power…" Lilly said somberly. She glanced over the shoulder of the now seemingly distracted Liz. "Hey, what's up with the phone?"

Liz swallowed hard. "Ehm…" she started. She looked suddenly. "Remember when you said it was best to not keep in touch with the others in Europe because it could be dangerous and could be used to track them and…"

"Yes…" Lilly dropped the backpack on the ground and started to slowly walk around Liz who had plopped herself on the ground. "Liz… What did you do?"

Liz broke out in a sweat. She grinned stupidly. "I…have kind of…been keeping in touch with Quincy this whole time they've been away…"

"*What?* And you didn't tell me?" Lilly shot toward the couch. "What does it say?"

"I didn't want you to worry!" Liz tried to explain.

Lilly growled like a dog having a fierce discussion with its favorite squeaky toy. "What. Does. It. Say, Lizbeth?"

Liz jumped at the sudden use of her full name, a name she kind of hated. "You better read this for yourself." She handed Lilly the phone. "Look, I just didn't want you to worry about him. I knew that if I kept you up to speed, you'd never be able to find some piece of mind and—"

"Well, what do you know?" Lilly scowled and snatched the phone from Liz's hand. Liz had never seen her this angry. Well, maybe once in the catacombs beneath Eldritch Island, but this was something else. *"In Sussex area in England now,"* Lilly read aloud.

"I hadn't heard anything for over a week, I was fearing the worst," Liz added.

Lilly slapped her hand on Liz's face without taking her eyes off the phone. "Hush," she said softly, and continued reading: *"Things aren't…good here. Something happened. We lost time. We've got less than a week.* Wait, I don't understand. What does he mean we've got less than a week? Do you know something more than I do?" Lilly snapped at Liz.

"No, I don't," Liz said, sounding dreary. "But I suspect they would know better than us. Look, I'm sorry Lilly, I didn't want to put you through this…"

Lilly read the rest of the messages in silence. *It's now or never. We're going to try and make this happen but it's going to be a close shave probably. Sky's red now too, looks pretty gnarly. I'm scared, Liz. We all are. You don't wanna know what's out here. We're trying our best. Tell her I love and miss her. Take care, Q.* Lilly dropped the phone and wiped away the upcoming tears.

"Lilly, I'm really—" Liz started.

"It's okay," Lilly interrupted her. She stood up, determined. "We've got to get out of this place. We've gotta get there somehow. It's never going to end otherwise… It's a damn curse…but it's never going to end."

A startled look appeared on Liz's face. "Wait, go where? What, Europe? How are we going to——"

Gunshots and the deafening sound of air raid sirens interrupted Liz. There was an outcry from the streets right outside of the house. Men, women, and children alike were crying out of fear or misunderstanding. More gunshots, and then the cries all ceased at once. The siren continued and a bright orange glow seeped through the small house's shuttered windows, cascading the cozy home's woodwork in a sickly bright glow. A knock at the front door brought Liz and Lilly back from the hazy state of mind they had experienced from the sudden shock and change of atmosphere.

"Open up in there!" A heavy voice rang from the other side of the shabby door. "This is official business approved by your local overseer. Now I'm going to ask you once again to open the goddamn door. You've got ten seconds to comply! Ten! Nine! Eight!"

Liz paced across the room in panic. With a swift swish of her hands, she telekinetically moved the couch, chairs, and bookcase against the door. "What are we going to do? Dammit, shit, what are we going to do?"

"Five! Four!" the voice barked.

"Eat shit, dirtbag!" Lilly yelled at the door. Liz looked at her in disbelief. "I didn't know what else to say!" Lilly said to her, throwing her hands in the air.

"Aha, we've got a clown, boys, you hear? Three! Two! You know what it means when we got a clown, right? One! It means someone's not *complicit.*"

For a moment there was nothing but silence. The sirens seemed like distant nightmares, swallowed by some kind of deep existential fog that obscured all sound. There were no gunshots, no shouting. Nothing. Just for a half of a second. Lilly watched several chess pieces fly across the broken board that lay on the stack of furniture piled against the front door. She heard the Ouija board's magnifying glass slide across the wood.

The letters formed together in her head and one by one she could visualize them clearly. C-H-E-C-K-M-A-T-E. A mocking reminder of her many cross-realm chess games with old man Mortimer who kept the Nearly Departed realm in check.

Lilly snapped out of the dazzling trance when Liz pulled hard on her arm in a to get her to move out of the way. An explosion blew away the house's entire front wall, and Haven agents were piling in. In the middle of the mass of soldiers clad in heavy combat gear and amid agents with slick black suits, stood a sinister looking figure dressed in a bright orange robe. The sky outside had turned red, and the black silhouettes of six-legged winged beings flew high above the town.

"Welcome to the end, Miss Swansong." The cultist grinned through broken black teeth.

BRIGHTON *& Hove Quarantine Zone, England — 5 days, 19 hours, and 31 minutes until the end of the world*

Quincy tapped away at his phone, let out a deep sigh, and broke it in half before throwing one piece in the bushes next to them and the other piece in the ocean.

"Was that—" Moira started.

"Our last message for…for I guess a long while, maybe even…" Quincy stopped and bit his lip. He felt the salt of his tears prick the corners of his eyes.

Moira held his hand and softly patted it. "You *will* see them again, Quincy. And we *will* make it through, I promise."

"They won't get away with it. Not this time. I've had enough of this inhumane bullshit for a dozen lifetimes." Sean grunted. He started rummaging through the duffel bag.

The three could only sit back and watch helplessly as the spectacle at the marina unfolded in front of them. The Final Dawn cultists, together with Haven, hand in hand like the absolute plague on the world that they were, had gathered another group of volunteers at the edge of the dock. More innocent people who had happily signed on for a chance at beautiful seaside resort living, but who were oblivious to the fact that whatever was on the other end of that rusty hatch would spell visceral decay for all of them. One by one, the smiling civilians lined up to be thrown into the protruding tube and, from what it looked like, be grinded into a fine paste to be fed to the murky red ocean, the water thick as syrup from all the blood and gore it had already absorbed. Flashes of orange lightning alighted the crimson red sky, already at peak 'apocalyptic,' accompanied nearly every sacrifice. Quincy, Sean, and Moira, jumped up every time it happened. The abhorrent sound of crunching gears and ripped apart flesh turned their stomachs time after time until only one volunteer was left. The little man grinned broadly, seeming to pay no attention to the strange sky above him and the carnage in front of him. He bowed to the robed figure, and Quincy could barely make out a 'thank you' as the man, nodding to the two Haven agents who helped open the hatch leading into the darkness below, jumped in headfirst, laughing. A sickening crunch followed.

The ground began to rumble. It felt like an earthquake but not quite. It was as if it did not come from the shifting of the tectonic plates but from some kind of sonar vibration deep beneath the Earth, perhaps even from the ocean.

The cultist cackled maniacally. "It is done, my children!" He turned toward the ocean. "You have all been judged. And most of you judged *worthy*!" Still standing at the edge of the platform, he raised his hands toward the unnatural red sky and looked out over the sea. Waves of heat were now rippling across the horizon. "The Infernal Machine…*is sated!*"

Sean watched everything unfold with the others. He scowled angrily and ripped open the last protective piece of foam from the bag. When he revealed to Quincy and Moira what he held in the bag, they were both taken aback.

"You brought a rocket launcher…" Quincy stammered. "A *rocket launcher?*" He resisted the urge to start feverishly pacing, fighting it off since the chance of discovery was too great. "Whatever happened to keeping out of trouble and being covert and all of that?" Quincy whispered to Sean, appalled. "That…*thing* isn't exactly playing it safe from the shadows now, is it?"

"Didn't you see what I just saw?" Sean's voice started to get louder the more the rumbling around them increased in volume. "Those poor people were led like lambs to the slaughter. They even *laughed* as they were butchered for whatever horrible goal Haven's working on here. That's pure evil, Quincy. You know it is. I can't stand on the sidelines and let this happen." Sean slung the huge cannon like device over his shoulder and started to take aim.

Quincy tried to argue but was cut off by Moira. "Don't get in the line of a rocket launcher, Quincy. It's not good for your health." She laughed cynically. "I get where Sean is coming from… I've worked with them in the past and even then, I have never seen such a display of wickedness as today and…" Moira stopped short and looked up toward the strange, almost pulsating sky as if a sudden change in arcana balance caught her off guard.

"What's up?" Quincy asked. He was shaking, visibly ill, and he also looked mentally exhausted. He was pale as a ghost. "What's happening?"

"Take cover!" Moira yelled and pushed Quincy down behind the stone wall. His face was pressed up against the depiction of a monstrous crab-like god that was spray-painted on the face of the wall. Moira jumped after him immediately. "Sean!" she pleaded. "Now!"

Sean stood at the top of the wall, balancing the rocket launcher on his shoulder. The rumbling beneath him was starting to get worse. He tried very hard but simply could not manage to aim so he could fire directly at his intended target: the dock, that 'machine' and, most important of all, the evil people standing around it. The wind suddenly started to pick up which threw him off even more. He heard Moira shout his name again. Whatever was happening he could not and would not relent and take cover until his target was obliterated. Sean finally had his shot, or so he thought. It was as if the stars lined up perfectly. The ground was still for a brief moment, and the gusts of ocean wind had relented too. But it was not the moment *he* was waiting for. It was the moment for something else. Sean didn't take the shot. He couldn't. His synapses were firing on all cylinders as he was trying his best to comprehend what was happening right in front of him.

From the shore came a sonic boom. The blast wave knocked Sean down off the wall and flat on the ground. Thunder and lightning boomed, lighting up the fire-red sky. On the horizon in the distance, something horrifying emerged from the ocean. Impossibly huge and sporting features which no earthly fauna could ever dream of possessing, the thing literally overshadowed the entire western Brighton coastline. It was incomprehensible to behold and impossible to describe. Sean left the rocket launcher behind and scrambled toward his friends and taking shelter with them. But Sean could not look away from the horrific scene in front of him. He desperately rubbed the sand and silt from his eyes as he tried to make sense of whatever it was that had emerged from the thick, red brine of the primordial sea. He felt panic rising in his gut as he realized the purpose of the so-called Infernal Machine. Sean crawled toward the edge of the wall; he dared not look back at his friends. He stretched out his hands in the hopes that either Quincy or Moira would grab on tight and pull him to safety. Sean watched the crazed cultist dance uncontrollably before the robed maniac calmly slit the throat of the two Haven agents, basking in the blood spattered all over the flowing orange fabric. Sean looked further ahead while blindly reaching for the wall above him.

The abhorrent shape in the distance, so incredibly alien and non-Euclidian, was closer still, and Sean could see a host of winged beings seemingly detach themselves from their hosts and fly toward the shore. Their silhouettes did not betray many of their features, but they had large bulbous heads and at least four wings, two on each side. Their legs were unnaturally elongated.

Sean felt the warm familiar embrace of his friends. Moira and Quincy pulled Sean carefully down the slope and eased their friend down so he could regain his composure; All color was leeched from Sean's face, and his features were twisted in horror at what he'd just seen.

"I think I may have stared at the edge of oblivion," Sean panted. He grabbed Quincy by the arm with pleading eyes and squeezed. "It's one of *them*, Quincy." He turned to Moira. "I have seen one. Holy hell, not even everything the Mind Flayer showed me could prepare me…" He felt bile rising at the back of his throat. He turned back to Quincy. "The chart at your parents' mansion, there was one in the Atlantic right?"

"Right." Quincy nodded. He thought he had prepared for the worst, but he never could have seen this coming.

Sean laughed in desperation. "I think… I think it's right off the shore… Quincy." Sean looked straight at him, deadly serious. "Can you feel this heat…whatever the numbers are in your head… I think, I think the Apocalypse isn't a week away, I think it may be starting right n—"

A crash of thunder and a wall of unearthly, deadly noise interrupted Sean. Quincy bit the inside of his cheek and stood up. He did not come this far just to watch the world go down in flames from behind a wall sporting mediocre graffiti. He peered over the wall and, to his shock, saw the gigantic *thing* that was one of the thirteen Gibbous Horde beings creeping ever closer to the shore. The docks were on fire. Two Haven agents' bodies hung just off the edge of the wood, but where the cultist once stood there was now a pile of ash. Quincy slinked back behind the wall. Drips of sweat trickled down his forehead and nose.

"Well?" Moira asked expectantly.

Quincy failed to look her in the eyes. "Yeah, it's definitely one of them." He shuddered. He managed to look away from the chaos in front of him and turned to Sean. "At least your orange friend seems to have bitten the dust."

"Oh?" Sean perked up. He could not help but smile.

Moira shook her head. "Whatever it is, boys…now is not the time. Just before this all happened, I felt something shift. A change in the electric current around us. I…"

Sean scoffed, "Yeah, no shit. The world's ending right now. Or at least a part of it is. What else is new?"

"This is something different. It's as if the Earth itself was…screaming. Begging for help. And now… Now…" She trailed off and her mouth fell open. It was impossible to keep her hand from shaking as she pointed to the surf shop right in front of them.

From among the rubble and the sticky green goo that stuck to everything, shambling and rotting corpses started to rise. Up above on the boulevard, the same thing was happening. Fresh kills and old dried out husks were rising everywhere around them. At first, the walking dead seemed confused or even scared, but a few moments later the innumerable amount of walking corpses, moaning or screeching gutturally, started to make their way toward the shore. To the three's total surprise, the dead did not pay any attention to the living. It was clear it was not brains or organic matter that they were after. This was definitely another sign of the end times. Soon, everything would go down in flames, and everything they had worked so hard for would have all been for nothing.

Moira took her turn to peek over the wall. "By the Crossroads…" she muttered as she laid eyes on the towering mass of doom now standing waist high in the middle of the marina. If it had something akin to a waist, that is. The flying creatures were also very close to the shore. Moira could see their large tumorlike growths that apparently functioned as heads with a mass of tentacles protruding from a hole shaped vaguely as a mouth. To her dismay, she knew what they were. It did not take long for Moira to pop back behind the wall. "Whatever is directing the zombies," she started. "It's directing them to fight with those Mi-Go…" She rubbed her arms nervously.

"Mi-Go, huh?" Sean chuckled as the situation became more and more ridiculous with each passing moment. "This is ridiculous," he said, thoughts that were echoed by the others.

"And it just got weirder," Quincy said. He had a hard time comprehending what exactly was happening around them, and it was all happening so fast. It was impossible to get a grasp on the situation.

Right in front of them, a black horse with a blazing mane of fire and eyes as red as the inner core of Mars or the inner shells of Unhallowed Chatturga materialized. On top of the nightmare steed sat a rider embraced in a darkness so deep it was practically a void. His cloak was like a portal to distant constellations and galaxies, for with every sway you could get a glimpse of some faraway place for just a few moments. The rider's face was obscured by a silver mask with a blue gleam that was shaped like a skull. His big black bushy beard hung off his chin and his eyes seemed to light up with a strange kind of yellow hue. The dark rider held a gigantic halberd decorated with unknown glyphs and what looked like lines of scripture. Strands of red velvet hung from the weapon along with a pair of decaying human heads.

The black horse reared up, but the mysterious rider kept perfectly balanced as he coolly calmed the majestic but terrifying creature back down on all fours. He threw a scroll at Quincy's feet, who was in such a state of awe that he could barely get himself to move a few inches.

"We can hold them off," the rider said suddenly. His voice was deep but sophisticated. Despite being just a few feet away from the group, it sounded as if it echoed from another plane of reality. Distant, but clear as day. "I will take it from here, Master Swansong. You three get to the Monastery of Saint John near Lewes right now!"

The three didn't move. There was a sentence forming on

Quincy's lips, but he was too slow, and far too mesmerized or perhaps too afraid, to speak up.

"GO!" the rider commanded. The flaming dark horse and its imposing rider jumped high and flew over the wall toward the shore where sounds of tearing flesh and the screams of zombies and Mi-Go fighting had started to rise.

The three were left stunned after so many mind-bending encounters and happenstances following one right after another. They were still alive during what started to look and feel like the actual apocalypse. Quincy snatched the rolled-up scroll from the ground and unfolded it with shaking hands. A crude map was drawn on the yellowed paper with an address scrawled next to it. The countryside near Lewes was their next destination. Everything so far had been what Quincy witnessed in his horrifying dreams. The only thing that was scarier to him than the prophetic nightmares that had been plaguing him becoming reality, was what came after. He did not know. For all he was knew, nothing came after.

Chapter 5

Tenebrae, WA, United States - 5 days, 19 hours, and 1 minute until the end of the world

THE HOLES LEFT in the bathroom wall by the Haven enforcers' enormous guns were the size of golf balls, or even bigger. The cabinet shoved against the flimsy door was shaking violently as the orange robes of the cultist leader became more visible through the gaps of the torn off wooden frames with each passing second. Lilly fiddled with the window frame in between panicked breaths. She tried to ignore—or at least not acknowledge—that the sky had turned a burgundy red with occasional flashes of bright yellow. Pink lightning was another one of those things that both Lilly and Liz thought should be ignored, at least up until they weren't in immediate danger of being shot. Outside, the harrowing screeches of some profoundly disturbing beasts and monsters echoed through the once calm and quiet streets of Tenebrae.

There were other cries too. Human cries. But whether they were the pleading voices of those poor individuals that did not know what in the hell was going on, or the muffled yelps of Haven agents being plucked away by things that even they might not be able to completely control was up for debate. So, while Liz kept herself busy holding up a force shield (not unlike the one a certain Fire Vampire named Tim once used to save the twins' bacon beneath the sands of New Mexico to keep a particular wall from crashing down on top of them), Lilly was in the process of jimmying a child-proof bathroom window lock even though they didn't actually have any kids running around. It would be a lot easier, Lilly thought, if the damn thing's plastic key would at least have been stored somewhere near the actual lock, instead of in the kitchen drawer which was now either buried in rubble or, by the sounds of it, in the stomach of some unnatural beast that was doing flybys over their house. Lilly gritted her teeth as she jammed the sharpened end of a plastic toothbrush between the two plastic lids and pulled. With a quick snap the poor thing cracked in two and Lilly, in a bout of annoyance, threw the makeshift tool on the ground, sighed deeply, and started to look around for a replacement.

Liz squinted as the droplets of sweat forming on her forehead started to sting the corners of her eyes. She squeezed her left hand for a moment to relieve some of the strain. The left side of the force field immediately weakened and a gap the size of a small coffee table blew out of the wall. Liz gulped and concentrated on balancing the electric current derived from the spark of magic and spreading it out across her entire body before letting it release quietly, peacefully, and correctly as it ran into the ground beneath her soles. *Stable, Balance, Zen,* she thought as she stared into the loop of the double-barreled shotgun that the Haven enforcer held through the gap in the wall a few feet away from her face. The enforcer squeezed the trigger. Metal and shrapnel released from the barrels into the little bathroom. That is, it would have if it wasn't stopped by Liz's magic. With each impact, she gasped for air. She was astonished she could hold on for as long as she did, but it would not take long for her to collapse on the ground and be done for. She knew this; Lilly knew it too, which was why she was trying so hard to arrange an escape. Liz was thankful for everything she had done and was doing.

"What the *hell* is taking so long?" Liz screeched over the sound of multiple gunshots trying to find their way through the invisible field of magic and into the fleshy underbellies of their intended targets.

Lilly threw her newest attempt at an improvised lock-opening device, a beard trimmer, toward the outer wall in frustration. "Why do we even *own* one of these?" she snarled. The cheap metal item ricocheted from the corner of the tiled wall to the rim of the bathtub and, with its surprisingly light build, bounced a third time from the edge of the tub straight through the window. Lilly saw the spectacle eunfold and for a nanosecond looked at the hole in the thin window with astonishment. "Eh, I'll take it." She shrugged and reached for the toilet brush. "Mind the splatter!" she yelled over to Liz.

From the hole in the wall, the sinister cultist leader peered into the bathroom and cackled at the weak display of frenetic activity. "You are too late, *far* too late!" he yelled.

"Although I must say we were *very* surprised to see you up and about," one of the Haven agents said with a sneer. "But let's just say we'll fix that right away." He grinned.

Another hellish sound came from above the house. The noise was such an assault on the senses in every single way that it was nearly impossible to describe. Imagine some deep-sea giant that dwells in the darkest most forgotten parts of our oceans. A leviathan with the power to swallow islands, cause tsunamis, and end civilizations. Now imagine the sound it would make. Just try to envision it, but ten times as horrible, ten times as foreboding. It would be but a fraction of the melancholic horror that was overheard above Lilly and Liz's small and cozy cottage. It was something so vile that even the Haven enforcers, agents and, most surprising of all, the leering cultist, whom the women now saw appeared to be blind, looked up in shock.

Lilly took the opportunity to jam the toilet brush into the

hole in the window and swerved it around, breaking the pane into little pieces. She was careful to remove the sharpest bits and pieces from the bottom of the frame and threw bath towels over it along with the soggy mat she slipped out from beneath Liz's feet.

"Come on!" she yelped toward Liz, stretching out her hand. Lilly was outside already. She wasn't ready to look at whatever carnage was happening around her, but she knew they had better chances here than in there. "Liz!" she yelled again.

Liz started to inch backward toward the window. At the last moment, she released her right hand from the center of the spell and took Lilly's. Immediately, the spell weakened as the enforcers and agents at the other side of the barely standing wall were ready to strike. Lilly used all her might to pull Liz through the window in a single swift motion. The shield fell and the bullet rain that followed was deafening, overshadowed only by whatever unknown horror was making its rounds above Tenebrae. Upon planting her feet on the soil outside, Liz used her last bit of energy to make a dash with Lilly for the edge of the woods. They did not look up, and with whatever was happening, the woods did not at all sound promising, but it would at least provide some sort of shelter, a place to hide and lay low until they could get a grasp on the situation.

"You know what I'm really curious about?" Lilly panted, her eyes locked with Liz's ever since she pulled her outside. "I wonder why they never thought of… I—" Lilly was the first one to look up. To try and explain, make sense of or otherwise fully describe the spectacle that was unfolding was a disservice to it, them, and whatever else was up there. "Holy sh—" was all Lilly could mutter before the women were plucked from the backyard lawn and into the flying carriage that flew past them.

Lilly and Liz were unable to speak from shock as they held on for dear life while they felt the familiar sensation of being lifted into the air. Familiar, because they experienced it on a plane and in a rollercoaster and less so, from being literally catapulted through the sky in a wooden cart with flames coming out from nowhere. Lilly squeezed Liz's hand tight and despite the wind and particles of ash and soot flying around, tried opening her eyes to see whatever it was that was dragging them to their inevitable fiery demise.

"M–Mortimer?" Lilly stammered, surprised that the weirdness of the day still had a few tricks up its sleeve.

In the front of the black wooden cart sat Mortimer. There were no more pretenses that withheld his true identity. He wore a long black cloak with a long hood that obscured most of his bony features. Under the hood two bright red eyes burned menacingly. In one skeletal hand, he held a long black and silver scythe which swished in the air as if it had a mind of its own. Any flying creatures, Mi-Go or otherwise, would be very unlucky if they were to pass too close to the carriage. The wrath of Mortimer's scythe was legendary, Lilly knew. Seeing it in action, cutting through beast after beast and ripping open whatever body part was closest and leaving it a bloody mess, Lilly felt a strange sense of admiration.

In his other hand, Mortimer held the reins for the two skeletal horses that pulled the flaming carriage through the sky. The beasts shrieked loudly every time he pulled the reins, but it was impossible to discern whether they were from pain or pleasure. Maybe being a skeleton and pulling forth a hell-fire burning carriage through the Apocalyptic red skies of Washington state held a lot of benefits. Who could tell, really?

"What are—" Lilly had to turn her head to gasp for breath a few times in between the words. "You doing–here?" she went on.

Liz pulled herself up to get back at Lilly's eyelevel. "Is this —" She gasped the same as Lilly. "*Him?*" she asked. "Mortimer?"

"Stop being so dramatic." Mortimer turned to the women. His voice wasn't what Lilly remembered. It was less human now, she thought. "The carriage has its own gravitational field and air bubble," he explained. "So either you're doing one of those high octane action set pieces like in the movies for the fun of it or—wait, excuse me." Mortimer swung the scythe dexterously to his left where it cleaved through two Mi-Go with one fell swoop. "As I was saying," he continued in a soothing voice, "sit up and calm down, there's no need for this. Then open your mouth and speak."

"Why are you…huh, yeah, that works." Lilly shrugged and tried her best to get into a more comfortable position. While the magic in the carriage certainly did its job, it was Lilly's brain that had to get used to the strange angled sitting position. "Why are you here? What's going on? Wait…are we dead? Like, *dead* dead this time?"

Mortimer or, let's make it official for a moment, *Death* growled. "No," he muttered. "Nothing like that. But it does seem that the Apocalypse has begun."

Lilly scoffed. "Oh great! Is that all?" she sarcastically remarked.

"It's quite the pickle!" Mortimer exclaimed. "It's too early, this is absolutely *not* in accordance with any of the prophecies that proclaim the world is coming to an end in our current year. Some come close, but it's still too early."

"So, what could be the earliest that the world would end?" Liz asked. She couldn't quite believe what was going on, where in the world they were, and why the rocking motions of the carriage weren't making her sick to her stomach. Although that last bit was a welcome change.

"The earliest?" Mortimer answered. "Well, that would be a few days from now, about five or six depending on where you are in the world or what your favorite constellation or color is."

"And where are you taking us?" Lilly asked. She glanced to the side for a moment and saw the faintest of smiles on Liz's face. Despite the grueling circumstances that came with the world ending, they were together, as she had promised and wished for. "And thanks," she added, turning back toward Mortimer.

"Don't mention it." The red lights in the skull's eye sockets flashed for a moment. "We need you now. We do not like a false start, just everyone else." His teeth clicked together. "As far as *where* we're going, we'll be landing in a poppy field in Flanders, that's Belgium by the way, in about an hour."

Lilly brushed her hands through her ash-filled curls. "Why there? I don't understand any of this, and who is we?"

Mortimer either ignored her rising frustration or it was just too difficult to express any emotion from the face of a white skull. In either case, he proceeded calmly. "We're going there because in the closest apocalyptic scenario that place is the very last to go down in flames and darkness." The scythe swished again and two more flying monsters were relieved of their heads. Thunder crashed around the carriage, but Mortimer remained motionless and focused. "And *we*," he continued, "means me and my fellow riders of the Apocalypse, of course. As well as your brother Quincy and his friends."

"Quincy is there?" Lilly gasped. She squeezed Liz's hands so hard she yelped.

The skeleton shook his head. "Not yet. First, they must procure the Cross of Saint John and then my…colleagues will make sure they arrive in Flanders in one piece. Believe me when I tell you that we're in this together. We're trying to stop whoever has kickstarted this early Apocalypse."

"Stop it how?" Liz spoke up. She was as curious as she was skeptical. Even while trying to lay low and outrun these horrible incidents, they had a knack for popping up anyway. She and Lilly were on the other side of the world to Quincy, Sean, and Moira, but here they were, ready to meet up again as if the first part of a scavenger hunt was coming to a close and break time was starting. "You mentioned a cross?"

Mortimer nodded. "There are a couple of holy relics that

are said to lead to the nesting place of the terrible fate that belies the world, as well as holding a key to stopping it."

See! Liz thought. *It* is *a scavenger hunt.*

"We have no idea if you will be on time to track all of them down before everything comes tumbling down," Mortimer continued. "But the poppy fields are the safest place now… And if there really is no time left, we'll have to send you back, and that's a whole mess on its own."

Lilly's ears pricked up. "Send us back?" She swiveled over to Mortimer and grabbed his robe. "Do you mean through time?"

"Yes," the robed skeleton answered reluctantly.

THOUSANDS, if not hundreds of thousands of years ago, immeasurable and unfathomable for us meek mortals and/or souls of the (near) afterlife, an event transpired in the location that would one day be a vast stretch of moorland in the Flanders part of a small country called Belgium where rows upon rows of countless poppy flowers would bloom as far as the eye could see. All that time ago, there was nothing but barren rock and lifeless ash. Numerous volcanoes littered the hot, gray landscape, their smoke bulging up into the stratosphere at all times of day and obscuring most of the life-giving sunshine. The Earth was a transitory planet among a group of planets inhabiting the Milky Way galaxy, as it would someday be called. Some of these planets remain, such as Mars, now vacant and empty but perhaps thriving with life not unlike our blue sphere is today. Others vanished long ago, such as the twins Tarook and Tebetha, also known as the Sulfur Giants. In that swirling vortex of primordial chaos, our planet was nothing more than a pit stop along the way for interstellar journeys of species so ancient even the Celestians would not dare to try and name them all.

However, when the Celestians came and planted the seed

that would one day sprout poor old humanity, the current and ever unfortunate denizens of Earth that we all know very well and perhaps are even a part of, there came into existence five more beings. Nobody knows who was responsible for their appearance. Maybe they were simply plopped into existence as some sort of cosmic joke set up by our wonderfully hostile and indifferent universe. A joke to some, an Apocalyptic event that ended entire civilizations to others. Anyway, these four plus one individual arrived almost simultaneously at that steaming wasteland about a hundred miles south of what would sometime in the far future become the Netherlands. They all rode in on a four-legged creature that would eventually be called a horse, but back then did not have a name because evolution had not yet set in enough for something like the gallant horse to first emerge. Horses are akin to a couple other Earthly creatures and their species actually originated somewhere else among the stars. But let's not open *that* particular can of worms.

Huh, funny story about worms…yes, but anyway. These four plus one mysterious and cloaked individual came together and, without even speaking a single word to each other, instinctively knew their purpose in existence. They were the custodians of the end times. Specifically, the end times that would one day befall this disastrously ugly speck of a planet they appeared on just now. When, some day in the far future, the time came for all life and existence to end on this planet called Earth, these four plus one individual would be called upon to make sure everything transpired as smoothly as possible. Four of them were then known as Death, Famine, War, and Plague. They were not given these names by anyone, nor did they decide on the names themselves. They simply came into being knowing how they should be addressed.

Immediately after defining their purpose of existence, the obviously existential questions arose. *Who am I? Where the hell did we come from? What is this place? What is a* Hell? *I feel like I know what that should be but why don't I—aaaah.* But alas there was not much time to speculate on these things, even though there was all the time in the world for it would be thousands of years until the Celestians would depart and leave room for humanity to be borne from the void of the distant stars. Straight to business these strange, cloaked riders went. To discuss anything else other than their duty, of which they had no idea who had instructed them and/or why they should follow up on it, was indeed a folly.

"What if… What if it starts too early? What if it is not yet time?" Death asked. Smoke bellowed from the darkness beneath his black hood.

War growled. "Easy. We hold whatever or whoever is the culprit back and make sure everything will transpire on time as it should."

"And when will that *time* be?" Plague asked. She shooed away the flying critters that we would come to know as flies that buzzed around her head.

"We will *just know!*" Famine interjected. She fumbled with the reins of her horse, who looked pale and as if it was starving but somehow also happy. "But the question Death poses is still valid. We'll know when it'll be too early, we'll know who or what caused it, but *how* will we stop it?" A smile formed on her shadowy visage, just barely able to be made out underneath her hood. "Do we starve whoever is responsible? Deprive them of food and water, drain the life force out of them?"

"Do we unleash sickness among their ranks, gutting them from the inside out and rendering them too weak to even lift the few scraps of food they *can* find to their disgusting mouths?" Plague gushed, excitement in her tone despite the horror she'd spread.

"Do we pit the remainder against each other, turning their petty quarrels into full blown mortal combat on the fields of strife and glory?" War bellowed. His eyes glowed wide underneath his blood red hood, and he nearly frothed at the mouth.

Death sighed. "Easy for all of you to say… Once they

croak, then it will be my problem, and I don't think I'll like taking on lots all at the same time. Besides, who says the premature apocalyptic scenarios will be the fault of this planet's future dwellers?"

Famine nodded. "Perhaps the answers to those questions lie somewhere beyond the stars. In any case, I would think for now we say we'll *cross that bridge when we get to it*, whatever that means. Anyway, what's with the furry thing?"

"I thought it was yours; it's not mine," War answered. "Death? Plague?"

Both shook their heads.

You might be wondering who the mysterious fifth entity was that appeared that day on the shimmering sulfur flats of prehistoric Earth together with what we now know are the four horsemen, and women, of the Apocalypse, right? There will be enough time to explain, hopefully. But for now, know this: my name is Henry, and I am what they call a cat.

MISKATONIC UNIVERSITY, *Arkham, MA, United States – 25-ish years until the end of the world*

William rubbed the stubble on his jawline as he straightened the tiny glasses on his nose. He turned to Tobias and Emily and cleared his throat. They were in awe of being present in such a historical and impactful place of learning as Miskatonic.

"It's really quite peculiar, isn't it, Tobias?" William eyed his nephew up and down and raised an eyebrow. "For Pete's sake you two, would you stop gawking as if you've never seen a university campus before and start paying attention to what's really important? See this, Tobias?" He pointed at the glass display case in one of the darker corners of Miskatonic University's famed library. "The back has elongated from three to three-and-a-half inches since we first found them in the hyperborean ruins in Nova Scotia."

However grateful he was for the opportunity to finally visit the ancient and weatherworn Arkham again, Tobias was underwhelmed by the findings his great uncle William had praised during their conversations on the phone earlier that week. "Are you sure they weren't just miscalculations on the part of your Canadian colleagues?" he asked rather bluntly. "I mean, the kilometer and the mile, kilo and pound, centimeter and inch. They've got all these different metrics and…" Tobias sighed, looking away from William's stern and annoyed face. "I mean…a lot can go wrong…"

"What Tobias is trying to say," Emily interjected, trying to sound as calm and nice as possible since she did not exactly enjoy the long drive over here. Especially if there wasn't much to show for it, not with her belly increasing in size and everything getting more laborious with each passing day. "What he's trying to say is that maybe you should wait for a few more days next time before we come over here. This isn't anything to write home about, William."

William scoffed at the two. "Oh, but it is, my dear nephew and niece. If you'd let me finish before interrupting with your petty non-explanations on inferior metrics, you'd have sooner laid your eyes on these." William took an envelope out of his outer coat pocket, opened it, revealing three photographs. "Let me tell you, it was a whole ordeal getting these tablets sent here from Marblehead, but it was worth it. These photos were taken a few minutes after uncovering the pieces, a day after, and then three days after that, respectively. See the progression near the bottom in the second and third photograph as the writing becomes more visible? How's that for miscalculation, hmm?"

Tobias's eyes widened at the revelation. Any doubt he held about the strangeness of the tablets now made way for genuine interest and fascination. Even Emily, who was not particularly dispositioned for a life of research into the history of occult and supernatural artifacts, had to admit the reveal left her awestruck.

"Have you managed any translations?" Tobias knelt next

to the glass case and held a magnifying glass as close to the edge as the barrier allowed.

"Nothing concrete, only a few loose passages. But get this, Tobias…there is a reason I had them shipped here, even though I do not teach here anymore."

"Oh?" Tobias looked up. He must have missed that news.

William grinned. "From what we can gather, the tablets speak of something old. Something very old, Tobias. Something already ancient when the universe was still young. And you know what? I think its secrets might be right under our noses for us to uncover. Right here in Arkham."

LEWES COUNTY, *England – 5 days, 16 hours, and 14 minutes until the end of the world*

If there is one thing that is fortunate when a large supernaturally infused hazardous event happens near where one needs to be and one does not want to be detected and shot at by the crazed agents of a malevolent organization, it's the fact that said agents are probably preoccupied elsewhere. Perhaps they were awaiting said event, or perhaps they are cowering in the corner of a forgotten basement somewhere, praying to a god they hadn't thought of for a long while, which they might not know is actually a machine built by an ancient race of benevolent extraterrestrials.

So when the dark rider showed up just when the dead were rising up all around Quincy, Moira and Sean and something so horrific it can't be described was waddling out of the sea, the trio saw their chance to get the hell out of Dodge as quickly and as nimbly as their feet would carry them. And no, it would *not* be a Swansong adventure without someone rigging a car and taking it for their own. After they got out of the immediate 'danger' area of the Brighton & Hove Quarantine Zone, Sean spared no expenses picking out a nice sedan which he hoped would take them up north quickly.

Given the situation, Quincy had a lot less trouble stealing someone's car than he had back when he and Lilly had to flee Lafayette some time back. It wasn't *that* long ago, Quincy realized, but it felt like a different lifetime altogether. He simply could not believe what was happening. Feeling sick to his stomach and weak, so very weak, he felt like he could sleep for months on end. Thus, when the border crossing into the gray zone was mercifully absent of any type of Haven personnel, it did not take long for Quincy to pass out. The trip wouldn't take very long, so as Moira watched her friend slump down in the seat next to her, she hoped his sleep was merciful and dreamless.

WAKE UP, *Quincy.*

The voice rang through Quincy's head as if it was a chainsaw digging its way into his inner ear canal. Quincy gasped and bolted upward. He was no longer in the car but lying on a wooden slab that was laid across an altar. Looking around at the small building, he realized it was not a full-blown church in terms of size or lavish ornaments, painted ceilings or stained-glass windows, but it was unmistakably a place of worship. Pews lined both sides of the room and between each set was a window, any glass now long gone. There was nothing to see outside of the windows except for a terrifying crimson glow that looked thick and impenetrable. The chapel, for Quincy decided that word best described the building, was also hot. It was so hot that the wood on which Quincy lay was soaked with his sweat. He could feel the dizziness and delirium of dehydration coming with any movement that was too quick or too sudden.

Why do you resist? You have lost, Quincy.

Quincy looked up to be greeted by a thousand eyes opening from the ceiling of the chapel. They were all bloodshot with a red iris and an elongated pitch-black pupil. Worst of all, they were all staring at him. "Who are you?" Quincy scowled. "Where am I?"

I am you, and you are me. For the same atoms that separated themselves from me eons past and drifted along the stars until they eventually settled on a barren rock dancing in space that would one day become known as Earth are the same atoms that make up your own biological and anatomical structure. We are all the same. And here we stand together, at the end.

"The end of *what?*" Quincy gritted his teeth. "Why do you concern yourselves with a puny planet such as ours? Leave us alone. Why should we be the ones to face oblivion?"

You think you are the only one.

"Aren't we?"

You are too late. We are at the end of everything. *The cosmos should not be seen as a grand ballet of beautiful chaos. Chaos yes. But raw, primordial, savage. You are too late. You are all that's left.*

"Wha– What?" Quincy stammered. He tried crying out for his sister and friends. But like all true nightmares, no sound could escape his lips.

Goodbye, Quincy Swansong.

～

"HE'S WAKING UP!" Sean's voice sounded garbled. Distant, but still close, as if being spoken through a broken megaphone. "Get him some water. I brought some in the bag… Hey!" Sean smiled as Quincy opened his eyes. "You had a nightmare again, buddy? It's okay, man, we're here. We'll always be here."

"We'll be with you until the end, Quince," Moira added.

Quincy's pupils grew wide. "The end?" He grabbed Sean's wrist and pulled hard. "The *end!*" he shrieked.

VI

. . .

LEWES COUNTY, *England — 5 days, 16 hours, and 14 minutes until the end of the world*

It took Quincy a little while to calm down and make sense of his strange premonition. That is, if it actually *was* a premonition and not some twisted nightmare that his own broken psyche had developed ever since he began realizing that reality was on the brink.

Quincy did not go into much detail about what had him so on edge. Sean and Moira were skeptical, but Quincy's Swansong persistence made sure that whatever they thought they could get out of him was a lost cause, at least for now. For one, he himself still didn't know what it was that he saw in his dreams or if it was some kind of vision of the future or indeed a horrific fictional depiction of what *could* happen that he had subconsciously created. Either way, he was dead tired and missed his sister, but he determined to finish whatever it was he needed to do. And for now, that was to find a way to get inside the monastery on the hill on the edge of the town where they were now, just in the shadow of the famous Lewes Castle, and get a holy relic that was, based on his dreams and speculation in his father's diary, hiding *some* kind of clue, and then… Then? Quincy had no idea, and neither did Sean or Moira. His only hope was that whatever he would find up on the hill would provide a decent enough clue to send them on their way to whatever destination they'd have to infiltrate and endure next.

There was another thing that addled Quincy's mind each time he tried to envision his recurring dream of visiting the monastery and ultimately getting chased out of it. Two things, actually. Every time he traced the steps from his dream, he wracked his brain about something he felt he forgot. There was an important distinction, something very important that lay just on the edge of his memory that Quincy simply couldn't put to words or explain but knew would have devastating consequences if forgotten or ignored. And secondly, there was the feeling of meeting a familiar, yet not familiar, 'face' inside of his dream. Quincy couldn't recall speaking to anyone in his visions of the monastery except for Sean and Moira through the walkie-talkie. Quincy felt his heart skip a beat when Sean handed him his walkie-talkie; it looked exactly like the one from his dreams. Quincy had the nagging feeling that there was someone else there, something that his mind erased from every single loop of the dream just as he woke up. Quincy could only hope that this individual was on the right side of the fight, but considering his only friends were in the U.S. orwith him at this moment or…well, dead, Quincy considered the chances to be slim. Only time would tell, as it would with everything, as it would be the only damn thing still *ticking* after all of this mess. Probably.

"Hello? Quincy, are you still there?" Moira waved a hand in front of his face. "Quincy, my exorcism skills are *very* limited and whatever thing could possess a headstrong Swansong like you would probably be *way* out of my league."

A drop of sweat plunged down from Quincy's brow and landed on the soggy soil below. The sky was overcast, only slight traces of the Apocalyptic red and orange they saw a few hours ago remaining, and a slight drizzle of rain had started falling.

"Hm, yeah," Quincy replied. He gripped the walkie-talkie tight. His coat felt uncomfortable in the humidity. "I'm fine," he lied, smiling insincerely.

"What is going on with you, man? I know things have been rough with the dreams and all that, but something is off. You took us here because you believed we had the power to change the fate of the world, right? We can't have you slacking off." Moira wasn't having any of it. "Quincy, listen, I know everything is going to shit at the moment, but we need your head clear in the game, yeah?"

"I said I'm fine!" he snapped at her. "I– I'm sorry, Moira. It's just hard. I'm so dead tired. This whole thing feels like such a burden, and the dreams… It can get to be too much, and it doesn't even feel like we're making any progress. If anything, everything is going to shit, as you like to put it, even faster than we had anticipated. We literally *lost* time. How does that even happen? It's just too much sometimes and when that happens, I tend to like, zone out, I guess. Find my happy place or whatever."

Sean rummaged through the trunk of the car for a bit before popping his head out. "Hey Quincy, if you want me to go in, you know that's fine by me, right?" He lifted the big duffel bag that once held the hidden bazooka out of the trunk and buried his hands inside. "I mean, why not? You could take time to get your head cleared up a bit, perhaps try to get more than half an hour of sleep for once, and maybe, just maybe, you might dream up something new that could help us get to wherever we need to go next once we've got what we're looking for. Hmm?"

Quincy looked sullen. "No, that won't work. I– It's like I have a map of this place inside my head when I've never been here before in my life. It's the strangest thing. Looking at it now…" Quincy lifted his head, gazing at the cobbled and dirt road of the narrow street, and looked past the rows of distinct English townhouses up toward the green hill rising over the rooftops that looked over the ancient ruins of Lewes Castle. The monastery stood like a silent guardian watching over the quiet and empty little town. It had nobody to speak to except for the few oak and willow trees that accompanied it on the grassy slope and the occasional townsperson who would hike over and chat up the friendly monks that lived there. *Used to live there*, Quincy thought. "Looking at it now" —he focused back on his friends— "I know exactly where everything is and where I'd want to go. It's only logical that I'm the one who can get the cross relic. Besides, it wouldn't make sense if I'm the one in my dreams that goes inside that I wouldn't be the one going in now."

"Maybe you shouldn't put all of your trust in your dreams, Quincy. I mean, we've gotten this far without them, right?" Moira asked carefully.

Quincy wanted to scoff but he controlled himself. *There was no reason to act like a jackass,* he thought. "We haven't gotten anywhere, really," he said dryly. "It's the best chance we've got, so I want to do this. Wait for me at the Woodland Inn, okay?" He turned to Sean who could see past the exhaustion and pain and noticed sincerity and perhaps even hope. "Please, let me do this. On my own, quickly in and out."

"What about the part in your dream where you're chased?" Moira asked. She was still in doubt, but even she could see that Quincy had made up his mind.

"I always make it out in one piece." Quincy smiled. "I exit at the churchyard where there's no opposition and all I have to do is sprint over to the road at the inn where you'll be waiting. Easy."

"Well." Sean grimaced as he pulled a large piece of orange cloth out of the duffel bag. "I knew it was a crazy idea but that it would turn out handy someday. I'm sure this'll fit ya."

Quincy grabbed the orange Final Dawn robes presented to him and pulled them over his regular clothes. "Like a glove, but it still feels terrible." He laughed. "See you two on the other side."

～

THE HILL WAS A STEEPER and longer climb than Quincy expected. The robe's large hood obscured most of his peripheral vision so most of the time he saw nothing but a little stretch of dirt road ahead of him and his own feet. The rest of the mission so far had been surprisingly easy and smooth, to Quincy's great relief. Up on the hill he found the monastery doors open and, after the unexpected shock of running into a couple of robed cultists, Quincy noticed that nobody paid any heed to him, and he was free to roam the grounds of a place he had never been but knew by heart. Just like that, Quincy stepped inside and found himself in a brown hallway with old bronze torches lining the roughly hewn walls. He was in.

Without delay, Quincy navigated the brown, moldy hallways with ease. His suspicions were confirmed as he felt like he had a map of the entire building in his head, just like someone could find their way to and navigate their childhood neighborhood in their head. He turned right at the second shadowy intersection and counted the old oaken doors on his left. *One, two, three, fo*— Quincy gasped. From the fourth door on the left emerged some kind of shadowy apparition. Its face was nearly indistinguishable but unmistakably in pure torment. It was pure black, but less like a shadow and more like an amalgamation of dark substances which dripped from its arms and legs. The thing appeared not to come through the door but rather…well, *through* it. It was sticking halfway out of the age-old woodwork with the mysterious and foul black liquid seeping throughout the seams of the wooden boards. Quincy instinctively bounced back three steps. He clutched the knob of the third door next to him with his left hand. Hesitation pricked at the back of his mind. Shaken and distraught, he was ready to turn and open the door, but he could not keep his eyes off this inhuman entity.

"Betrayer…" the thing said with a low guttural moan. "*Betrayer!*" The thing held out its hand. It was almost entirely through the door.

Quincy bit so hard on the inside of his cheek the coppery taste of blood filled his mouth.

"*Betrayer!*" the thing yammered again. Only his left leg was now inside the door. The entire square foot in front of the door was drenched in dark liquid.

Quincy felt salty tears stinging the corners of his eyes. *Betrayal*—he most definitely felt it. But not in the way that this damned thing sniffed him out. Rather, he felt betrayed by his gift of foresight. Not once in all the times he walked this very hallway in his dreams did he encounter whatever unholy apparition this was. The thing was just standing there. Was it watching him? Was *he* the betrayer? The thing did nothing, but Quincy knew that their plan, flimsy and uncertain as it already was, was balancing on the edge even more than it was before. It was like an omen. One wrong step and everything would be for nothing and everything and *everyone* would perish. He knew he had to get out of here and find some other, perhaps more unfamiliar, path to the anti-chamber that held the cross relic he sought.

Quincy took a deep, silent breath and started to turn the knob of the third door. To his surprise, the knob turned all by itself, and the door swung open, nearly flinging Quincy inward. On the other side, one of the orange-robed cultists stood with a sacrificial dagger in his hand. Quincy could see what looked like a stone altar behind him, all bloody.

The cultist paid little attention to Quincy, who was again thankful for Sean's skill at procuring items of vital importance. The cultist peered into the hallway at the thing, which was now entirely out of the door and stood motionless in the hall. "Oh, there he goes, 'ere he goes again!" The cultist turned to Quincy. "He's at it again, innit? The bloody scamp, should've never been summoning on a Tuesday, that's what me mother used to say."

"I—uh, yeah, it's at it again. Damn...*scamp*," Quincy stammered.

"Oi!" the cultist yelled at the thing. "Betrayer this, all is lost that! You get your betrayer arse back in that room this instant or else there'll be hell to pay!" He shook his fist at the dark entity. "And I knows yer not too keen on getting back there!"

The cultist took a few steps into the hall and the entity started to make its way back through the door into the room. Quincy peered into the room for just an instant. He saw a couple of human fingers strewn about on the makeshift altar. It was then that he saw his new cultist friend missed a couple of digits on the hand he liked to use for making threats.

"There 'e goes," the cultist said to Quincy, not paying any

attention to the bloody stumps that were gushing blood all over his robe. "Are ye new here, lad? I noticed the accent. Not from around here, are ye?"

"That's right," Quincy lied. "I just got here last Friday for the…the big event, you know. Just a couple more days, heh heh." He hoped his eyebrow would stop twitching before it got too out of hand. He knew he was just saying stuff without context, but would this moron take the bait so easily?

"Right!" the man answered. "I am very excited. Very excited indeed."

Yes. Yes, he would.

"Best be on my way." Quincy smiled dryly. "I was supposed to meet a brother in the south anti-chamber, that's the fifth door left and then the second right, right?"

"Just the one right at the end, hehehe!" the bloodied man joked, and Quincy was ready to die inside. "But, ahem, that's correct, yes," the cultist eventually admitted.

Quincy gave a little wave and walked on for a bit before he halted one last time because sheer curiosity stopped him dead in his track. "One more thing, by the way…eh?"

"Larry."

"Larry! One more thing. What the hell was that thing?" Quincy asked. "I've never seen such a strange haunting before."

Larry scoffed. "That's no haunting, lad. That's Magog, second lieutenant to Baal, Lord of the Flies, and a real stinker when it comes to personal hygiene as well, bah!"

"Ah… Thanks," Quincy said, already regretting asking and resisting the urge to ask why Magog was here. Without looking back, he moved on.

To his relief, Quincy did not find any other kind of opposition on his way to the monastery's southern anti-chamber. His eyes flicked around nervously as he grasped for the final door's handle, turned it, and went inside.

The room looked just like it did in his dreams. There were the same drab walls, the same old-time religious paintings, and the same dingy desk with the same nonsensically written essays on pseudo-religion and the occult strewn about. If there was any doubt lingering in his mind that his dreams meant nothing, the significance of this room would dispel them completely. Quincy wandered over to the desk and pulled out the middle drawer on the left-hand side. His eyes grew wide as he gazed upon the shining cross, the Cross of Saint John. Very carefully, he reached pick it up while simultaneously bringing the walkie-talkie he had hidden inside the cultist robe up to his lips.

"I've got it," he quietly mumbled into the device. He gently caressed the gold and silver cross. Quincy was relieved; he had found what they came here for, but he felt as if something was still missing. A sliver of a thought hung somewhere in front of his face, waiting to be uncovered.

The walkie-talkie buzzed back. On the lowest volume setting, Quincy could barely make out Sean's voice on the other end. "Copy that, eyes on the prize. Load it in, Quince, we're ready for you at the rendezvous."

The doubt in Quincy's mind grew larger. Something wasn't right. He lowered the orange hood so his peripheral vision was less obstructed and checked back with his friends. "Any opposition on your end?" he asked.

"We ran into a couple of red hoods earlier, but since we've been laying low for the most part, they had no idea who we were, so they just walked by," Sean answered.

Something in Quincy's head snapped when he heard Sean mention *red hoods*. He suddenly remembered his entire dream vividly. In just about all of the scenarios, he did *not* steal the cross relic from the monastery. Moira and Sean did...every time. Quincy stole the book.

Quincy gasped as he pulled on the bottom right drawer and saw the enormous leather-bound tome laying inside. Golden and maroon letters spelled out *Arklay's Treatise on 'The Void.'* Quincy shook his head.

"No, no, no," he yammered. "This is all wrong."

"Come again? I didn't get that last part." Sean's voice rang through the walkie-talkie much louder this time. Quincy had apparently pushed on the volume button in a stupor upon his revelations.

"This isn't right," he spoke quickly and in a panic. "*You* are supposed to get this thing. *I* should be getting a book. This book right here…" Quincy groaned in frustration. "I can't take them both, but we *need* them both! We don't know what happens if things don't exactly go as I saw… This is all wrong!"

"Quincy, listen to me." It was Moira's voice that came through the device now. "Quincy, remember how you said your father's notes mentioned this cross several times?"

"Yes…" Quincy answered through gritted teeth.

He could hear Moira softly breathing out. "Okay," she went on. "Did his journals ever mention a book? They must, of course, but was it ever a book by the title you have before you, or something that fits its description?"

Quincy sighed with a labored breath. "No," he told her.

"Has everything up to this point been exactly as you remembered in your dream?" Moira went on.

"No," he admitted. "No, there were things that were… different. Also, there are still some black spots I can't quite remember or make out."

"Listen to me very carefully, Quincy. Don't take this the wrong way, but I don't think you can rely on your dreams to take us all the way home anymore. It's good that they help you, help us, but we've got to let go sometime, are you getting this? Am I coming across?"

Quincy's eyes shot from left to right. Was that painting always there? Were there three or four drawers on the left-hand side of the desk? Why hadn't Moira and Sean gone inside earlier to take the cross? Was the cross even inside? "None of this makes sense," Quincy whispered. He started taking off the robes; he was much more comfortable without them. Besides, he was sure he didn't have them on in his dreams. Really sure. "These don't belong," he said angrily as he pulled them off and squeezed the walkie-talkie even tighter.

"Quincy," Sean interjected. The speaker was at full volume now. "Grab the cross and get over here, man. Do not put your faith in what your subconscious tells you. Your own head can tell you lies, man. I've been there, with the Mind-flayer... I..."

A scuffle sounded and then Moira was back on the other side. "You've got to make a choice. But you've got to do it now. We just saw three cultists run by on their way up the hill. Come on, Quincy."

"I– I don't know what to do," Quincy stammered.

The door slammed open with a huge bang and two cultists, large and broad shouldered, stood inside the opening. "Who the hell are you?" one of them groaned.

The other one grinned. Quincy could make out his black and yellowed teeth peeking out just under the hood. "He's fucking *dead*," that one said.

OVER DUNKIRK, *Flanders, Belgium — 5 days, 15 hours, and 38 minutes until the end of the world*

Lilly breathed a sigh of relief. The air was cooler here and a lot less stagnant. The sky was less deep red and more of a pink or lighter shade of indigo. It reminded her of her friend Tim, who would often display a similar color when brought to embarrassment or shyness. The skeletal horses pulling the fiery cart snapped their jaws gleefully whenever Mortimer pulled the reins or cracked the whip; the pain seemed to excite them. The whole contraption shot through the air like a hot knife through butter.

Lilly watched Liz sleeping next to her with her head buried in her lap. She barely made any noise, but Lilly could see clear that her mind was troubled and uneasy. Who could blame her? It was not every day that a doomsday cult working hand in hand with a despicable secret organization came crashing down at your doorstep and you got whisked away on a flaming cart by your friend Mortimer, who not only was the custodian of the realm of wayward souls but Death itself, and thus a horseman of the Apocalypse to boot. An Apocalypse that seemed to be very much happening right now or was at least *well* on its way.

"Ugh, what a mess…" Lilly quietly mumbled. To top it all off, her ears closed up and she was trying the moving the jaw trick to get them to pop, but it wasn't working at all.

"We are almost there," Mortimer said quietly from the front of the bobbing cart. "I know it all seems grim now, but…have faith."

"Faith in what?" Lilly scoffed. "The God-machine?" She peeked over the side of the carriage and gazed down. She couldn't see a lot through the low hanging clouds except for the coastline and some forest and farmland. "What's happening down there now? Like, everywhere?"

"Chaos," Mortimer answered grimly. "But like I said, have faith. We are fighting back. The riders and their power, but also the people, are fighting back. *Your* people, as a matter of fact: monster hunters, paranormal investigators, witches, occultists, and everyone else fits somewhere along those lines."

"A rebellion…" Lilly murmured. "To stop the end of the world… To stop mass extinction."

Mortimer cackled. "That's right. Stop it or die trying, and believe me, I am not ready for that kind of workload," he said with a laugh. "So, rebellion it is."

"An Apocalypse rebellion," Liz said with a smile on her face, still half asleep. "Fucking awesome."

THE MONASTERY OF ST. *John, England — 5 days, 14 hours, and 23 minutes until the end of the world*

Quincy dashed down the flight of stairs with such incredible speed he had to restrain himself and think rationally before he decided not to jump out of a window for an even faster, and more painful getaway.

"Stop right there, *scum!*" The burly but very agile man dressed in red robes ran after him. The man with the yellowed teeth was behind him, screeching in the hallway. Fast and unrelenting, they trailed Quincy by mere inches, grabbing and snatching at his collar with one hand and holding a shining cross in his other. "Drop that cross this instant!" the broad-shouldered cultist yelled. "You have no idea how valuable that is!"

Quincy, panting and sweating, looked behind him and threw a sly smile at the angry face beneath the bright colored robe. "Trust me, shit for brains. There's little to nothing that can faze me anymore. I have died and have experienced rebirthof my frail body and my soul. I have seen the black abyss yawning and churning beneath the wobbling thin thread that separates rational human thought and utter and complete madness." *Wow!* Quincy thought. *I always thought that sounded cool before, but I never expected I'd recite it from the top of my head!* He ran out into the broader, open monastery hallway that over-looked the inner garden. Again, he somehow knew exactly where to go and, despite the growing number of inconsisten-cies, he was on his way in his escape.

The weather was typically English—gray and drab. Quincy looked behind him to see the man with the yellowed teeth losing distance on him. The other one, the gorilla type, wasn't anywhere to be seen. Quincy smirked. Perhaps being big and strong didn't mean you were automatically fit as a fiddle. Or perhaps his words really did resonate with the guy? He always wondered how it would be to just make the most terrible and cursed statements regarding to humanity's survival and the crisis of existentialism. At that moment, Quincy remembered part of his dream and quickly wondered if his words really *did* have some sort of profound impact on the somewhat frailer members of the Esoteric Order of the Final Dawn, but only for a second or two, right before several more cultists appeared in front of him, menacingly waving shining silver daggers toward his face.

"You're out of yer league, boy," one of them spat. "Shoulda stayed across the pond," another one added.

"Ah shit!" Quincy exclaimed before jumping and diving through one of the open arches that lined the right side of the half-open hallway. He landed painfully on his shoulder but managed to roll through most of the impact, a maneuver Lilly once taught him to, in her words, *"You know, not die so quickly."* Not before long, Quincy was back on his feet, adrenaline pumping through his veins. He convinced himself he was still on track. Just a few meters more and he'd be out in the fresh air, into the getaway car and off into the sunset, presumably.

He diagonally crossed the courtyard and was on the other side in a matter of seconds. The bright mass of orange and red-cloaked individuals scampered over the little knee-high wall but with a lot more trouble than Quincy had anticipated. *Right on cue*, he thought, right before he remembered to duck. At that very moment, he saw the glimmer of a mace swinging toward his face. Quincy dashed right and pushed the somewhat clumsy mace-wielding cultist back. Putting all of his weight into it, Quincy managed to knock the guy on his butt. The heavy mace landed right onto the large man's chest as he released a gust of strained breath. The cultist was knocked out cold. Quincy waited a couple of seconds. His eyes darted from left to right. Nothing.

Good, he thought again, and brought the walkie-talkie speaker to his lips. "Okay, I– I understand. I—" He panted, still dashing toward any possible exit. "I took the cross, and I left the book. You were right! I have to trust what Dad left for us, not whatever it is that's affecting me and my dreams." He looked back again. Still nothing. It was as expected, but Quincy still felt relieved. "Did you two run into any trouble?"

"Nothing really," Moira answered quickly. "The guys we told you about earlier were just about the most exciting thing we ran across. We're ready to pick you up at the parallel road next to the Woodland Inn, right on cue." Moira's familiar voice was comforting and filled Quincy with warmth. He felt calmer. "That all right with you, Quince?" she double-checked.

"Sure, I…"

Quincy sped through an apparent servant's corridor and emerged outside on the north-facing side of the old structure. There he found a quiet graveyard full of weathered and overgrown graves and headstones was found, surrounded by a rusty iron fence and thick oak trees. This was not the most peculiar thing, however. Because there was something that instantly shut Quincy up. In the middle of the old graveyard stood a strange man. He was of average height, sported an impressive but finely kept beard, wore peculiar seventeenth century nobleman's clothing and, this is the big one, was literally ripping Final Dawn cultists in half and spreading their viscera all across the yard.

"Come out and fight, do not stand on ceremony in front of *me*, evildoers. You slick orange lapdogs of Satan, you swine of Beelzebub, come forth and face the wrath of your Maker!" The man's face contorted for a moment before speaking again. "BLOOD FOR THE GOD OF DEATH, FACE ME MORTALS AND TREMBLE IN FEAR, YOU KNOW NOTHING!" he yelled, shook his head in confusion and closed his eyes for a bit. "You cannot control me, demon! For the righteous will always prevail."

Quincy looked behind him. There was a distinct lack of any pursuers. In fact, he saw one of the windows above him slam close and heard what sounded like boards being nailed over it from the other side.

"Quince? Are you still there?" the walkie-talkie crackled.

"Oh, no. Oh, crap. It's *you*. I forgot all about you. *You're the one*. The familiar face." Quincy eyed the old timey gentleman up and down. "Well, kind of familiar."

The crazy man's eyes flashed toward Quincy who was sweating profusely. "Who stands before me now? Another pawn of the Antichrist? Perhaps another shadowy denizen of Carcosa in disguise, flaunting itself like a scholarly individual, hmm?" His eyes grew wide. "GO ON, GASH OUT HIS EYES AND HIS TEETH AND HIS... MASTER SWANSONG?"

Quincy gritted his teeth. This was indeed who he thought it was, thus confirming that the world had just officially started to end, because nothing in his wildest dreams except actual prophetic abilities would conjure up such a ridiculous scenario of a living and incredibly dangerous Fire Vampire once again descending upon the Earth. "Yes, Tim. It's me. It's good to see you," Quincy said carefully. "Tim, can you tell me how you got here? And what you are doing here?"

"RIDING THE COATTAILS OF THIS ONE, A MOST PECULIAR ONE I'D S—" The man stuck out his tongue, started blowing raspberries while looking crooked eyed. He then spoke again, only it was in the other voice. "Do not listen to that devil that has attached itself to me and is trying to trick me into using my glory for nothing else but its own nefarious ways. I have returned from very far away, for evil once again walks the land of old Europa, and it is up to me to cleanse it. In the name of our Lord, I am a warrior of God Almighty, and nothing will stand in my way. Jolly good times, old chap, I'd say!"

Quincy suddenly remembered everything, but he had no idea what to say or think about any of this. He looked hard at the pale, somewhat flaky skin. He gazed deep into the cold lifeless pupils that bore into his soul. This man was dead. Or at least he had been. Quincy cleared his throat. "And who...*are* you, exactly?" He presented the question as lightly as possible.

"FEEBLE M— frail youth, how can anyone not recognize the master in front of them, *pip pip*. My name is Matthew Hopkins, Witchfynder General and— HE IS WEAK FLESH AND BONE, MOTTLED I am pleased to make your acquaintance. Will you ride with me, youth AND ONCE

AGAIN BASK IN THE GLORY OF TIMAXOATI-LACILUZIPTA BANE OF THE ANCIENT COSMOS and become my apprentice in banishing evil from this land? AND KILL EVERYONE THAT STANDS IN OUR WAY."

Quincy scratched the back of his head and let out a big sigh. "Oof, well this is very peculiar indeed."

"Quincy? Are you okay?" Sean yelled through the walkie-talkie. "Do you need a pick up? Quince?"

Quincy held the speaker to his lips. "Yeah! I'm fine, I just ran into… Eh, long story I– I um… Say, I don't *feel* so good. How are you?"

Red and pink spots appeared in Quincy's peripheral vision. The world around him was going blurry and it seemed as if, but he wasn't quite certain, that Tim was somehow fading in and out of existence. Well not Tim, *exactly*, but rather the essence of Timaxoatilaciluzipta, or Tim, the Fire Vampire who was currently possessing the decomposing corpse of Matthew Hopkins, a witch hunter from the seventeenth century who decided to just *show up* in the back garden of a British place of worship because he felt like it. And yes, that is one of the weirdest sentences I ever uttered, and I am an immortal space cat. But Quincy started to feel *really* ill at this point. He made the unfortunate mistake of looking down at his own hands to experience the strange sensation of one's own atoms being torn apart to be reconnected and built back from the ground up somewhere else. Something else was happening to the group right at that very moment.

"What is happening?" Moira's voice rang out from the walkie-talkie. "Everything is wobbly and distorted. Is some-thing messing with us? Is– *Hello!* Who is that? Who's talking to me! Sean, where are you? Quincy? Are you there? Quincy! Qu—"

The walkie-talkie dropped to the grass. The churchyard was empty. Quincy and Tim/Matthew Hopkins were already gone. Sean was gone too. And before she could summon a last desperate cry from her vocal cords, they too, along with the rest of Moira's body, was gone. Gone, and shot through time and space to end up exactly where they needed to be at exactly the right time with exactly the right people.

A POPPY FIELD IN FLANDERS, *Belgium – 5 days, 13 hours, and 59 minutes until the end of the world*

The group fell onto the grass at the same time. Lilly and Liz felt a distinct force push them gently out of the carriage, and Moira, Sean, and Quincy appeared from what looked like a miniature black hole that opened three and a half feet above the ground. The possessed body of Matthew Hopkins didn't appear from anywhere but rose up from the taller grass with a profoundly creepy grin on its face. A disturbingly exposed decaying nipple poked through the rotting fabric of the four-hundred-year old colonial garb.

The trio that was hurled across the English Channel with extradimensional speed and accuracy had the worst of it. Quincy was green just everywhere but most of all in his face. He vomited for a few minutes before regaining his composure and assessing their current situation. They were at the threshold of what looked like a small chapel, an abandoned and isolated former place of worship. The chapel stood silently along the edge of a vast wood to the north and a huge open field filled with thousands, if not hundreds of thousands, of poppy flowers to the south. The air was a light shade of orange, and dark clouds gathered all around them, with flashes of pink lightning and the intermittent roar of other-worldly thunder.

However, there was nothing about the strange scene that could prepare Quincy for the next few words that reached his ears.

"Hey bro, how are you?"

Quincy looked and his eyes meet with those of his sister. She smiled wide, tears running off her cheeks and mixing with her make up to create a pink, red and black mess. She buried her head in his shoulder. Her arms reached around him, and she squeezed until it was hard for him to breathe; even so, he did not want her to let go. "You look like shit," she whispered and giggled before finally releasing him.

"What are you doing here? How'd you get here, I—" Quincy saw Liz walking up now as well. "Man, it's good to see you," he told her.

Moira and Sean joined them. "Good to see you all," Sean stammered, appearing very confused. "Can someone tell me what the hell is going on?"

"A very good question," a somewhat familiar voice called out. At least, familiar to Lilly and Quincy, and now Liz as well.

A dark shape, like a pitch-black floating cloak sitting on top of a very thin looking horse, descended from the bright orange and yellow heavens. Another rider followed. This one Moira, Sean, and Quincy knew, for it was the masked warlord on the ferocious steed they had seen earlier at the Brighton marina. The thunderous thump when he landed blew dirt and broken stalks of grass all around him and his horse. Almost as if it was expected, a third rider soon joined them, landing next to the giant warlord. Their horse was even thinner and more sickly looking than the first, and the rider sported a yellow, disgusting looking cape. It looked like a giant scab. They were followed by a horde of flies. Lastly, one more horse arrived. It was just as agile and quick as the ones before it, but it looked terribly famished. The rider accompanying it was crawling with locusts and other insects and smelled of rotten meat.

"Mortimer?" Quincy asked carefully. "What are you doing here? Who are all of you, what is going on?"

The bony apparition beneath the void-black cloak laughed and the white, glistening, ever grinning teeth revealed themselves for a few seconds from underneath the hood. "All in due time, Quincy. We're glad to have you all together now so that we might finally begin."

"Begin what?"

Mortimer chuckled again. "Begin stopping the Apocalypse. That's why we are here, Quincy." A bony hand pointed toward each of the riders individually. "Allow me to introduce Marty, Aila, and Cookie, or as you might better know them from all your fancy religious texts, War, Pestilence, and Famine." Mortimer turned to Moira and Sean. "I believe we haven't had the pleasure. I'm Mortimer, but you might say I'm better known as—"

"Death," Moira gasped. "Mort..."

Mortimer snapped his phalanges. "Like I said...pleasure." He shuffled on top of the skeletal horse and held his large silvery scythe between his arm and torso as he cracked his knuckles. "There's a lot to discuss and a lot to take in, I'm sure. But I'm afraid our time, however infinite it might seem, is quite limited. For now, let the talk on how we're going to not let the heat death of the universe commence."

PART II

Revelations on the End Times

Chapter 6

WHAT A CURSED PLACE.

I mean really. Of the sixty-five plus million years that our spinning blue (but once hot pink) globe has been dangling around in our solar system between the once mighty fortified Elder Race of Mars and the deadly acid storms of grandiose and hidden Venus, it has faced approximately thirty-three thousand, eight hundred and ninety-two world or universe-spanning extinction events. Six-thousand of these had to do with hostile alien races or aberrations hailing from deep space; around seventeen thousand were to blame on that strange power emanating from the center of the universe, bulging and brewing and spewing chaotic energy all the time that can easily rip the fabric of reality in two. The rest are to blame on humanity themselves, sticking their noses into things they have absolutely no business with. Speaking of which...

From the time that time first began, there have been around five hundred and forty-one billion, yes billion, anomalous events that took place on or around Earth. Each of these events had consequences so severe and catastrophic that reality had no choice but to split, resulting in diverging timelines whenever an anomalous occurrence took place.

You may understand that keeping track of all those different realities and diverging dimensional planes is hopeless, so we try to just keep an eye out on our favorites. One of which is this one, the Swansong one. You may wonder why choose this obviously terrifying and doomed reality, I understand. But you need to know things can get far, *far* worse. What they found during the 1969 moon landing over on the 7543.12204.0689 timeline… *Oof*, no, you really do not want to know. And the consequences? Even worse.

Still, our Swansong timeline, up to this point, has played host to about seven hundred and seventy-nine thousand occurrences of what is popularly known as supernatural, paranormal, or anomalous activity. Eighty-one percent of which happened after the so-called Awakening, of course. A rather interesting, dare I say exciting, happenstance that is as rare and convoluted as it is dangerously deadly as well as an immediate threat to society and humankind as we know it. Of the remaining nineteen percent, about half were extinction-level threats that were carefully and meticulously, often at the very last moment, prevented by either an enormously clever human being or group of human beings or, a lot more likely, an outside force willing to spare Earth because they needed the planet for whatever plans they had cooked up. Did you really think a Spider-god from distant and horrid Ckoontk capable of creating a black hole the size of a football stadium would simply *give up* if a couple of pesky humans strode toward it with a semi-automatic and some incense sticks? Because that's exactly what some tried over on the 8102.55682.1190 timeline, and it ended in catastrophe. A literal one. Everyone died. That is to say, it's not like the Gibbous Horde are anything to sneeze at. They are as deadly and extinction driven as the lot of them.

What a horrid, horrid thing. And what a horrid curse.

So why? Why do it? Try to save Earth at all. Why not let the Swansong timeline, the Apocalyptic Swansong timeline, die together with the doomed Earth that inhabits it?

Perhaps because hope is a beautiful thing? Perhaps I have become attached to these peculiar young people, these Swan-songs, in an emotional and spiritual way. Perhaps because however rotten humanity might be, this Earth really *is* worth fighting for, unlike that Earth on which all mammals turned into lawn chairs. Perhaps I just want one last actually good *Highlander* movie.

But what do I know? I am just the spacefaring, prophesizing, bender of time and space and apparent fifth member of the horse(wo)men of the Apocalypse in this timeline. And a cat as well.

A POPPY FIELD IN FLANDERS, *Belgium — 5 days, 11 hours, and 17 minutes until the end of the world*

"Why does that cat keep staring at me?" Lilly whispered to her brother. She leapt off the aged wooden fence surrounding the overgrown chapel garden. A low, menacing rumble in the distance made her ears prick up. "So, that's that then?" She turned toward her friends, but her gaze landed on Mortimer's patient and grinning skull. "Infinite timelines and all that jazz, and we're the one with the lucky lottery number that got us murdered parents, a world with death around every corner, and now the literal end of days with gigantic space alien assholes rising up in every corner of the globe." She cocked her head. "Am I missing something here?"

"Oh, I think you are well on your way." Mortimer's lower jaw clacked hard against the upper one. "I know this news comes sudden, or perhaps not, considering you knew of the Horde for quite a while before we arrived at this point."

"Four months, two weeks, thirteen hours, two minutes and thirty-seven seconds to be exact," Cookie, also known as Famine, chimed in. "No wait, thirty-eight. Oh—nine…forty!"

A low growl from Marty, the horseman of War, made Cookie count out the rest in the silence.

"Anyway," Mortimer continued, the grim visage of skeletal

death still making the group uneasy, even though they knew they probably had nothing to fear from him. "I know for a fact that these revelations of a more cosmic and interdimensional sort will have caught you off guard. Excuse us for the perhaps sudden onset of existential dread you may face…"

"Yeah, no shit." Sean sighed and plucked a poppy from the field at the edge of the road.

Mortimer's eyes flashed bright red. "Please refrain from that," he growled. "As I was saying. My colleagues and I apologize for the onset of any uncomfortableness you may experience. But we assure you, all is not lost. A lot of our solution has to do with that silver relic you hold in your hands right there, Quincy. Good job. We are already well on our way."

Moira cleared her throat. "Please excuse my French, but what the fuck? Up until now you have only revealed two things. One, the Earth or even the universe is always screwed in one way or another, and two, *our* Earth is in the process of making way for the intergalactic highway of ultimate fuckery *right now* and we are sitting here doing what? Waxing philosophically on if the Quincy, Lilly, Moira, Liz, and Sean of this timeline make it or not? This is beyond fucked."

Marty slumped off his horse and gently walked it to one of the trees on the wood's outskirts. He gestured for the other riders to do the same. "You are right that we mostly seem to ponder the current state of the universe rather than be direct about what you can add to the effort of saving it." He glanced toward Mortimer, then to Aila and finally to Cookie. They all nodded in agreement. "Okay." Marty's lumbering shape knelt in front of the five mortals and gave off the slightest 'sort of' smile he could. "Ask." He stared at them. "Ask us anything and we will answer. There is work to do, but you need to be informed. So, ask."

Lilly and Quincy exchanged glances, and so did their friends. They had just a little while to bring each other up to speed, but both groups revealed things that shocked the other. "Okay," Quincy started. "First of all, the Final Dawn cult seems to be in the business of sacrificing a lot of innocent people. Why? We know they aren't technically a part of Haven, but they do seem to be in league with each other, but even Haven has never been this cruel before. What's going on?"

Aila hissed. "You are mistaken. The Final Dawn is Haven through and through. They are just the most zealous and crazed within their ranks that created an offshoot from the main organization. Their goals are the same. They want to annihilate the human race entirely, with only their own to take its place." Aila spat on the ground. "Sinister sacks of meat. They all need to rot."

"As far as the sacrifices go," Marty spoke up. "Things like the ceremony Lilly and Lizbeth saw broadcasted, the entirety of the town of Tenebrae as well as the thresher machine in the Brighton Marina that Quincy, Moira, and Sean witnessed, are ploys to harness the soul energy of the meekest humans— those that have already succumbed to the mind scrambling powers of the slumbering, now awakening, Gibbous Horde."

"Does that mean that the blatant blindness toward supernatural events that we witnessed last year all have to do with the Horde increasing their power over the weaker minded humans?" Lilly asked.

"Correct," Marty confirmed.

Lilly turned toward the others in shock. "They're like lambs…lambs to the slaughter." She was visibly shaken.

"They were smiling and laughing," Moira said, wide eyed. "Laughing…right before that infernal machine ripped them to pieces and colored the waters blood red…"

"These sacrifices give the Horde their power. They have been going on for years," Mortimer added grimly. "I have known for a while…the influx of souls in the Afterlives… Broken souls, incomplete."

"Then why didn't you do anything?" Lilly gasped. "If you have known all along, then all of this could have been prevented!"

Mortimer shook his bones. "I am afraid it is not that easy. We, as a group, can only interfere in a scenario in which the world is threatened on an apocalyptic level. We cannot prevent anything beforehand."

Sean scoffed. "You probably just didn't try hard enough!" He turned to the rest. "We have got to stop them. We can't let them get away with this. We've got to find where they congregate next and strike. We—"

"You cannot!" Cookie yelled. "There is simply no way and there is no time for such trifling matters. You, *you*, my friends, have other parts to play. You can stop them, but only by finding the right tools for the job." She conjured a kind of rolling pin in her left hand and threw it at a nearby tree along the forest's edge. The pin pressed into the wood for a second before falling down, the hole where it had stuck now oozing maple syrup. Cookie grinned.

Quincy looked down at the cross relic in his hands and gripped it tightly. "Which brings us to this, right?"

Mortimer's bleak grinning skull nodded in approval, along with the other three riders. The curious cat blinked understandably as well, much to Quincy's discomfort.

Aila pointed at the cross. "What you are holding is the Holy Cross of St. John. It is one of the *three* relics that will lead to—and be able to open—the Ark of the Covenant."

"Excuse me?" Liz's eyes grew wide. "*The* Ark of the Covenant? Since when did this become a biblical thing?"

Lilly scratched her head. "It's kind of always been one I guess?" She looked over to her brother who nodded in agreement.

"It's kind of a given with the whole four Horsemen and women of the Apocalypse thing and so on," Mortimer added.

"Eh…right. So, Ark of the Covenant." Sean flicked his fingers. "Totally normal, really. We find two more of these things" —he pointed at the cross— "and we open that sucker right up. And what will we find inside? Some old slabs of primitive concrete? The answer to the first and last question ever revealed? Life, the Universe, and everything?"

Quincy couldn't help but chuckle. "I have a suspicion that that's *exactly* what we'll find in there." He looked into Mortimer's darkened dead eye sockets. "It's the Celestians, isn't it?"

Mortimer nodded. "That is correct. Inside the Ark you will find the secret last method of contacting the Ancient Race of Celeste that exists and will ever exist on Earth. They have the technology to destroy the Horde. They are the only ones." The four Horse(wo)men and the cat looked toward the twins and their friends. "The relics must be found," Mortimer pleaded. "It is the only way."

"Well, that sounds simple enough," Sean said sarcastically. "And how long do we have to travel all over the world to find these things and get them back here to open what could very well be Pandora's Box?"

"Very good question," Liz added.

Aila smacked her lips and cracked her knuckles. She appeared to be deep in thought. "Around…five days? Perhaps a bit more?" she said.

Quincy rubbed his temples as his friends let out audible groans of amazement. "Five…*five* days," Quincy groaned. "That's…not a lot of time, is it?"

"We have the means to play with that *a little bit*," Mortimer said. "But we'd rather not. It's very finicky, and it could result in numerous paradoxes. Not recommended. Not at all."

"Unless absolutely necessary. Like with the Cross," Marty added clumsily, to Mortimer's dismay.

Moira's mouth fell open. "That–the lost time… That was *you? You* robbed us? We had two weeks at the minimum, *two weeks!* What the hell?"

"I can't believe this is happening… Why would you ever do that?" Quincy was shocked.

"We're doomed. You doomed us all," Moira added dismayed.

Mortimer shrugged. "Don't be such a Doomer, Miss LaGrande, there was nothing left for us to do. You arrived too early in East Sussex. The Cross was not where it should've been. We needed a quick, albeit I admit a sloppy, solution."

"Oh, this is the gift that keeps on giving," Lilly said.

In the corner of the chapel garden, between the gnarled thorns and the nettle shrubbery, something emerged. It was the strange figure of Matthew Hopkins, awakening from his 'after slaughter nap,' as he liked to call it. The man yawned, and his jaw made a sickly sound as it unhinged. A second yawn pushed the rotten thing back into place. "Ah, what a lovely day. God be praised, He has granted us a long and bright twilight to act out His will against the evil knaves of Hell's deepest crags. Where shall we go ne–*RIP AND TEAR, RIP AND. TEAR. Lovely to see you Mistress Swansong,* I want to *CRUSH A SKULL AND DRINK TO ETERNAL YUGGOTH TONIGHT, Huzzah! Mwuahhahahahahahahha!*"

"Right, I think I'm up." Liz started and gave a weak and less than genuine smile. "So, question number, I dunno, twelve? What the *fuck* is that thing and why is it jittering like that?"

"Matthew Hopkins is actually mine," War admitted and started to pace around the group. "One of the fail-safes I implemented. When the world appears to face imminent destruction, the spirits and corporeal forms of long dead occultists, monster hunters, and slayers of evil-doers will rise up as my generals to lead my armies of undeath into battle against the threat. Hopkins, portrayed in history as a foul name accompanied with the unjust deaths of scores of women tried as witches, suffers from an unfortunate case of mostly being exactly like the stories describe him. Tales of the vile dens of witches and warlocks he sniffed out were conveniently left out of the history books. The man was too eccentric and trigger happy to separate reality from his own cursed fantasies however, which led to his eventual downfall. Nevertheless, he was a fine addition to my armies. The single-handed brute force he showed at the cult hideout is but one example. Best to keep an eye on him, though."

Matthew Hopkins turned his nose up. "Preposterous you might think I am nothing less than the perfect evil-slaying machine, my liege."

"At ease, general. I am just as much a king as you are a literal machine—not at all. So shut your trap and plan your next assault accordingly."

Hopkins's eyes lit up as if tiny fires of orange and indigo were lit just behind the thin film of the vulnerable iris. "HIS BRAIN IS BUT ROTTEN MUSH AND BUGS AND THAT WHITE FLOOF THAT APPEARS WHEN YOUR BREAD IS ONLY A FEW DAYS OLD BUT YOU LEFT IT IN A WARM, HUMID ENVIRONMENT FOR TOO LONG. BETTER YOU HEED LESS THE CALL OF THE ROTTEN ONES BURIED BENEATH YOUR DOOMED EARTH'S SOIL AND YOU HEED THE ADVICE I GIVE TO YOU NOW, AS IMMORTAL KIN OF THE COSMOS."

"That only answers half of our question." Quincy fumbled with some loose change in his coat pocket. He gestured again at the intimidating, yet sad, appearance of the resurrected form of the famed Witchfynder General. "Why is Tim– Let me rephrase that, why is a highly dangerous extraterrestrial entity…"

"A cogni-memetic hazard, as they would say in the Global Defense Force," Lilly added playfully. She winked at the inter-stellar consciousness behind Hopkins' dead eyes. She was happy to 'see' Tim.

"A *Fire Vampire*," Quincy went on, "why is it possessing one your generals, Marty?"

War shrugged. "That I do not know. And frankly, I do not much care either. It's doing good work against the Final Dawn. So, I don't see why I should care."

Mortimer tapped his scythe. "I have a theory," he started as he rubbed his phalange-bones against the cool steel of the scythe. "Perhaps whenever he arrived on the planet, he was automatically drawn to a soul with more conviction on pursuing their goal than anyone else."

"More conviction than *us*?" Moira asked, slightly insulted. "Why would any of us, especially Quincy and Lilly who *came back from the dead*, have less conviction than that thing?"

"Well, to start, your hearts are a lot purer and thus harder to possess, I imagine." Mortimer pulled his cloak a bit tighter. "Also, I doubt your goals align, but the process differs. Unless you also try to fight evil by meticulously ripping the head off of anyone even *close* to just *thinking* about summoning something bad into the world."

"I guess he's right," Sean told Moira. "Even though the thought once went through my mind with those fucked up agents that tortured the hell out of me, that just isn't us."

The shuffling figure of Matthew Hopkins slowly inched its way forward into the sort of semi-circle that had unconsciously formed as all of the individuals talked about stopping the end of the world. "Why don't you…" Hopkins's eyes narrowed. "Why don't you ask him yourseeeeellaaaaaah! IT'S NOT HARD TO IMAGINE. I ONCE OWED MASTER AND MISTRESS SWANSONG A BOON FOR FREEING ME FROM THAT ACCURSED PRISON OF ETERNAL TORMENT THAT BALD TOAD PUT ME IN."

"You mean Aleister Crowley, right?" Lilly fished for confirmation.

"FUCK *ALEISTER CROWLEY*," Tim went on. "*EITHER WAY, THE BOON HAD BEEN REPAID WHEN THE GOD-IN-THE-MACHINE LIVED ONCE MORE. THE PROTECTION YOUR PUNY LITTLE PLANET ENJOYED WAS BACK, AND BEFORE I WAS STUCK IN THIS MISERABLE HELL FOREVER, I SLIPPED THROUGH THE CRACKS AND WENT BACK INTO THE ETERNAL BLACK VOID OF ENDLESS SPACE. OH, HOW I ENJOYED THOSE TIMES.*"

Quincy scratched the stubble on his chin. "Tim, you sound kind of depressed. What happened?"

"WHAT IS THIS THING, DEPRESSED? I WAS MERELY DISDAINED BY THE FACT THAT WHEN I NOTICED THE BARRIER FADING AWAY AGAIN, THAT MY WORK HAD BEEN UNDONE."

Lilly gasped. "Oh no! Are we vulnerable again?"

"A RATHER LARGE SPECIMEN OF THE GIBBOUS HORDE LAY SLEEPING RIGHT BENEATH THE CELESTIAN CITY IN ANTARCTICA. IT DESTROYED EVERYTHING. I COULD NOT STAND THAT EVERYTHING WE… UH I HAD BEEN WORKING SO HARD FOR WAS SQUANDERED. SO, HEHEHEHEHE, I CAME BACK. FOR VENGEANCE…"

"And because you like us, don't you?" Lilly giggled. "Go on, admit it, you couldn't bear to see your favorite human flesh bag twins die without putting up a fight yourself."

Tim growled. *"I SHALL NEVER ADMIT WEAKNESS. I AM THE ETERNAL FLAME OF CTHUGHA MADE SENTIENT, I AM THE THOUSAND YOUNG WRAPPED INTO ONE, I AM THE VOID, THE IMMORTAL TERROR. I RETURN WHEN YOU LEAST EXPECT IT, IN A FORM YOU WOULD HAVE NEVER GUESSED. I AM THE BEGINNING AND THE END. THE FATE WORSE THAN DEATH. I AM TIMAXOATILACILUZIPTA AND THIS WORLD IS MINE! MUAHAHAHAHAHAHAHAAAA!"*

Even Quincy couldn't hold back his smile. "There we go. That's the Tim we all know and love."

"This is a lot weirder than you two described it," Moira told him.

Liz nodded. "Uh huh, a lot."

The group watched the jittering form of Matthew Hopkins, walking as unnaturally and alien as it could, head back to its patch between the dirt and vines in the chapel garden, plop down, and begin to snore loudly.

Lilly twirled one of her curls. "Oh, how I envy some of my alternative timeline selves who would still consider that the absolute weirdest thing she ever saw."

"*Now* you're thinking infinite-dimensionally! Good job!" Aila told her.

Quincy looked around the semi-circle. "Okay. So now that we're literally doing the whole council of Elrond in Rivendell thing here, what with the exposition and the discussion on how we're going to beat the big evil guys against all odds—"

Liz laughed. "Nerd," she whispered to Lilly, and they both giggled.

Quincy ignored the playful jab. "Before we discuss our next task, I've got one last question of my own."

"Go ahead." Cookie smiled slyly, and the rest of the riders followed.

Quincy rubbed his eyes and took a few deep breaths. "These dreams, these supposed prophetic dreams, they're killing me. Almost literally. I can't sleep for more than an hour at a time, and it's slowly driving me mad. What do they mean? Please, help me to understand what they mean."

"Cursed child of the Swansong bloodline, listen very carefully to me now. Set your face upon my horrid façade and feast your eyes upon those of my sister and brethren," Cookie started. Her bright green, deep sunken eyes grew wide and serious. She took two steps forward. Quincy stood frozen in place. "Do not heed the call of the dreams, not now, not ever."

"You have experienced firsthand the terror that one Gibbous Being can bring with it. The thing known as Mother manipulated your minds and showed you things that did not actually exist or poisoned your mind with memories of things that never really happened," Mortimer addressed Quincy and Lilly. "Merely *one* of them almost led to your ultimate demise, and it would have if not for Miss LaGrande here."

"Do *not* trust the things they show you!" Aila wailed. "Think back on how the Mother thing took everything from you, now imagine that thirteen-fold. All centered around *you*, Quincy Swansong, all centered around you."

"Why me! Why is it always one of us?" Quincy let out. Feeling defeated, he dropped his head.

Marty stepped forward and pulled Quincy's chin up. "Because they know you have the power to call upon the Ancient Race of Celeste and stop them. You five aren't just unlucky bystanders caught in a net. Collectively, you have the power to stop them."

"Compassion, the power of benevolent arcana, and control over the occult…" Aila looked at, and nodded, toward Liz and Moira.

"Grand cognitive resistance and sheer force of will…" Cookie winked at Sean.

"Brilliant minds, persevering strength, and the power to overcome any and all odds." Mortimer faced Lilly and Quincy and grinned. Which kind of always happened considering he had no skin or lips.

Marty smiled. "The only thing they fear is you."

Sean clenched his fist in anticipation. "That's freaking bad ass."

"I did not come up with it," Marty admitted. "But I could not wait until I could use that line."

Quincy watched the sun slowly set. The bright orange ball of flame sank behind a distant hill on which five lonely trees stood in tranquil silence. In the distance, the deep red sky flickered now and again. Quincy swore that on more than one occasion a deep shadow could be seen behind the clouds on the far horizon. It was vague and unclear, but it might just be the end times catching up with them. "I will try to pay no heed to what my dreams show me," he sighed, still gazing off toward the distance. "They helped show me the way before, but I realize they could have been a trap. It was actually you, War… Marty who *actually* showed us the way. You gave us an actual location."

"That's right," Marty acknowledged.

Lilly smiled weakly. She saw hope creeping back onto her brother's face. She hadn't seen hope in him for a long time. It started when they saw each other again here in the Flanders poppy fields but more returned now. "So, what's next on the agenda?" She looked at Mortimer and Marty, then to Aila and Cookie, and finally to the cat who was still present, sitting on the little wooden windowsill of the chapel.

"You cannot face the Horde headfirst, of course. For you would surely perish," Cookie told her.

Mortimer clacked his jaws. "And this time it would be permanent," he added.

"Yeah, we got that from all of the messed-up things we heard about and already saw… So, we take the fight to the cult?" Sean asked.

Liz shook her head. "No, we've got to find the last two keys to the Ark of the Covenant. It's the only way to get an interplanetary beacon running so the Ancient Race can come and sweep all of the Gibbous Horde off the planet." She laughed at herself. "Now, there's a sentence I never dreamed of saying in a million years."

Marty walked toward the flaming stallion tied to a tree near the forest edge and patted it gently. "You are both correct, I think," he told Sean and Liz. "Finding the next relic will require you to do what you do best. Going back to the basics."

"The basics?" Moira asked.

Cookie rubbed her hands together. "The next relic is actually very close. It is a chalice with a mossy emerald stone embedded in the bottom. It's in a shrine deep within the Sonian woods, the forest that stretches out right in front of us."

"Lucky! So, what's the catch?" Liz asked.

"The catch, as you rightfully surmised, is that the Haven woman known as Agent Black, together with her subordinates and her Final Dawn comrade Brother Azael, are scouring the woods for it as we speak," Cookie told them.

Sean nodded along with the words. "Hmm hmm, okay okay. That's doable. Anything else we should know?"

Aila raised her hand. "Perhaps it is wise to know that an

extremely dangerous malevolent entity called Deogen, also known as Old Red Eyes, stalks the woods and is famous for being the perpetrator of multiple deaths, as well as numerous disappearances and people returning disorientated and in states of panic."

Moira whistled. "Now there's a catch and a half! I like this whole studying ancient and evil supernatural entities thing we've got going on, just too bad the situation's always so dire." She winked at Liz, who also recalled their run in with a primordial hag not too long ago in New Orleans.

"Following clues to find an important item within hostile territory while escaping the clutches of evil organizations and supernatural threats." Lilly smiled widely. She nudged her brother.

"The basics," Quincy agreed.

Liz raised an eyebrow. "You make it all sound so easy. I'm sure nothing bad will happen at all," she added sarcastically. "No, but seriously. Regarding the world ending scenarios playing out everywhere else, I'll take my Blair Witch hike into the woods. I'm ready."

"Alright," Marty told them. "I'm glad we've got that sorted. Now we can begin working on a strategy." He breathed in extravagantly. "*Hopkins*! Wake up and start setting up the table! We're going to talk guerilla tactics!"

The peculiar stinking corpse of Matthew Hopkins flew up once again. He saluted Marty and headed into the chapel, slamming the door closed behind him.

Sean cracked his knuckles. "Alright, let's do this."

"Hey, can I ask one last thing before everyone starts making preparations?" Lilly pulled Mortimer's cloak as he turned toward the chapel with the others.

He turned to her and lowered his head. "Of course. What is it?"

"I can't shake the question of why. If the timelines are infinite and we are just a speck of dust amidst a desert of different worlds, then why? Why all of this trouble for one version of an infinite amount of the same thing?"

"That's because this timeline…" Mortimer watched the cat leap off the window and disappear into the shrubbery from the corner of his eye socket. "This timeline is the original."

Chapter 7

*A poppy field in Flanders, Belgium – 5 days, 9 hours, and
49 minutes until the end of the world*

QUINCY SAT on the crooked fence and lightly tapped his heel on the post beneath him. He watched the others gather supplies and discuss possible approaches for surveying the forest and getting to their destination as quickly as possible before Haven, Final Dawn, or Old Red Eyes got a chance to respond. Peering over the field of endless poppy flowers in front of him, he watched the horizon stretch out across the hills in the distance. In his mind's eye, he could see and feel the grotesque, world-ending horrors lavish in the fresh blood and tears of innocents. Emotions ranging from melancholic, suicidal depression to absolute seething rage whirled through him. But try as he might, he simply could not get the images out. It was as if he had a 24/7 live feed of the most disturbing and horrifying show imaginable running through his head. Closing his eyes would only make it worse. The poppies were a nice distraction though. As was the idea that the end of the world might be the best for everyone involved. But he tried to dismiss those particular thoughts. He was shocked to even entertain the idea, and he knew Lilly would absolutely scold him for it. Speaking of which…

"Fancy meeting you here," she told him and hopped onto the fence, joining him. Lilly scooted closer to him and smiled. However, it was not her usual happy-go-lucky smile, the optimistic and fun-loving expression of someone who always tries to pull the best out of people. It was a smile that held sadness and regret. She made an empathetic gesture that said, 'I am sorry to hear everything in your life is terrible, but rest assured so is everything in mine.'

"If there ever was a more fitting setting for the reunion of the 'famed' Swansong twins than the literal Apocalypse then I doubt I'd want to hear about it," she continued.

Quincy chuckled. "How are you, sis? I've missed you."

"Well everything is fine and dandy in the land of getting kicked out of your home by the community of a quaint little town you and your girlfriend fell in love with because the entire town was basically *Truman Show*-ing us from the start, getting swept up by *Death* himself, and answering the age-old call of *saving* the world at the *end* of the world… So yeah, absolutely wonderful." However bad the situation, Quincy still recognized the slight sparkle of mischief in Lilly's eyes that was always there. "And I've missed you too, you big oaf!" She playfully punched him on the arm. "I truly have, Quince…" she reassured him.

"I heard about that business up in the northwest." He nodded. "I'm sorry that happened to you two. I truly am. More than anything in the world I wish I could have solved this entire mess on my own without bringing anyone else into the fray. But it seems forces beyond our control won't let me do that."

Lilly shook her head. "Don't be. Sorry, I mean. There was nothing you could do. If anything, I can't help but be overjoyed to see you here safe and sound. I was worried sick, day in and day out. When it comes down to it, I cannot imagine saving the world without you, bro. Or dying trying, for that matter." She laughed.

"I'm sorry for being so mad, and not understanding that your lot in life and mine are not one and the same forever."

"Quincy…"

"Even though we went through hell and back together, I was an absolute idiot thinking you'd follow me to the ends of the earth for a slight chance of overcoming this terrifying evil. Especially after what we went through before. Especially now that— I mean, you don't deserve any of this." Quincy slurred his last words, as if he was trailing off into sleep, or somewhere else, somewhere horrible. He thought again of the flashes of horrifying things presenting themselves to him. He hoped they were just that, images, and not some terrible live feed of horrid things happening across the world.

Lilly waved her hand in front of his face, snapping him somewhat back to reality. "You know *you* don't deserve this either, right?" She shuffled uncomfortably back and forth on the fence. "None of us do. But however the cookie crumbles…" Lilly looked up at Famine leaning against a tree in the distance who turned around at the sound of her nickname. "Just a figure of speech," Lilly reassured her and waved, then turned her attention back to Quincy. "*Wow*, she's got good hearing. Anyway. Whatever happens, we're here now, and even though there was an ocean between us, it still wasn't far enough for this crap to leave us alone. So, we're here. We might as well try to fix it."

Quincy looked surprised. He had not expected this to come from Lilly. She had determination in the face of odds tremendously out of their league. Even though he could feel the tiredness and anger radiating from her, he felt inspired. "You mean that?" he asked her.

"Yeah, of course," she said. "But rest assured that once all of this is over, and if by some grand miracle we're still standing, then I'm out. Actually out. For life. I mean it." She laughed.

"You and me both," he told her with a smile. "I'm *so* done with this."

Lilly's lips curled into another smile. "Say, I have what might be a strange question."

"It's getting stale to say, but I don't think there's much left that can surprise me. What's up?"

"Is a part of you also really glad that Tim's back?" she asked carefully. She wasn't quite sure what Quincy's first reaction had been, if there was one at all, at the presence of their old 'friend.'

"Yeah, it's the strangest thing, isn't it?" he answered, much to Lilly's relief. "It's like having your old homicidal uncle who only visits like once every three or four years stop by. Like he scares the hell out of you, but you're still *kind of* enjoying his company?"

Lilly laughed. "Exactly like that!" But then Lilly's face turned grim. "Well," she started, "the end of the world, huh? Even though we've been on the brink for years, I always hoped things would work out, just like they always have." She looked puzzled. "Or is that just wishful thinking, luck, whatever you'd want to call it?"

"I don't know," Quincy muttered. "A few months ago, we were all full of life, energy, and whatnot. Me, Sean, Moira. We felt like we could take on the world and anything it would throw at us." He glanced sideways toward Sean and Moira. "Look at them now. Dead tired and afraid, not knowing that anytime I wake up from whatever night terrors that decided to plague me, I can see them shivering in their beds just as much as I do. *They* really don't deserve any of this. They could have left everything alone. Sean leaving forever after Lafayette, Moira fading into quiet obscurity after her forced Haven partnership. Yet they decided to put themselves right into harm's way. Why?"

Lilly watched Sean attempting to have a conversation with Tim, inhabiting the undead body of the witch hunter, and couldn't help but laugh. "It's because they have good hearts," she told Quincy. "It's that simple. They help us, stay with us through thick and thin because they see merit in helping people when no one else can." She looked at Liz sitting next to Moira, cradling her scratched up and bruised arm. Little by little the wounds closed and the skin returned to its natural brown glow. "It's kinship. They say we can't choose our family, but I think all of us did. Look at Sean, an orphan who once enrolled into the GDF because he literally had nothing left to lose. Moira defied the black magic roots of her family, which resulted in their pursuit and vilification. Liz's family…" Lilly took a deep breath. "She lost everyone in the first year after the Awakening. The Night Lights gave her a new place and new meaning. And now she's still here, with us. Not just because I love her, but because she believes in what you do, in what *we* do."

"Kinship…" Quincy whispered. "It used to be just the two of us… The last Swansongs against the entire world. Figuratively and literally," he said with a laugh. "And now——"

"And now you roped in three suckers to go down in flames with you two until the very end," Sean said as he walked up and laughed. "Just kidding. But either way, I couldn't help but overhear what Lilly said, and she's right." Sean sighed. "I signed up for the army because I didn't belong anywhere else, and I had nowhere to go. Even in the force, I never clicked with anyone else beyond supporting them in the line of duty. Plus, anyone I ever remotely started liking died soon enough. Before I met you guys, my best *friend*, if you can call him that, was an old creepy dude called Uncle Scooter I met on a bus on my way to New Orleans. Subsequently, as you know, *he* died too. Huh, maybe you guys would be better off without me." He grinned. "Seriously though, I value your friendship more than anything I have left here; I'd follow you to the ends of the earth. Or the Earth's end. Depending on where we're going, I'm very curious to find out what comes first."

Red lightning flashed in the distance. The thunder that followed was louder and stranger than any kind of thunderstorm any of them had ever experienced. It sounded like an unearthly roar, as if something awoke far and deep within the outer reaches of the cosmos. "I have my suspicions though." Sean grimaced and pulled the duffel bag over his shoulder.

During the conversation, Moira and Liz had quietly joined and listened. Now they too saw a chance to speak up.

"I don't want to make a whole thing out of this," Moira said, "but yeah, I heard you too, Lilly. Thanks to you two, I feel like there's some kind of meaning, some kind of strain of normalcy and reason in my life. You did not choose to judge me and condemn me because of mistakes I made and the things my family roped me into. For that, I'll always be thankful."

"I'm just happy I found someone just as weird and floaty as me." Liz laughed and squeezed Lilly's arm. Liz knew there was a lot more she wanted to say, but for now it felt best to just leave it at that.

Quincy scratched behind an ear and looked surprised; he felt a distinct sense of relief. Even though they had always been there, some sort of veil had been lifted, and he knew he was less alone. "So, all of you?"

"It's a fool's errand, but it should be fun." Sean nodded.

"I'd never give up without a fight," Liz told him.

Lilly grasped Quincy's hand. "Whatever it is you saw, whatever it is, we'll face it together at the very end. We'll be here with you."

Moira smiled warmly. "Are you ready?"

"Yes," Quincy told them. "Yes, I think I am."

MISKATONIC UNIVERSITY, *Arkham, MA, United States – 25-ish years until the end of the world*

"It is said that cats have some sort of profound outlook on existentialism, Tobias. Their role in history…the occult, spirituality, ancient religion. Extremely interesting, wouldn't you think?"

The cat plopped off William's lap and tip-toed calmly out of the hotel lounge and into the dark and stormy Arkham night. Emily smiled as she watched it go.

The room was dimly lit but fairly cozy. A nice sofa, some very comfortable chairs, and a couple of fine oaken tables on which to place one's drink filled the room. The rain softly clattered on the windows.

Tobias sat up straight. "You still haven't told me…us rather, why you stopped teaching at the university, William. Something the matter? Finally retired? Or is it your health, perhaps?"

"Oh no, nothing so serious," William countered. "No, I struck a rather luxurious deal with a publisher right here in Arkham. Although I've been told they'll be moving down to Boston soon. My short stories are going to be printed and sold in three separate bundles which will be released about one year from now."

Emily's eyes narrowed. "That old dribble you used to write for those pulp magazines in the '20s and '30s?"

William chuckled. "Call it whatever you want. I know I might have never achieved peak literary genius, but I always felt I put my heart and soul into those stories. It's what elevates them, I think."

"Elevates them into what?" Tobias smirked as he lifted the wine glass to his lips.

The light of the candle cast eerie shadows on William's face as he crept closer to it. "Into something *more* than simply stories, Tobias. You should know more than anyone that to ponder existentialism is to ponder *all* of the possibilities, however frightening they may be."

Emily stood up, softly caressing her belly. "And you think your stories are the perfect way to convey those philosophical questions?" She raised an eyebrow. "You are a scholar, William, why not write an actual book on the subject? Something more scientific, peer reviewed, something less fiction?"

"Pah, Emily. I am afraid you lack understanding of the

more careful nuances that come with the academic fields in this day and age."

"Oh really?" Emily replied. She tried hiding her grin. She enjoyed the occasional back and forth with William, and even though she would never admit it to his face, she admired his tenacity on the subject.

"Without sufficient proof, I would be heralded as a phony and ridiculed. No college would have me lecture ever again. The pulp tales are more subtle. They are as amusing to the casual reader as they are food for thought and research for the other. Perhaps in another time, another day and age, the wonderfully dark things that I see in the universe will be made manifest so everyone can see. I can only dream."

"And so can I." Emily smiled and made an attempt at a gallant bow. She groaned as she lifted herself up, which made her laugh. "Off to dreamland for me. All this extra weight and food to eat makes my bones creak. Good night."

Tobias watched his wife disappear from view. He smiled. She had that pregnancy 'glow' he heard so much about. It was the warm smile and expectant eyes of a mother to be. A great mother, he thought.

"Of course, keeping in mind that the Leng Plateau actually *exists* in Antarctica, we can…" William had started up on one of his wilder theories. *The Ancient Aliens Sleeping on Earth* theory, he called it. Tobias was only half listening. He hadn't quite realized that while Emily said her goodbyes for the night that William had continued ranting about his research and beliefs. Research and, sort of, beliefs Tobias shared to a certain extent. Still, Tobias felt William could sometimes go on and on about the same subject, often a boring one, without much regard for potential listeners.

"Of course, with modern satellite technology we can almost certainly say that the government is covering up *something*, same goes for the Russians by the way." William droned. He didn't notice Tobias's lack of any real attention.

Perhaps it was this that led to the decline in attendees at

William's lectures while he still taught at Miskatonic University, Tobias wondered.

"...Energy readings right here in Arkham, but for that matter..." William went on.

Tobias snapped out of his own thoughts and his ears pricked up now. "Excuse me, what? What was that, William?"

William scoffed, apparently annoyed at Tobias's lack of attention. "Like I said," he continued. "A call came from the museum that the tablets are somehow responding to strange energy readings coming from right here in Arkham."

Tobias's eyes lit up. "Very interesting indeed. Any idea where the readings are coming from? I take it we've got the geology department on this?"

William nodded.

"And? What did they say?" Tobias had a hard time holding in his enthusiasm. In contrast to William, he shared less of the appreciation for vague stories and make believe and was drawn to actual physical evidence. And thus, whenever such evidence presented itself, especially on a platter ready to be dug into like it did now, Tobias could hardly contain himself.

"Do you know that old boarding house on the corner of Parsonage and Pickman?" William said with a smug smile, already knowing the answer. Despite his preference for the scientific method, it was hard for Tobias to forget his favorite stories of old.

"Do you mean..." Tobias stammered. "The Witch-house? *The* Witch-house, from *The Dreams in the Witch-house*?"

"By old Howard Lovecraft himself, yes." William grinned, satisfied. "That, and also the small island in the Miskatonic east of the first bridge."

"Where the death lights dwell..." Tobias didn't know what hit him. Here was William telling him only one, but two infamous Arkham hotspots for supposed supernatural activity. Both of which had little to do with each other, but both of which simultaneously drew the attention of just about every earth-scientist and occultist alike in all of Arkham. And what of the tablets? It was a mystery too juicy not to pursue. In fact, for Tobias it was personal. For a man who dedicated his life to pursuits of science, the attraction of the paranormal always drew him in, but it also tore him apart; his rational mind could not make heads or tails of the wild tales he so desperately wanted to believe. He knew Emily was the same way, perhaps even more so than himself. Was this their chance? A chance to experience *something*?

"This is your chance," William echoed as if he could read Tobias's mind. "Now, go and sleep. We've got a long day ahead."

Chapter 8

The Sonian Woods, Flanders, Belgium - 5 days, 4 hours, and 11 minutes until the end of the world

A FEW HOURS of rest was all the group could afford before they had to leave. Whatever the real reason the four horse(wo)men had for speeding up the flow of time to this moment was something to bring up later, Quincy thought. Even though it supposedly helped them, it had still taken nearly two weeks of their lives; time had just disappeared into the ether. When you acknowledged that time was even more precious with everything going on, he couldn't help but feel robbed. Then again, he was robbed of a normal life from the get-go, wasn't he?

If there was one thing Quincy *was* thankful for, however, it was that the past four or so hours of sleep he had were mercifully dreamless. In fact, he could not recount the last time he slept *so* well. Perhaps it was the intervention of their newfound 'friends' that gave him some much-needed relief, or maybe it was the sacred ground of the poppy fields and the small chapel, the last bastion of humankind's design and influence on the world in the eye of an all-devouring apocalypse.

Perhaps it was just dumb luck. Whatever it was, he was thankful and glad. Those four hours of nothing gave him back more energy than he could ever ask for, and he felt empowered and driven to find whatever they needed to find here as quickly as possible so they could hurry on back and end this living nightmare for better or for worse.

At the cusp of the end of the world, the group stood in a vast wilderness that was as old as the world's beginning. With every gust of wind, the ancient trees creaked and groaned. Leaves lay across the entire bed of earth beneath their feet. With each step they took, the underbrush rustled as if awoken from slumber, for they had been there for as long as they could remember, until they too would fade into nothing. Life, all kinds of life, stirred between the ancient bark and emerald-green moss. Even now in the twilight years of the Earth, owls hooted, mice squeaked and scurried between the broken twigs, frogs croaked and insects, well, insects had their own world entirely. Beneath every stone or log and in between every bush and reed was an ecosystem all on its own, blissfully unaware of what was going on outside of it.

Liz was enamored with the place. Her attunement to nature and the white life magic made the Sonian Woods, a primordial place strongly emanating the deep, dark wilderness, a true temple. However, she also felt uneasy because she remembered her conversations with Moira on the so-called *old world*. No matter how strange and terrifying American folklore was, many of the tales stemmed from the 1600s or 1700s at the earliest, this forest was much older. Even counting the tales of indigenous people, their true origins difficult to place, it wasn't much further back than a thousand years. But Europe was different. For centuries it was seen as the center of the world, the universe even. There were tales hailing from Europe that went back as far as time immemorial. There were tales of entire civilizations thriving there before mankind was so much as a passing thought. The tales Quincy and Lilly told confirmed that. The stories of the Ancient Celestians made the entire adventure even more frightening. In this spectrum of the waking world, everything felt darker in this old country. Even the trees and the woods itself. The old hag Liz and Moira had fought in the New Orleans library was merely a taste of what secrets could be uncovered here. The question was, why would they want to do that? And what would happen if they did?

The wobbly bag of green meat and bones that once resembled a pilgrim of old turned witch-hunter started to shamble next to Liz. His gaze was intrusive, for as much as she could gather from staring into the cold dead eyes of what should have been and should have stayed a corpse. "There is something about you, girl..." His jaw clicked as he spoke. "God has granted me the power, and the task, to rid the world of the evildoers of Satan. I smell it on you... Brimstone and sulfur... Are you perhaps..." —he took a deep whiff— "a *witch?*" Hopkins's eyes grew large and there was a spark behind those age-old stony marbles.

Liz shrugged and with one quick motion shot out her hand and grabbed zombie-Hopkins's nose. Pulling hard, she separated the rotting flesh from its brittle skull with ease and tossed the gross, lumpy thing on the ground. "I don't smell anything, do you?" She frowned at Moira, who played along and threw up her hands.

"Only moss and damp swamp. Feels a bit like home," she told Liz and winked.

Liz turned back to the thing that was once a man and pushed him in the chest, which almost made him lose his balance. "I suggest you *smell again*," she insisted angrily.

"HEY," an obvious Tim answered from behind the dead glassy eyes. "HOW DARE YOU DAMAGE THE VESSEL FOR WHICH I AM SO GRATEFUL TO HAVE DESIG-NATED FOR ME, AN OUTSIDER OF YOUR PUNY WATER WORLD? WHO ARE YOU TO DEFY ME? THE GLORIOUS, THE ETERNAL, THE..."

"...the absolute forever doomed puny Fire Vampire if you

ever so much as speak to Liz that way again," Lilly answered as she butted in from the back. "Don't think me and Quincy haven't done our research, Tim. We *know* how to bind a Fire Vampire now, and you can be sure we'll do so easily if you even so much as think of harassing our friends. We'll find a nice pocket watch or chamber lamp for you to eke out a miserable existence for all eternity, no fail-safe. How does that sound for you? Hm?"

"BUT," Tim stammered.

"No buts," Lilly responded firmly. "As of now, you either behave yourself, and you keep that disgusting thing you inhabit in linel, or you'll have to face *my* wrath and Quincy's. And I'm telling you he's grown awfully fond of that old oil lamp you used to live in."

The Matthew Hopkins thing's jaw dropped, and it shuddered. "NO!" Tim yelled. "ANYTHING BUT THAT!"

"Didn't that thing sink into the—" Sean started but was silenced with a quick jab in the ribs by Quincy. "Right," Sean wheezed. "Always loved that lamp."

"A-AGREED," Tim stuttered. "I AM SORRY… MISTRESS BORDEN, MISTRESS LAGRANDE, MASTER COOPER."

"Oh, this is rich," Liz told Lilly. "Thanks, but you didn't have to stick up for me, I can handle annoying men just fine." She chuckled.

"And I am somewhat an expert in the resurrected dead," added Moira happily.

"Oh, one hundred percent absolutely!" Lilly told them. "But look at it this way, you are now the proud co-owners of a being so horrible that if he ever got loose who knows what kind of havoc he could wreak on poor unsuspecting bystanders. Isn't that fun?"

Liz smiled. "Glorious."

But Liz's smile soon turned into a frown. She looked past her friends toward the darker bank of the little river they were following deeper into the woods. She had started to see figures staring at them from behind the thicker trees. Some were merely dark shapes, outlines of something vaguely human. Others were unmistakably human-like in appearance. They never got closer. They were always just there. Watching from a distance.

"I see them," Moira whispered to her. "They've been there for a while, coming in and out of sight ever since we entered the woods. I do not know what to make of it. My guess is they are merely spirits, souls of the departed that still echo through these ancient woods like an old tape player constantly rewinding itself, or a radio broadcast that was once sent out into the ether and endlessly repeats forever."

"They do not appear malevolent," Sean said. "But I've got to say, the staring creeps me the hell out." He pointed to a cluster of lights not far from the riverbank where they stood. "You see those will-o-the-wisps? I heard the stories, the legends and what not. So long as we're not obviously following them into whatever trap they might've laid out for us, we should be fine. But those things staring… I don't know what to make of it."

"Perhaps they are the images fading in and out of existence of people just like us, but in different dimensions or timelines. Perhaps they see us the same way we do them, and they are scared, but just as fascinated by what they see before them," Liz wondered aloud. "Ever heard of that one?"

"I've read some research on the subject." Quincy nodded. "Quite a fascinating subject, really. They remind me more of the legend of the Dark Watchers. Figures atop high mountains or hills watching down and keeping an eye on travelers. Keeping them out of trouble, you know? Perhaps we've stumbled on their European equivalent. Who knows."

Sean sighed. "As long as they keep their distance, I'm good. This place is something else. This stuff about whatever malevolent entity should be roaming about this place has got my hair on end. *Old Red Eyes*—it sounds so simple, yet so eerie. Anyone seen anything fitting its description yet?"

Lilly looked toward what appeared to be an abandoned camp site just up ahead. "No…not yet but…" She nudged Quincy and Liz. "What's that over there? Appears to be… Yeah, it's human made, surely?"

The remains of a fire were still smoldering inside a small circle of stones. The wood was still smoking, and the group could see embers glowing between the blackened logs. Next to it were a couple of flat spots in the grass, indicating that a tent or at the very least a couple of air mattresses had been laid on the ground for a while.

Sean looked about. "This is fresh, very fresh. Haven must be close. Agent Black and whatever his freaky cult name is shouldn't be far. Including a couple of those goons they no doubt took with them."

"Hey, over here," Moira shouted from nearby. She stood next to a rock at the riverbank, the rock splattered with blood and bits of fleshy tissue.

Liz and Quincy cringed as they got closer. At the base of the rock, they could see a white light emanating from the loose dirt.

Sean dug in to reveal a quietly beeping device. "Some sort of GPS tracker maybe or, hmm." He tapped on the little three-inch screen for a few seconds. There was a message displayed which said: *Audio-Visual Transcript successfully delivered. Click here to review your file and our additional findings.* "The Haven team sent some kind of status update to their HQ or something," Sean muttered.

"That could be interesting and helpful," Quincy told him. "Can we check it out?"

Sean scrolled through the word-processing feed. "Yeah, yeah…" he said absentmindedly. "I mean, it's probably mostly dull transcription from what appears to be a head mounted camera but let's see…"

The rest of the group gathered around him as they started to read the transcription together.

. . .

TEAM: *ST-004 consisting of Agent Devon, Agent Nightingale, Agent Peterson and led by Agent Black. Add: Brother Azael of the Final Dawn*

Date and Location: 05/16/13, Sonian Woods, Belgium

Primary Mission: Extract relic from destination before Class-09 Wanted Subjects reach it.

Secondary Mission: Neutralize Class-09 Wanted Subjects: Swansong, Q.S; Swansong, L.E; Cooper, S; LaGrande, M.M; and Borden, L.S.

HEAD MOUNTED *camera worn by Agent Peterson is activated. Team has cleared up their camp and gear-check has been initiated.*

Agent Black: Team, status report and confirm gear-check.

Agent Peterson: Nothing to report, weapons online.

Agent Nightingale: Nothing to report, weapons online.

Agent Devon: Those creepy ghost children were back again behind the trees. But, everything seems quiet. Weapons are online.

Agent Peterson: Now that you mention it. Saw them too. Little fuckers give me the creeps.

Agent Peterson's camera feed flickers for an instant and there appear to be three distinct shadowy shapes looming from the tree line just north of the team's initial camp site.

Agent Black: Brother Azael, please report your status.

Brother Azael: My word, so formal, all of you. My status is this: I am still alive and so are you, but if we do not find the relic, the clock will keep on ticking for all of us.

Agent Black: Eh... Okay. Gear check....?

Brother Azael: Ugh. Yes, yes. Look, sharp knife. Now, let us go.

A rustling in the shrubbery nearby alerts Agent Peterson as the cam swings widely to the left, 90 degrees of original orientation.

Agent Peterson: What the hell is that? Can you...can you hear this too?

A low growling can be heard very close to Agent Peterson's microphone, as if it were no more than three to four inches away.

Agent Nightingale: What are you on about, P? I hear jack shit.

Agent Devon: Except for those frogs that never appear to shut up.

Agent Peterson: Keep quiet! Both of you.

Agent Peterson takes four steps toward the waterline and keeps quiet as he appears to listen intently. The previously heard growling is no longer present.

Agent Peterson: Shit, I can't hear it anymore. Fuck, whatever it was it was something different… Spooked the hell out of me.

Agent Devon: Pussy.

Agent Peterson: Hey, fuck you.

Agent Black: Both of you need to call it quits right now before I keep this whole little spiel in our official transcript instead of redacting it. Grow up.

Agent Peterson turns back to his original position to face Agent Black. For a little while, two piercing red eyes in the wooded background are visible just over Agent Black's shoulder. Neither Agent Peterson nor any other operatives seem to notice this at first.

Agent Nightingale: Hey, have a look at this.

Agent Peterson takes a couple of steps forward. Agent Nightingale stands near a dark and thick oak tree where several bodies of forest and marsh critters hang tied by ropes. Rabbits, Frogs, Birds, and

[Redacted]

Agent Devon: Shit, man. Think we've got another Crones of Cappadocia case going on here?

Brother Azael: Why are we dallying? Every minute we waste on these petty non-hazard creatures is time wasted in finding the relic. If the Swansongs get there first…

Agent Black steps up to Brother Azael, holding up her hand.

Agent Black: Brother Azael, although I share the sentiment, I would like to ask you to refrain from ordering my team around.

The camera starts swerving from left to right and back again. Vital statistics show Agent Peterson's heartrate increasing exponentially over the course of several seconds.

Agent Peterson: There's… There's that growling again.

Brother Azael: I sincerely apologize, Agent Black. I was merely commenting on the urgency of the matter.

Agent Devon: The world's falling apart, Brother. The urgency is pretty much a given.

Agent Peterson: Can't stop. Won't stop.

Let the record show that on the initial live feed there was an intense growling heard coming from Agent Peterson's speaker feed. However, on subsequent playback of the audio and video, none of it seems present.

Agent Nightingale: Hey, hey what's with him.

Agent Peterson appears to walk backward toward the water's edge at an increasing pace. Over Agent Devon's shoulders, we see piercing red eyes in the distance for about three to four seconds before they appear to dart out of the immediate vicinity.

Agent Peterson: Get it out... Out of my head!

Agent Black: Peterson...snap out of it now. Come here, that's an order.

Agent Devon: What's with his eyes, man? He looks all **[Redacted]** *and holy shit he* **[Redacted]**

Agent Peterson: No...no! Nonononono!

The camera turns to the edge of the swamp where a black shape with piercing red eyes and a gaping mouth filled with approximately five to six rows of razor-sharp teeth peers out of the water. Any other details are not possible to describe due to camera malfunction and static interference. We hear Agent Peterson scream in anguish as the camera begins shaking wildly before falling to the ground. Blood and viscera are seen pooling **[Redacted]** *...whereupon the* **[Redacted]** *after having* **[Redacted]** *appear to all be missing. Agent Peterson has by all accounts expired.*

Agent Black: HQ, I don't know if you just witnessed that entire shit show, but we lost Peterson. Type and Class of hazard unknown. Agent Nightingale will install a new cam. Proceeding with mission as planned. Taking extra precautionary measures for a physical— possible cognitive hazardous entity of at least Class B8, perhaps even **[Redacted]**

[End of Transcription]

"WELL, THAT'S CERTAINLY VERY NICE," Sean said as he tried scrolling down the log once or twice to make sure they hadn't missed anything. "So, this blood huh." He gazed at the bloody rock next to the riverbank.

Lilly silently watched the water wary that something could leap out from the edge and pull her into the murky deep below. Which, to be fair, isn't a very *out there* thing to fear in this day and age. Liz and Moira nearly experienced it in Bywater, New Orleans, where the deadliest of marine life converges into one very messed-up pool party.

Moira looked around the edges of the dark wood. She tried her best to get in tune with the place and its old, old spirits. But so far, to no avail. "This place…it feels like a graveyard," Moira said aloud, but it was meant for Liz, who was standing right next to her.

Quincy turned toward her. "What do you mean? Like, there could be a lot of dead people buried beneath the soil here?"

"I have no doubt that is the case here," Liz said. "But I think what Moira means is that this place feels like it should be left alone, undisturbed, so whatever denizens dwell here can roam in peace."

Moira nodded. "Exactly."

Lilly held up one of the notebooks she had been scribbling in ever since she and Liz had first 'landed' in Flanders. There was a lot of writing and a few drawings. One of a black dog, one of a ghostly shape between the trees, and another of a group of horsemen riding in the sky, chasing after a black beast below. "When Marty first mentioned Old Red Eyes, I was reminded of some of the old tales about the creepy Deogen that my Belgian companions in the GDF used to tell me about," Lilly started. "Old Red Eyes or, even better, The Beast of Flanders, is supposed to be this ancient entity tied to the woods here. Besides the numerous stories of people gone missing and people dying under mysterious circumstances, there are also sightings of a huge black dog. Some say it's Old Red Eyes's companion while others say it's literally the same thing but in a different disguise so to speak."

"Let me get at them, and I will positively *slay* anything that gets in our way, milady!" the living slab of green meat that was Matthew Hopkins announced.

Quincy grabbed the notebook and was impressed at his sister's drawing skills. "You did these? They're great," he remarked, and Lilly blushed gratefully. "So, do you think whatever killed that Haven agent is…the same thing?"

"Tales about these kinds of ancient nature spirits or guardians or what have you are a staple of Old European and Slavic folklore," Liz told them. "It's possible this thing is some kind of Leshy, or grand Fairy. Which wouldn't make it any less deadly."

Lilly pointed to the drawing of the riders in the sky. "There's something else though. In some tales, Old Red Eyes has ties to the so-called Wild Hunt."

"Ghost riders in the sky, oh I heard the tales." Moira smiled. "They hunt this…dog form of Old Red Eyes, right?"

"Exactly." Lilly nodded. "These guys" —she pointed at the drawing— "these spectral horsemen often have stories linked to bad omens, portents of doom, and you guessed it, end of the world and apocalypse scenarios."

"Considering the world is ending that all lines up pretty nicely," Quincy said. "But there's not anything we can really do with that information, except try and stay the hell away from this thing."

"Yeah, that's our best bet," Sean agreed. "We need to focus on finding that relic pronto, and I think the best course of action would be to follow that Haven Squad closely. While you were talking, I managed to derive a couple of coordinates from the Haven device. I think that might be where they're going. I can use the thing as GPS too, which is good because I don't think normal burner phones have any sort of reception here."

Moira snapped her own mobile phone shut. "That's correct, we do not."

Lilly turned her head to the side fast enough to see a figure dart behind the trees. "We are still being watched…" she told the group. "I think it's best to move on."

"Onward into battle, unto the Lord I dedicate this strife!" the disheveled man-thing that was Hopkins shouted. "RIP AND TEAR," Tim yelled from the same mouth hole.

Chapter 9

?? - ?? days, ?? hours, and ?? minutes until the end of the world

FOR EONS UPON EONS, I have hopped between the fissures of time, space, and beyond. Even now, I am not necessarily here talking to you, but then again, I might be. You don't know. I don't really know, nobody does. The only one who would know is me. There is not a single atom in existence that I have not seen or touched. I was there when the world began in the volatile chaos of time before time actually existed. Existence was little more than a fleeting thought before the slivers of primordial stardust exploded the universe into being. Yet, I was already there. Across a sea of infinity, of endless timelines and variations and worlds beginning and ending there is but one constant and that constant is me. I am the one. The alpha and the omega. The dark and the light. The beginning and the end. I am the beacon, the icon, the idol, and the curator. I am the eerie gust of wind blowing in from the abandoned churchyard, the shiver up your spine as you feel eyes on the back of your neck, the doubt in your mind whether the things you've seen and heard are actually there or just a figment of your poor, fleeting imagination. I am everything. I am life and death. I am the cycle, the sowing and the reaping, the lone wolf in the night. Time is a construct; Space is just an idea. I am the architect. I am forever. I am eternal.

Do you really think you can win, Swansongs?

THE BANKS *of the Miskatonic River, Arkham, MA, United States — 25-ish years until the end of the world*

"Are you alright, Tobias?" Emily asked as she groaned, pulling her left boot from the thick puddle of mud.

"Hm?" Tobias responded distantly. "Oh, yes. I'm sorry. I had drifted off in thought for a bit there. I was reminded of a dream I had once. It might have even repeated itself last night. Must be the anticipation."

Emily raised an eyebrow. "What was it about?"

Tobias scratched his head and stared off into the fog floating on the edge of the bank. "You know, I don't quite know. It's less a dream, or perhaps even a nightmare, about things happening and more of a feeling. Like someone telling you to feel a certain way."

William paused his hike for a moment and peered back. "What way, Tobias? How did your dream make you feel?"

Tobias waited for a moment. "Powerless," he eventually answered. "Small and insignificant," he added. "But let us not dwell on this, please. I must be tired, and my mind may still be a bit fuzzy, but we did get up at an ungodly hour to hike through this soggy river land, so there's that."

It was early in the morning, very early, and the sun had been up for about half an hour. It wasn't a long hike from the town, and the river crossed through it rather than pass by, making this quiet streak of nature an odd but beautiful getaway from the bustling and busy life of Arkham. The trees along the bank of the Miskatonic River consisted of birches and willows, the latter drearily overhanging the water's edge so close that some touched the water. A bridge from one ecosystem to another, William had said. All around them, the thick morning fog did not waver. It was quite harrowing to traverse the banks. A shiver of cold air emanated from the dark water and the peculiar bubbling noises of water were loud and clear at all times.

"What do you expect to find down here, William?" Emily asked as she oversaw the sorry state of her favorite boots, contemplating why on earth she even agreed to go on this 'brisk morning walk' in the first place.

William shrugged. "I don't rightly know, my dear," he admitted, holding the bag containing two tablets temporarily on loan from Arkham's museum for 'field studies,' whatever that entailed.

"Perfect," Emily replied. She clutched her growing belly carefully with love and care and whispered, "Our day is ruined, my children..." There was no way of knowing yet, but somehow Emily knew she was pregnant with twins—a boy and a girl. She would bet her life on it. And as we know, she was right. "But don't you fret," she continued. "We will get some ice cream in town later and then our day will be saved. There are always answers, even in the darkest of times."

"What are you doing, Emily?" William yelled back. "Come on, keep up."

Emily sighed. She knew she wasn't showing *that* much, but it still hurt that he did not seem to notice she was pregnant. Even the grocery store clerk, a barely mobile little lady of approximately a hundred-and-ninety-years-old, gave her a warm smile and nod the moment Emily stepped inside. "I'm coming," she told William.

"Fascinating tales about the so-called death-lights here," Tobias lectured, mostly to himself. "Not unlike other *will-o-the-wisp* tales from folklore, they are often found on the edges of swamps and riverbanks, but these are particularly haunting. Legend says they can cause severe burn wounds before leading enraptured victims down into the river to drown."

William nodded along. "Over the years, over half of the

population of Arkham has claimed to have witnessed these spectral lights. Especially at night."

Emily couldn't help but stifle a laugh. "Are you sure they aren't just fireflies, William? They *are* native to the area, as you know."

"That's a very good observation, my dear." Tobias smiled. "Another great example of how real-world things and events lead to the creation and spread of folklore."

William scoffed. "Pah! Be that as it may, I have never seen fireflies granted the ability to do what the Death Lights are said to do right before appearing. They are said to create—"

"Eerie circles upon the waters…" Emily interrupted him. She stood flabbergasted on the edge of the bank, staring at the strange ripples making tiny waves in the water. A shiver went down her spine.

THE SONIAN WOODS, *Flanders, Belgium – 2 days, 15 hours, and 44 minutes until the end of the world*

"Something is very wrong." Moira turned around in panic. "Did anyone else feel that just now? Please tell me it wasn't just me."

Liz bit her lip. "It wasn't just you," she responded, downcast. "It was as if a veil was lifted, or parted a little, and we all went through it." She reached out her hands through the tree line where they had just come from. "Nothing… Whatever it was…we can't go back. *Shit*."

Sean groaned softly. "I felt nothing." He looked over at Quincy and Lilly, who both shook their heads as well. "If Moira and Liz are the only ones who felt it, it must have been magical in some sort of capacity. And Liz rightfully called out 'shit', that's not good. Not good at all."

They were deep into the woods now. Whatever few traces of light used to shine through the canopy above were absent as the forest, like the entire world, was clad in an unsettling eternal twilight with the sky in perpetual shades of red, from bright fire red to deep crimson and burgundy. The whispers from the edge of the wood increased in volume and number as time went on. Lilly wasn't sure if they were responding to visitors from the outside in the only way they knew or if it was some kind of warning, but it was, to say the least, extremely unsettling to listen to. Especially since, as Liz had told her earlier, she couldn't make out any kind of Anglo-Saxon language in the flow of moaning and fleeting whispers. Likewise, Moira, who dabbled in foreign speech and had some familiarity with Asian languages, also drew a complete blank. Whatever the spirits tried to tell them, it was in a language or speech far outdating anything resembling modern language. It was enough to put them on edge.

"Are we any closer, you think?" Quincy carefully asked.

Sean shook his head. "I don't know, I—" He started rapping on the tracker. "The device has been acting up ever since…ever since we walked through whatever it was that Liz and Moira noticed."

Something cracked and swished. "Master… Swans…"

The resurrected rotting husk of Hopkins nearly collapsed under its own weight. It was as if the entire decomposing process had started anew at a much-accelerated rate. Even Tim, who was once again bound to a vessel on Earth, struggled to hang on.

Liz knelt beside the now crawling abomination. "Everything is going so quickly. It's only a matter of hours, a day or two at most, before all of Hopkins will return to the dirt. Ash and dust."

"Where he belongs," Moira spat. "I for one wouldn't mind at all if the soul of that fiend were to be cast right back into Hell. I never thought I'd see the day where I prefer the presence of a malevolent space creature like Tim than the decrepit remains of one of the vilest men in history. All those lives taken for nothing. All those innocent warlocks and witches."

Lilly could not help but agree. "Hell *is* where Matthew Hopkins belongs. There is no doubt about that. But Tim?

Yeah, Tim is infinitely more useful when he's down here, working whatever trickery he's good at, rather than up there, where's he's just another blink in the ever-changing tide of the universe."

"I…resent that…" Tim complained through Matthew Hopkins's muffled body, which was lying face down in the mud.

Quincy rubbed his eyes. "He's no good to us in this state. What are we going to do with him?"

"N-Nothing, I can stand," the shambling mess said. For the first time, it was unclear whether it was the resolve of Matthew Hopkins or that of Tim that uttered the words. Nevertheless, the promise was not in vain. The body stood up with relatively few pieces of meat falling to the wayside. "I… am…ready," the thing groaned.

Moira rolled her eyes. "Just about ready for a funeral in your honor."

"Hey," Sean broke through the bantering. All heads immediately turned toward him as he knelt next to a wide oak splattered with rust-colored liquid. There was no doubt about the origin of the dripping goo; it had once belonged to a person, and it seemed to be fresh. "I picked up another transcription. I'm uploading it to the tracker now but… Huh, that's weird."

"We've got to start forbidding the words *that is weird* in our communication because it never leads to anything good," Quincy groaned. "What's going on? What's weird?"

Sean tapped the device a few times. "The date on this transcription is wrong. It's…" Sean looked up and seemed lost in thought for a few seconds. "Maybe it was later than… Eh, never mind."

Moira swallowed. "I don't like this one but…"

"None of us do, but here we are." She grasped Liz's hand tight as they gathered around Sean.

Sean hit the play button.

· · ·

TEAM: *ST-004 consisting of Agent Devon (Missing), Agent Nightingale, Agent Peterson (KIA) and led by Agent Black. Add: Brother Azael of the Final Dawn*

Date and Location: 05/19/13, Sonian Woods, Belgium

Primary Mission: Extract relic from destination before Class-09 Wanted Subjects reach it. Extract Brother Azael, status elevated to VIP.

Secondary Mission: Neutralize Class-09 Wanted Subjects: Swansong, Q.S; Swansong, L.E; Cooper, S; LaGrande, M.M; and Borden, L.S.

Tertiary Mission: Extract the remainder of Team ST-004

A RIFLE MOUNTED *camera is attached by Agent Nightingale. Agent Black is seen bandaging her right knee. A brownish substance stains her entire right leg; a green substance appears to ooze out of several wounds.*

Brother Azael: I can feel the power emanating from just beyond those trees in the distance, it is not far, my friends.

Agent Nightingale: Heh, who gives a flying fuck anymore, man. We're all going to die in here. This rotten and forgotten cesspool of mud and grime... How can you sit there and say we're close to our goals as if this place will magically let us leave without any repercussions when we get the relic? And who are these wanted folks anyway, huh? I heard they're just some youngsters man, why aren't they telling us shit, they're not even telling you *shit, Black. You know this!*

Agent Black: We have a mission, Agent Nightingale. Have you forgotten your oath? Have you forgotten your duties? If so, gladly remind me, for you know what we have to do to those that desert in the middle of a mission.

Agent Nightingale: It is a greater mercy than what happened to Peterson, or even Devon, who I am sure is having an excellent time dancing with the little fairies in the woods right now.

Brother Azael: Such animosity, such ferociousness. Whatever troubles you, young brother Nightingale, you should rejoice in the fact that you were one of the lucky few to have assisted in ushering in a new age. An age of absolute enlightenment.

Agent Nightingale: So I hear everyone say, yet nobody tells me fucking anything about what's actually going on. I've heard some of the boys and girls talk about how the higher ups are gearing up to travel onto a different—

Agent Black: Agent Nightingale, enough. I order you to hold your tongue right now or you will force my hand.

Agent Nightingale: They're leaving. They're trying to destroy the goddamn planet man. Arma-fucking-geddon.

Agent Black: Agent Nightingale, this is your last chance. Stop, or I will be forced to terminate you.

Agent Nightingale: You're not important enough, Black! You can't go with them. You will die, just like the rest of—

The camera flips onto its side as Agent Black brandishes her handgun and shoots four nine-millimeter bullets toward Agent Nightingale. Agent Nightingale's head falls down in front of the camera, covering half of the frame. Agent Nightingale appears to have expired. Two bullet wounds are visible in the frontal lobe area and through the right eye.

Agent Black: Fuck, fuck! Why the fuck did you make me do that, Jon? Why, why? You know what the hell is up, you know the protocol and you know the risks involved.

Brother Azael: It was inevitable.

Agent Black is seen pacing in and out of the frame, audibly frustrated. We hear a low growling turning into very faint guttural laughter emanating from the left speaker. It seems neither Agent Black nor Brother Azael acknowledged or even heard the sounds.

[Redacted]   [Redacted]   [Redacted]   [Redacted] [Redacted]   [Redacted]   [Redacted] *…Agent Nightingale's body away. A spray of blood and tissue spatters against the tree. From outside the frame gunshots are heard.*

Agent Black: **[Redacted]**

Brother Azael: Whatever suits you, Agent Black, this is your mission.

Agent Black: It's ducking back into the tree line, move now. Now!

A cracking sound is heard very close to the camera microphone. We hear a few light taps.

Unknown Voice: Are you in there?

[Redacted]

Unknown Voice: I see you.

[End of transcription]

SEAN CLOSED the log and turned off the screen without a word.

"Killing your own for not following an order is a positively *maniacal* thing to do." The horrid tongue of Hopkins's corpse waggled nauseatingly. "I APPROVE," Tim spoke. "YOU HUMANS ARE *RAVING MAD* SOMETIMES; I KNEW IT WAS A GOOD IDEA TO STICK AROUND SOME MORE. MUAHAHAHAHHAAACK, ACCCK, *AAACK*!"

Sean punched the slithering Hopkins-thing in the face. "Lockjaw?"

The corpse gave something akin to a twitchy nod and went quiet.

Liz bit the inside of her cheek. "These special agents are getting picked off one by one, and *they're* the ones with the gear to fight whatever is out there."

"You don't know that," Lilly reassured her. "You can have all the guns in the world, but some fiends require more force of will to resist than bullets. You can never know for sure."

Quincy scoffed. "That's true, but in this case…the fresh blood spatter on the trees might give us a clue on what is effective against them. Mental fortitude won't do anything against sharp claws that can slice you open like a can of meat. Although I can hardly deny the thing is messing with us. Even now."

In the distance, branches cracked followed by the sound of something panting and running around on four legs. Following Quincy's suspicions, it was as if it came right on cue.

Quincy didn't budge at the sound, although he noticed it startled the rest of them. "I've been living with monsters in my head for quite some time now," he blurted, prompting some worried faces. "It's like, it's not just the dreams. Sleep deprivation is a thing, and everything that comes with it. But every time I close my eyes, I can see them grinning at me in my mind. It's as if I make myself extra vulnerable, not only in reality, but also my mental space." He cleared his throat. However troubling the message was, Quincy did look somewhat determined. "But with all of the bad stuff," he continued. "I've learned to somewhat use it against them. The story of 'The Boy Who Cried Wolf,' screwed me up time and time again, and soon I'll know exactly what is going on just by the subtle clues."

Lilly sat down and crossed her legs. "Eh, I'm trying to figure out what exactly you're going for, Quince. Are you saying you can *tell* whenever we're in danger?"

"Something like that. Not really danger perhaps, but I can kind of figure out when we're being messed with. I can distinguish reality from fiction," Quincy told her, but there was still a lot of doubt hanging from his words. Was he really sure of all this or was it just a simple reassurance so his friends would spend the remainder of their short lives feeling just a tad safer than before? Even Lilly had trouble reading her brother.

"And this?" Sean finally spoke up. "What do you call all of this?"

"Oh, it's definitely screwing with us. I haven't got a doubt in my mind that it's not a coincidence that we keep finding these *should-have-been-encrypted* Haven transcriptions everywhere," Moira spoke up and turned to Quincy for confirmation.

Quincy slowly closed his eyes and opened them back up. "True, but there's one thing that really bothers me about this."

"What's that?" Liz asked.

"Time," he answered. "The date on the transcription, the sky becoming darker with every passing hour, the dilapidation of Tim's vessel..."

Liz nodded. "It's true," she agreed. "Even the wildlife, however precious little there is, keeps getting more and more quiet. As if their lives are being snuffed out one by one in secret."

Quincy looked grim. "Something is coming, and I'm not sure if it has anything to do with Old Red Eyes. It appears as if time is catching up with us."

"What do you mean? That that veil we went through, what Liz and I felt, you think that was another time… mishap?" Moira asked.

Lilly sighed. "In the GDF we used to call it Temporal Displacement Zones, but they were usually temporary, and involved time slowing down or speeding up."

"That's right," Sean told her. "This is different. This feels permanent, as if we're being pushed ahead through time."

"Or like we were pulled back with a rubber band, and then shot toward the actual real-time space," Moira theorized.

Quincy shrugged. "Could be, could be."

"All this talk about time and space is making my head hurt," Liz sighed. "Thinking about it too much is also making me deathly afraid. What if… What if we were indeed just pulled back on a string, hanging on for dear life for just a couple more days while…"

Lilly shivered. "Don't say it…just don't."

"The futility of it all," Quincy voiced the realization.

Liz continued, "What if the world already ended and we're just playing catch-up?"

———————————————

Chapter 10

———————————————

5 minutes until the end of the world

COOKIE PUFFED OUT HER CHEST, taking in a deep breath. Her eyes nearly rolled into the back of her head as she released the noxious clouds building up in her stomach out into the world. It was one of the loudest burps she had ever let out, but the sound was drowned out by the unmistakable noise of collapsing tectonic plates all around them. "Do you think they will succeed this time?"

Marty politely shook his head and laughed. "There is no this time or that time. My word, Famine, where have you stuck your head these past eons? We're here, at the cusp as we were, as we've always been, as we always will be."

The sky had all but turned to a black void over the Earth as the atmosphere was starting to become swallowed up by the true cosmic malevolence that was the ultimate power of the Gibbous Horde. Aila sat restlessly on her steed. She was clipping her fingernails and licking off every bit of dirt and grime before she meticulously placed each torn nail into a leather bag for safekeeping. "I agree with her, War. Would be nice to have a change of scenery now and again. To have something *actually* happen."

"Why don't you close those crusty eyes of yours and just go back a couple of days?" Marty told Aila. "That Hopkins fellow is always a good laugh, isn't he?"

Aila pondered the notion for a while but ultimately shook her head. "Eh, it gets old really quick. Besides, I have a teatime get together with the Wild Hunt in about" —she looked up to the sky— "four to six flashes of Death Lightning, so."

"I don't see the problem," Mortimer told her, the sound of his lower jaw eerily clackingbut faded with the gathering storm of un-life. "That may very well be an eternity or a few milliseconds, if we're still on that whole time thing, anyway."

Marty sighed, "Please don't get them started, Death. We've got work to do soon."

"Do we?" Aila questioned.

"I'm bored," Cookie complained.

A small plop made the four horse(wo)men turn their eyes to the cat who had just jumped down from the windowsill of the little chapel, which was starting to catch on fire. The cat calmly wandered from the cobbled path leading from the burning chapel to the middle of the clearing of poppy flowers where the four riders sat in conclave. It looked up to each of them and spoke. "The twins are reaching the shrine and Old Red Eyes. It appears the cogs of the First Testament of Terra have been set into motion." The cat then dove into the shrubbery between the poppies, where it started to roll around and sniff the flowers.

The horse(wo)men looked at each other with a combination of confusion and general excitement.

"Well, that's different at least," Cookie said, smiling wide.

THE SONIAN WOODS, *Flanders, Belgium — 1 hour and 17 minutes until the end of the world*

"There's that feeling again," Liz panted. "The 'rubber-banding' is back."

Quincy's eyes darted around. "I felt it too this time." He looked over at his friends for confirmation. Sean, Lilly, and Moira all nodded in agreement. Matthew Hopkins's bloated and pus-filled silhouette tried to nod as well, but his lower jaw fell off and sank into a deep pool of water and mud on the forest floor.

"*Curses!*" was the word that Tim tried to form from whatever means of verbal communication he had left. The actual noise that came out was more akin to "Chhhhgggggg"

"I hear something further up," Lilly exclaimed in a furtive whisper. "It sounds like…panting, but no beast or monster this time, it's a person!"

They had arrived in a clearing deep within the woods. A group of ancient oaks reached into the dark canopy above them, accompanied by mighty willows whose branches hung low, the foliage acting like a curtain to slightly obscure what was to be found on the other side. There was a small shrine, about half Lilly's average height. It was made entirely of wood and overgrown with moss. In a world rife with modern technology and scientific mindsets, it was out of another time, a small altar of nature built for the ancient gods of the Earth from long ago and set in a pantheon of oak deep within the wood. Inside the shrine, beneath a flimsy roof of twigs, sat a wood-carved chalice embedded with a beautiful moss-green emerald. But much to the group's dismay and shock, there was something else in the clearing, something Lilly had already suspected they would find.

Slumped against one of the tree's trunks not far from the altar was a woman dressed in black. Everyone immediately recognized the distinct attire of a Haven field agent. She appeared to be slipping in and out of consciousness, which was not surprising given that she was missing one leg. Lilly heard the soft moaning and grunting of their enemy as she sat wounded and helpless, waiting to be devoured or killed.

But the group did not perceive this woman as an enemy. Despite feeling that Haven's personnel were blank slates without emotion and terrible people that do terrible things, all they felt now was pity. They clearly knew who she was, and from what they gathered from the transcripts, Agent Black wasn't some evil mastermind hell bent on accomplishing evil things. She was a person in a horrible position, forced to complete a hazardous suicidal mission in a dangerous and unknown world or suffer the consequences if she failed to comply or failed to execute her orders perfectly.

"Come to finish the job, have you?" Agent Black groaned as she watched the group approach from the opposite tree line. In the distance, she saw the vaguely human shapes of the forest's other denizens inching closer. At least she thought it was the spirits of the forest, it could very well be the souls of demons coming to drag her to Hell personally. It wouldn't surprise her.

"No…" Quincy answered. He noticed Lilly trying to form words, but they wouldn't come out, so he took it upon himself. "I don't know what you heard, or what your orders were concerning me, my sister, and my friends but…" He paused for a moment, staring at the sorry sight of the once proud Haven woman lying on the ground in defeat. When he came closer, she tried scurrying away like a cat; she was deathly afraid. Quincy reached out. "We're not your enemies…Agent Black."

"H–how did you…" Blood poured from her mouth as she tried to speak.

Quincy shook his head. "That's not important. What is, is that I want you to know that you have been lied to, all of you have."

Sean stared at her steadfast. "The world is ending, Agent Black, and Haven and the Final Dawn are directly responsible for doing so. Whatever the higher ups have told you and your colleagues, and your brothers and sisters in arms on the front lines, about why you fight and for what cause, know that they have been lying." There was hatred in Sean's eyes, hatred for everything Haven had ever done to him, but he knew in his heart that not everyone inside the organization was like this. Just like civilians were easily led astray or brainwashed, and people like Quincy were plagued with nightmares that made them question the world around them, who was to say that Haven did not do the same to those in their own ranks?

Agent Black tried sitting up. She held her side, from which more blood spilled onto the mossy ground, and pointed toward the wooden shrine not far from her. "The chalice is… It's an illusion. Brother Azael—" More blood spattered to the ground as she coughed and gagged. "Get him… The Deep Wood Chalice, he…has it…" Agent Black's eyes glazed over, and they saw the spark of life leave her body. She was dead, the last member of expedition team ST-004, who were sent on a mission where they only knew half the story and which they were never meant to come back from.

"MASTER AND MISTRESS SWANSONG?" The incredible weird noise of Tim's voice sounding scared of all things broke the silence that followed. "THERE IS SOME-THING NEAR– *AARH!*" was all that Tim could mutter from the broken-down body of Matthew Hopkins which was pulled violently into the woods. "For God's sake, *help me!*" is what the group would have heard if the mangled Hopkins's jaw had not once again come loose from the remainder of his body. Instead, they simply heard more gargling noises and the very disconcerting sounds of a body being torn to absolute pieces.

"Run!" Moira yelled, distraught, and she pulled Liz and Sean with her toward the middle of the clearing where the shrine stood.

Quincy and Lilly followed suit. But a very strange sensation settled over them both as they started to make a run for it. It was the same kind of falling sensation when you're dead tired and are falling asleep but are then shaken awake by your own body. Lasting only half a second or less, Quincy and Lilly felt weightless and paralyzed. In that moment, they were not inside the Sonian Woods at the end of the world, they were somewhere else, standing along the edge of a river inside a thick fogbank with peculiar yet somewhat familiar voices calling out incoherent things.

With a bright red flash a heartbeat later, the twins were pulled back to where they physically were. A loud, angry voice screamed from somewhere in the air and there was a streak of red, orange, and indigo light phasing through and swirling around the treetops, drifting upward until it eventually disappeared into the air. And then there was silence.

For a little while.

The twins scurried toward their friends in the middle of the clearing while staring at the edge of the deep dark woods in fright. A pair of bright red eyes peered at them from the darkness just beyond. There was heavy breathing, laughter from all around them, and most of all, there was the feeling of absolute defeat. Then, something else entirely.

"Well done, well done. Swansongs and friends… You have found it, the Chalice of the Deep Wood, the embodiment of Paganism, the 'old' ways, the ancient gods…" A man dressed in bright orange robes sporting a filthy beard and a crazy look in his eyes appeared in the clearing as well. He applauded them mockingly. "You have done it, my children. Now let me, Brother Azael, be your guide to the Apocalypse. For it all ends here…"

THE BANKS *of the Miskatonic River, Arkham, MA, United States — 25-ish years until the end of the world*

An unnatural gust of wind blew through the reeds of the Miskatonic riverbank. Emily, Tobias, and William stood awestruck as they watched the peculiar ripples on the water grow wider and wider. They did not know if what happened after was a product of their tired minds or if it was indeed a true supernatural event.

"Look, over there!" William spouted with all the enthusiasm of a young man's spirit trapped in an old man's body. "The lights Tobias, look Emily, dancing lights!"

There was no denying that just above the surface of the water, lights floated up into the air and disappeared inside the fog bank. They were magnificent, William thought to himself. For all the wonders that had left the minds of men in a quickly evolving industrial world, he could not help but smile at the supernatural spectacle in front of him.

Absolutely extraordinary, thought Tobias. He had always believed in the realm of the fantastical, but to see something this bright and gorgeous in front of him filled him with amazement. He savored every moment.

Beautiful, thought Emily. Perhaps she had been the most rational of the trio present that early morning, but she too could not help but gaze at the wondrous ballet of lights in front of them. She was overtaken by feelings she could not help but describe as partially divine and partially nostalgic.

They were all sorts of hues, but most of them seemed to fixate on the warmer color spectrum. Orange, red, crimson, indigo, and a shade darker than indigo were prolific.

"Look at them go," Emily gasped. "Can you see them, Tobias? They're twirling around as if each and every one of them is alive, like fireflies! I have never seen anything like it. I simply can't put it into words!"

Tobias grinned watching the mystical event. "I see them, Emily. Beautiful things in their individual right, but can you see it too? In their movement?"

"What do you mean, Tobias?" William asked. "Can you discern a pattern?"

"They twirl and dance around each other as separate entities yet if you look at the broader picture, you can almost see a kind of…a hive mentality. On a bigger scale they *do* seem to follow a single trajectory inside of the…" Tobias squeezed his eyes shut then gasped. "Wait, look over there! Do you see it in the fogbank?"

"What do you mean?" William asked, distraught, for he could not see anything at all. It annoyed him. "What is there?"

Emily sucked in her breath, "Are those…people?" She waved, but it felt in vain. "Hello? Who's there? Can you see me?"

Tobias shook his head. "They're gone. I can't see them anymore." He looked around. "The lights are dissipating as well." He balled his hands into fists. He felt defeated, being so close to experiencing *something* but having been left high and dry without definitive answers.

"It doesn't seem like it's coming back now, Tobias," Emily said with a sad tone in her voice. "Whatever it was, it's really gone now."

William huffed. "I know enough, and I've seen enough. Something reacted to the tablets here, and as far as we know we've got at least *one* more place to go."

"Let's go." Tobias turned around. "Off to the Witch-House then."

———————————————

Chapter 11

———————————————

The Sonian Woods, Flanders, Belgium – 31 minutes until the end of the world

"QUINCE...LOOK," Lilly whispered to her brother as Azael's harrowing shape crept closer. Above the treetops, the jellyfish-like Migrators were seen floating upward in droves. Their appearance lit up the sky like a Christmas tree. Where there was used to be only pure darkness, now their glistening shapes dotted the black void above them with beautiful shades of turquoise, purple, dark blues, and metallic sheens.

"Beginning of the end," Quincy whispered and squeezed her hand. "They're all leaving, each and every one of them." He could not help but chuckle in defeat.

Moira sighed. "Leaving this world in search of a better one. If only we could do that for all of us..."

The group shuffled closer together.

"What are you whispering about? Hm?" Brother Azael grunted. "Do you not understand the full scope of what is going on? We're the last ones left, my children. Don't you see? The Horde controls everything, and as such, so do *I*. The world has already come to an end... You're just a few tiny, teeny minutes on the other side … Do you want to count them down together?"

The black shape of something indescribable and unspeakably vile and evil loomed behind Brother Azael. The red eyes of this malevolent entity of pure wickedness shone so bright it was as if they could peer into their souls.

Brother Azael laughed. "Deogen, my friend. The stage is yours… Would you like to do the honors?"

The ground started to rumble and crack beneath their feet as Brother Azeal's body rose into the air. The sinister shadow, the void with the bright red eyes, floated up with him and embraced the cultist. When Azael fell with a smack, he gripped his hands into the loose dirt before throwing up blood. Azael began to laugh, an inhuman laugh so repulsive it could have never been produced by normal vocal cords. The trees around the group began to bend and crack as the swirling vortex of nonexistence kept creeping ever closer. Azael took a step forward, the ground shaking as he did, another indication of this unholy possession. "You fools, all of you," Azael went on. "Can't you see what a fool's errand you have been on? Can't you see the kinds of unlimited power one can achieve by causing un-creation and striking bargains with entities older than you, me or even this world?"

"But why?" Liz cried. "What is there to gain if everything you know and love is gone and nothing is left except for ash, grime, and misery?"

Azael cackled madly. "A chance…" he said. "A chance to start again, under a new rule. There are others like me… We could start over, turn the world into the glorious shrine to the ancient gods it should always have been."

"You're mad!" Quincy shouted. "All this and you're still nothing but an errand boy. A weak, pathetic maggot groveling in front of his masters."

"Am I?" Azael laughed and with those words he seemed to grow taller, his limbs elongating into illogical size and measurement. "A wise man once said, 'This is the last chance to evacuate planet Earth before it is recycled.'" Azael quivered in anticipation. "Now." He stretched out his no longer Euclidian hand. "Will…you…join…me?"

Sean took a step forward. "I think I speak for all of us when I say we'd rather die than—"

In a flash Azael wrapped his enlarged claws over Sean's face and twisted. There was a sick snap, and Sean's body fell lifelessly to the floor.

"Nooooooo!" Lilly fell to the ground in anguish. Liz dropped down beside her and cradled Lilly's head in her arms. Tears rolled down both of their cheeks.

Quincy froze, tears biting at the back of his eyes. What would they do now? What could they possibly do? It was as if all hope was crushed from him, as if the cold hand of death's icy grip wrung him out like an old rotten sponge.

Next to them, Moira was waving her hands to form a spell. She was seething with anger. So much so that she did not even seem to notice she was scratching and cutting up her arms to fuel the spell. She peeled away flesh and blood, nearly to the bone.

When she was ready to cast it, Azael could not help but cackle. "Go ahead, do your worst, Miss LaGrande!"

Moira tried to ignore the biting pain of her arms and waved her hands in anticipation. The time was now. She concentrated all of her energy into her fingertips and released. But the spell did not go far. The last thing Moira saw before her body burst into flames and almost instantaneously evaporated into ash and bone was the grinning face of the mad, possessed cultist. *No chance*, she thought. And then she was gone. Like Sean before her, Moira was gone in a flash. No goodbyes, no chance to help or to take action. Just gone.

Quincy, Lilly, and Liz lay on the forest floor, mortified. Lilly was sick to her stomach. Liz was shaking and hyperventilating. Quincy was quiet. The guilt building up in his mind was maddening. To see his loved ones die in front of him… It was enough to drive anyone insane. But for Quincy, it was enough to drive him over the edge of reason.

It was as if time stood still. He sat on the forest floor looking out into the great nothing that crept up to them and which would arrive in only a few moments. *None of this is real,* he thought to himself. *You are all messing with my head. You are not here, that…thing is not here. My friends are safe and alive. My sister is safe.*

"Quincy! Help!" Lilly stammered. She shoved her brother out of his trance. Next to her, Liz screamed in terror. Vines and tree roots had wrapped themselves around her and were squeezing her so tightly that she was moments away from not being able to breathe. "Quince! Please!"

Quincy turned around in shock and without thinking he went over and tried tearing off the vegetation one branch at a time. "This…isn't happening," he panted. "This is not real."

"Please…" Liz looked him in the eye, her voice almost a whisper, drained entirely of breathable air. "You have to…" The vines and roots pulled tighter and another ghastly crack was heard. The light of life dissipated from Liz's eyes and her body was unceremoniously dragged off into the void of unreality.

Lilly went pale as a ghost. She had no more tears to cry, she had no more voice to speak. It was futile in the grand scheme of things. She was done with it.

Quincy held his hands over his head and bawled his eyes out. "It's not real… These are just nightmares. They are all okay!" he shouted.

Brother Azael crept up to Quincy with a nauseating smile. "Oh, but it *is* real, Mister Swansong. All of it…" Azael laughed maniacally. "And it's *your* fault! Mmm, how sweet is the taste of pure anguish." Azael licked his lips. "I've never known a demonic bargain to bear this much fruit so fast, to have so much control, such quick results."

"You are nothing but a lapdog, fiend," a voice rang out from above.

Descending from the air were the four horse(wo)men of the Apocalypse on their celestial steeds. Clad in full armor and brandishing their favorite end-time weapons, they were well and truly ready for the end. War dropped down into the clearing between the possessed Azael and the twins.

"Know your place, dog," he said.

Azael took a few steps back in shock and shuddered to the ground. His eyes flashed red for a moment and then an inhuman voice rang out from his mouth. "No! No, it is not so!"

Death dropped from his skeletal warhorse next to War and nodded; his hollow skull clacked eerily. "Oh, but it is, my old red eyed friend. You know the rules."

"But… But this is different, this mortal was not part of the prophecies," Old Red Eyes spoke through the garbled voice and with the half-severed tongue of Brother Azael.

"Neither were these two, or five for that matter, but that didn't seem to stop the world from ending, did it?" Famine appeared and told the stammering entity.

Plague appeared behind Azael and swiftly took the chalice, the real relic, the real Chalice of the Deep Wood, from him and threw it to Death, who dropped it in an awestruck Lilly's lap. "Now, be a good boy, Deogen. Sit. Staaaay…" Plague told him.

"No! No, this cannot be," Deogen stammered.

"Good gods man, are you a grown-up timeless entity or are you a child? Man up and take the loss. It's time," War told him.

Lilly and Quincy still had no idea what was going on. Their minds were positively flipping between all kinds of emotions. Everything felt so useless, so incredibly futile. It was hard to even open their eyes because the world they knew and loved would be gone in a flash. Lilly did manage to look over to her brother. He was mortified at what had happened to their friends and he felt so guilty. How could he have possibly been so foolish to think it was all part of some elaborate illusion? The guilt dulled him. It weighed down on him like an anchor. He felt like he was slowly sinking deep beneath the surface of a chaotic twirling ocean. It was like a storm roared in his head, never stopping. Even looking Lilly in the eyes felt too hard.

But when Quincy did, he didn't find anger or resentment there. Rather, he saw compassion, love, and understanding. With her last bits of strength, Lilly reached out for him and squeezed his hand. She did not speak, but her eyes told him everything he needed to know. *It's okay, it's not your fault.*

From out of nowhere, the strange but somehow familiar cat flew out of the bushes. It plopped into Lilly's lap, startling her.

"What the..." she yelped.

Don't speak, the cat told her. Not directly of course, cats don't possess the right physiology to be able to speak the human tongue, don't be silly. She heard the voice in her mind. And glancing at her wide-eyed brother, Quincy did too. *There is no time. Know that there is still a chance. Your friends and this world can be saved.*

"Alright, that's it!" War shouted to the now crying Azael on the forest floor. "Ody!" he then yelled toward the sky. "Take it away, my friend!"

From high up above, a group of green see-through spectral riders descended from the dark clouds. They were riding on top of flying horses that were half-decomposed, but transparent, with rotting organs and decaying muscles shining through. The riders shouted in an unknown language that sounded terrifying and wondrous. It was like a rare, once in a lifetime dangerous weather anomaly, only with more bones and lucent specters.

Brother Azael's eyes flashed red for a moment before his body exploded in a shower of blood and viscera. It came so quickly and so unexpectedly that neither Lilly nor Quincy had any time to react. They just sat there wide-eyed, Quincy squeezing his sister's left hand tight, Lilly grasping back and holding the cat with her right. The black, red-eyed shadow emerged from Azael's body. But what was once an imposing, terrifying entity was a literal shadow of its former self. The thing yelped and ran into the woods on all fours. It even barked in fright.

"There we go!" Famine called out after it, "Are you the Beast of Flanders, or just a scared little puppy?" she laughed. Death, War, and Plague laughed with her. In the sky, the ghostly riders hollered and cackled as they flew after the fleeing thing.

War turned around to the twins. "The Wild Hunt will take it from here." He squinted at them and then at the cat. "We don't have very long, only a few minutes. You best hurry."

War is right, the cat told Quincy and Lilly. *I am glad to see that the plan succeeded for the most part. You now have two of the three relics.*

"But we have no time to find the third. Like, at all," Lilly answered. "What can we possibly do?"

Like I said, there is still a chance. The plan to take the vessel was a risky one, but one that paid off.

Quincy stretched his legs. "The vessel? Wait… You don't mean—"

A colored thick vapor swirled around the twins. The mist shone brightly in beautiful shades of red, orange, velvet, and indigo. It sparkled, not like glitter, but like something hidden inside the mist was a gateway to distant stars.

"Tim? Tim, is that you?"

FINALLY FREE, another disembodied voice said. IT TOOK SOME TIME TO REFORM BUT BEHOLD MY TRUE UNRELENTING FORM.

You are no longer needed here, the cat told the twins. *Your friend has the power to take you where you are needed. You are needed elsewhere not only to save this timeline but another one.*

READY MASTERS? Tim yelped in anticipation.

Quincy turned to the cat and looked it straight in the eyes. "Who *are* you reall—" but Quincy could not finish asking his question. He was lost for a moment, quite lost in time and space.

THE END *of the world*

A mass of creeping darkness covered the sun. A veil of eternal shadow was cast upon the last remnants of a dying world. Whole plots of land rumbled and tumbled into the oceans; ancient forests and mountain ranges collapsed into each other, and despicable monstrosities with countless other horrifying apparitions and monsters, freely roamed the earth, reveling in the chaos. Each flash of red and pink lightning was immediately followed by a roar of thunder that sounded so far removed from any earthly sound that it may very well have been the bellows of a primordial god awakening from slumber from the bowels deep beneath the surface. The unspeakable Gibbous Horde entities slowly awoke and arose from the oceans, deserts, and marshes around the world. Their hideousness was only masked by the fact that merely trying to describe them was just cause for anyone to go completely insane. To behold them was usually enough to make someone want to scoop their eyes out with a disher just for the sake of a precious wave of relief. Not that it mattered. Through it all, the enduring chaos of a world entirely collapsing in on itself, there was little to no indication that anyone on the planet was alive anywhere to behold the spectacle of destruction that pertained to everything and everyone they loved. It was not even clear whether or not Haven or the Final Dawn cult had any survivors left amidst their Armageddon, their Apocalypse, their *request* for total and utter deletion of everything.

Around a small chapel at the edge of the Sonian Woods, now on fire, four individuals riding on horseback gathered around the waist-high wooden fence of the age-old structure. Even with the entire world ending around them, the general expression on their faces was one of satisfaction and, in the case of the ever-grinning Death, also joy.

"That went a lot better than I initially thought," Plague sighed. She ran a dirty finger through her slimy hair a few times then proceeded to scratch her head like crazy. "Ooh, that one has been a long time coming," she exclaimed. "Eh, yeah anyway. What now?"

Death shrugged, the clacking of the bones underneath his black robes was barely audible above the sounds of existence ending. "We wait as long as we have to. But also, it should be instantaneous, like thirty minutes ago, if you are keen to check."

Plague let out a long yawn. "Eh, I can wait. This whole stopping the Apocalypse from happening has gotten me kind of drained."

"Yeah, about that," Famine intervened. "Don't any of you feel kind of odd?"

War turned toward his colleague. "Whatever do you mean?" His armor, splattered with mud and blood, still shone beautifully in the red afterglow of life on Earth.

"It's just…" Famine hesitated. "With the entire *stopping* the Apocalypse thing. The rebellion…our minions fighting the evil things around the world, holding the Horde back. All that effort…"

War chuckled. "I think I know where you're going with this."

"Why is it that the world is still ending, even though we're standing here in triumph?" Famine asked.

Plague plopped off her disease riddled horse with boredom streaked across her face. "It's not that hard, Cookie. All that stuff went to the effort of getting those twins and that Fire Vampire where they needed to be. The lost time thing was a bit of a close call, but eventually it worked. If what the cat said is true, they should return with the third relic in hand and stop everything."

"I just realized you never truly got the entire gist of it." Death swiveled his skull apologetically. "I believe you were in the kitchen at the time, making that delicious three course gourmet meal on the night of the meeting."

Famine swallowed hard, taken aback. "You mean that night millions of years ago on Primordial Earth when the cat first appeared? Jeez, thanks for the memo, people." She rolled her eyes; they made a disgusting squishy sound, kind of like dried up jelly.

War stared down at the floor. "Eh, sorry about that."

"Yeah," Plague concurred. "That's our bad… But hey, you know now, right?" She smiled in a nauseating way. "Let's just forget about it for now. Any of you want to play some cards or something? Or are we heading back right away?"

"It's alright." Famine nodded. "But hey…"

"Yes?" Death trotted around on his skeletal horse.

Famine raised an eyebrow. "Where did the Fire Vampire take those two?"

THE WITCH-HOUSE, *Arkham, MA, United States − 25-ish years until the end of the world*

Lilly awoke to the sound of creaking floorboards and muffled voices. She was laying on a bed with soft, old-fashioned blankets beneath her. They were brown and orange and looked straight out of the '70s. Quincy was in the bed next to her, fast asleep. They were in what appeared to be some kind of attic room. Everything looked dull, if a little dusty. The sloped roof ended in an oddly angled nook clad in shadow. With the exception of a particularly colorful fire roaring in the hearth, everything seemed very normal. Sunlight seeped in through a small window to their left. Lilly could just make out the spire of a church in the distance from where she was sitting up on the bed. She could not help but wonder long at the strangeness of the situation— appearing here in an ordinary guest room when the world was ending just a few moments ago. She was distracted and startled by voices coming closer toward the door on their right.

Lilly scooted off the bed and carefully inched closer to Quincy. "Hey," she whispered. "Quince?"

"What an odd contraption…" Quincy mumbled in his sleep. "Peculiar, almost impossible geography. The walls, perhaps?"

Lilly blew away one of her curls dangling in front of her face. Quincy finally seemed to be at peace. No nightmares, no cold sweats. Just dreams. Weird science stuff dreams, probably, Lilly thought. But pleasant ones, she was sure. She sighed and whispered, "I'm sorry, bro." She almost couldn't do it. Then she slapped him hard in the face.

"Aaauuuch! What did you do that for?" Quincy flew up out of the bed holding his cheek.

At the same time, the door to their right creaked open. Two men and a woman, who all looked very familiar, stood in the doorway.

"Oh, my. I am dreadfully sorry," the younger man exclaimed immediately. "We were informed that the attic area was vacant. But that appears to not be the case, please do excuse us." The man was in the process of turning around and leaving with the woman and older man in tow.

"Hey, wait." Lilly squinted; these people looked very familiar. "It's…okay, really."

Quincy seemed to share the sentiment. "We had a long trip…eh, were so exhausted we don't know where exactly we ended up."

The man smiled and turned back around. "Oh, I know all about those long trips." He chuckled. "They can really take it out of you. You're in Arkham, Arkham, Massachusetts." He held out his hand. "My name is Tobias Swansong, this here is my wife, Emily Swansong, and my uncle, William Swansong."

The room went deadly silent.

Emily blinked a few times. "Hey… Are you sure you're alright? Tobias…" She turned around. "They've turned white as a sheet."

PART III

Echoes of an Eternity

Chapter 12

*The Witch-house, Arkham, MA, United States – 25-ish
years until the end of the world*

"HOW ARE YOU FEELING NOW?" Lilly saw the beautiful visage of Emily Swansong hover over her. She was glowing like a proud mother, but that was because of her pregnancy, and not the impossibility that lay before her: her twenty-something daughter that was catapulted from the apocalypse to this here and now, lost in time and space.

Lilly looked over to where Quincy sat watching her from the other bed. He had a flabbergasted look on his face. She knew he felt the same, but not on all accounts. There was doubt lingering in his eyes; she could see the fear and anger on his face that Lilly was sure had to do with all of Quincy's powerful hallucinations thanks to the Horde. He was in doubt if any of what he saw now was even real. Lilly understood of course, she had been under the influence once before, but this was different. Lilly knew that this was, in fact, very real. She felt her mother's warm hands rest in her own palms, she saw her beautiful friendly face smile softly as she waited patiently for her answer. Behind her, Lilly saw Tobias, her father, peering out the window wondering about all of the strange and peculiar things in the world, as he was inclined to do. Next to him was W.A. Swansong himself, perhaps the most imposing Swansong that ever lived. Lilly never heard her mother talk about him, which had made Lilly believe he passed away long before she had ever met Tobias. Was it wrong to make that assumption? Were they really in the past or was there something else going on here? Lilly knew she needed answers quickly and, looking at her brother, he needed them even faster. It was all very overwhelming, and they both did not know how to react.

"I am fine," Lilly answered finally. She smiled warmly at Emily and deep inside her, her heart leaped. She tried to hold back her tears as best as she could.

Emily stood up, a shade of worry written on her face. "Poor girl, whatever happened that put you two in such a state…"

Lilly thought back to where they had just come from. She thought of Sean, Moira, and Liz and her heart ripped open a little bit more as each of their faces appeared in her mind's eye.

Next to her, Quincy's gaze fell on the fireplace. For a single moment, he could see the roaring hearth's fire flicker from its natural yellows, oranges, and little blues at the bottom to familiar shades of burgundy, crimson, dark pink, and countless others. There were sparkles amidst the cinders. And two distinct alien-looking yet familiar eyes popped up to stare at him for just one quick moment, a single heartbeat, a blink of an eye, a sigh from the cosmos. "Could you," Quincy started. "Could you excuse us for a minute please?"

Emily nodded. "Of course." Together with Tobias and William, she made for the door, but as she clutched the handle, she turned around. "I hope you wouldn't mind our company; we were hoping to ask you two for tea this afternoon?"

Quincy swallowed hard. "That would be lovely. Yes." He

blushed. He looked over at Lilly, but she seemed frozen again. It was hard, he agreed. But to get to the bottom of this, why they were here and if it was all real or some kind of disgusting trick, they had to play along, he thought.

"Oh, and I never got your names?" Emily suddenly asked. "How rude of me to have to ask."

Lilly started sweating. It was so obvious this would come up at some point, but why hadn't she thought of this before? She knew Quincy hadn't either because he seemed to have the same panicked reaction.

"My name is…" Lilly started. "Eh, my name is… Katniss. Katniss… Potter…" Lilly looked over to her brother, who looked just about ready to bury his head in the pillow. "And this," Lilly continued. "Is my brother…eh, Marty."

"Katniss, that's a peculiar name," Tobias said bluntly, but he tried to salvage his somewhat rude reply. "But I like it, though! Nothing wrong with it, ha ha."

Lilly couldn't believe how much of their father's loving awkwardness had carried over to Quincy.

"I like it too." Emily smiled. "And Marty, that's a nice name as well. Like Marty McFly in *Back to the Future*, I loved that one."

Lilly laughed hesitantly. "I loved it too!" she exclaimed. *It's also the nickname of one of the four horsemen of the Apocalypse*, she thought.

Quincy raised an eyebrow. This was a good idea for a little test, he thought. For a little covert info gathering. "Oh yes, great movie. It came out recently, right?"

Tobias scratched his head. "Well, if you'd want to call three years ago recently, then yes."

1988, Quincy thought. *Okay. The fire in the hearth…winter? If it almost 1989 then…* Quincy looked at Emily's belly. *This is so weird. That's…us. Right in there. Well, everything seems to add up so far and…*

"Hey." Lilly snapped his fingers at him. "Are you still here?"

Emily chuckled. "We will leave you two alone then, Katniss, Marty. Or maybe you should have called yourself Clint Eastwood?" She winked and then left.

A shiver went down Quincy's spine. He could read the same reaction from Lilly's face. Did Emily merely reference *Back to the Future* just now, or was she implying that she knew these weren't their real names? Perhaps it was both? She didn't seem to mind, but Quincy wasn't keen on having these paranoid thoughts enter his mind on a whim every time they had a conversation with past versions of their parents.

The twins listened for the sound of footsteps vanishing before speaking. After sitting in silence for a few minutes, Quincy spoke first.

"Well. This is certainly something," he said, not knowing how or where to start. He thought about their friends and what happened to them, but he tried his best to put a lock and key on those thoughts, those flashes of memories, and bury them forever beneath the sands of his scattered mind.

Lilly pulled her knees up to her chin and drew the blanket over herself. She was still twitching from cold and fright after everything they had just gone through. It was as if they were in an entirely different world altogether. This was partially true, of course, but there was no denying that mere hours before, they were facing the end of life, the universe, and everything. "It all happened so fast," Lilly said with a melancholy tone in her voice. "I don't even know where to start," she sighed. "We were there, and everyone was gone…and now we are here. Our parents appear to be here as well and… Well, I don't know what to think anymore."

Quincy nodded. "We appear to have gone back in time to 1988, if I'm not mistaken."

"You saw Mom was pregnant too?" Lilly asked.

"Eh, right. That was my immediate conclusion as well, yeah," he answered hastily. He saw no need to discuss his somewhat wild theories on this all being a shared hallucinatory fever dream yet. "Tobias…eh Dad, mentioned we're in

Arkham, Massachusetts, right? Doesn't that sound very strange to you?"

Lilly wracked her brain for a few seconds. "Eh… Is it because so many people consider Arkham to be…fictional?" she asked carefully, not wanting to sound uneducated or stupid.

"Exactly!" Quincy told her.

"Oh." Lilly let out a weak smile. "But wait, that doesn't bode well for all of this, right?"

Quincy rubbed his temples. "It doesn't do anything to move the authenticity of this experience forward, no, but—"

"RAAAARGGH, MASTER SWANSONG, WITH ALL DUE RESPECT YOU HUMANS ARE A FICKLE AND DOOMED SPECIES AS YOU ALWAYS WERE! NOT UNLIKE I, THE GREAT TIMAXOATILACILUZIPTA, EATER OF LESSER NEBULAS! MUAHAHAHHAHA!" The extremely loud and slightly authoritative voice came booming from the hearth's fire.

"Tim?" Lilly was surprised, yet at the same time not surprised at all. "I remember you being with us when we… flew? You were there, weren't you?"

"YES, IT WAS ME!" Tim exclaimed proudly. "IT WAS I THAT TOOK YOU BACK THROUGH THE ANNALS OF HISTORY TO THE YEAR OF STUPID WRETCHED HUMANITY, 1988. BACK ALL THE WAY TO SHAD-OWY, GLOOMY AND DOOMED ARKHAM WHERE THE SUNDERING TOOK PLACE. WHAT A GLORIOUS DAY, MWUHAHAHAHAH!"

Quincy winced. "First of all, can you *please* lower your voice, I bet everyone can hear you downstairs."

The flame from the hearth looked as if it shook its 'head.' "I AM ONLY AUDIBLE TO THOSE WHO I CHOOSE TO CURSE WITH THE EVERLASTING TORMENT THAT IS MY TRUE TONGUE! MUAHAHAHA!"

"Well, aren't you in a good mood?" Lilly said. "Perhaps you can enlighten us further?"

"Yes," Quincy agreed. "What's this about a Sundering? And why are we in a place that doesn't exist? Is this one of those alternative timelines? Oh, and for the love of the Celestians, please turn down the volume anyway, I'm getting a headache."

"WHY DO YOU INSIST THAT ARKHAM DOES NOT EXIST?" Tim wondered aloud. "INTERESTING, MASTER SWANSONG, YOUR SPECIES REALLY IS REMARKABLE FOR HAVING MADE IT THIS FAR, HEEHEHEHEE."

"Out with it, Tim," Quincy told him, annoyed.

The fire flickered red and black for a moment before returning to its normal state. "FINE," Tim relented. "THERE HAVE BEEN MANY RUMORS ABOUT THE STRANGE TOWN OF ARKHAM OVER THE YEARS... SOME SAY A DIMENSIONAL SHAMBLER SWALLOWED IT WHOLE AT THE TURN OF THE CENTURY. OTHERS SAY IT SANK INTO THE MUD SOMEWHERE AROUND THE 1930S AND THE EVENT WAS COVERED UP BY THE AMERICAN GOVERNMENT. THEN THERE ARE THOSE THAT SPEAK OF ARKHAM ONLY IN QUIET, FURTIVE WHISPERS, AS IF THE TOWN ITSELF IS SOME ANCIENT EVIL THAT NOBODY SHOULD EVER SPEAK ABOUT." Flames licked the top of the fireplace mantel. "I PERSONALLY LOVE THAT ONE MOST, MWUHAHAA. ANYWAY, THE MOST COMMON IDEA ON ANCIENT ARKHAM IS THAT THE TOWN NEVER EXISTED AT ALL... THE FICTIONAL TALES OF ONE MR. H.P. LOVECRAFT COLLECTIVELY ADDED TO THAT BELIEF, RENDERING THE ENTIRE TOWN A FICTIONAL PLACE OF ABSURDITY AND COSMIC MALEVOLENCE."

"And yet, we are here. In 1988, no less," Quincy said.

"THAT IS CORRECT, MASTER..." Tim wondered for a moment why he still called Lilly and Quincy his masters even though he was set free from the oil lamp years ago. He concluded it must be sentimental. "ARKHAM WAS VERY MUCH A REAL PLACE," he continued. "IT WAS IN FACT AN EVENT WE NOW CALL THE SUNDERING THAT SIMULTANEOUSLY EVAPORATED THE ENTIRE TOWN FROM EXISTENCE AND ERASED IT FROM THE MINDS AND HEARTS OF THE ENTIRE CIVILIZED EARTH. WHATEVER THAT MEANS, HAHAHAHAHA."

"Wait," Quincy stopped him. "Go back a few. There's that word again. You mentioned the Sundering? And this is different from the Awakening?"

"CORRECT."

Lilly pulled the blanket closer. "What happened?"

The fire grew bigger again. "AN ARTIFACT, TWO OF THEM. I BELIEVE YOU CALL THEM RELICS."

Quincy and Lilly looked at each other.

"THEY WERE BROUGHT HERE, WHILE THEY DO NOT BELONG. IN FACT, THEY DO NOT BELONG ANYWHERE BUT THEIR INITIAL RESTING PLACE OF ORIGIN *AND* THE POPPY FIELDS OF FLANDERS AT THE EXACT TIME YOU LEFT, OR ELSE THEY WILL BECOME UNSTABLE, AS WILL THEIR PLACE OF ORIGIN IF THEY DO NO GO EXACTLY TO THE FIELDS AT THE CORRECT MOMENT IN SPACE AND TIME."

"Where were they before?" Quincy asked. He felt like his head was spinning. After everything, this was still something akin to 'too much information'.

"I BELIEVE IT WAS IN A PLACE YOU NOW CALL NOVA...SCOTIA?" Tim answered.

Lilly gasped. "Quince... The Abyss? The big flood? Did it happen because these relics left there at the wrong time?"

"Let's not jump to conclusions," Quincy told her, although he believed it was very smart of Lilly to figure that out. It may very well have been so. Somehow this terrifying news made him feel a bit more at ease, since it would explain two things. One, it gave them a reason to be here and two, it explained the Arkham thing, kind of. "When is this Sundering supposed to take place?"

"EH…ABOUT EH, TOMORROW…ISH," Tim answered sheepishly. "I am afraid we do not have much time."

Quincy scoffed in disbelief. "Oh, great. From one end time scenario right into another. I'm sick and tired of hearing the word *time* strewn about everywhere. If anything, *time* has shown us it's utterly meaningless. But whatever, we'll play along."

"What happens to the people of Arkham?" Lilly asked carefully. "Do they…die?"

"NOTHING AS GRISLY AS THAT, UNFORTUNATELY, HEHEHE," Tim answered. "NO, I BELIEVE THEY SIMPLY CEASE TO BE. ERASED FROM EXISTENCE, JUST LIKE THE TOWN, AS IF THEY WERE NEVER THERE AT ALL."

"That might be a fate even worse than death," Lilly said. "Imagine being there one day and gone the next with no one ever knowing you were alive at all. Nobody to remember your face, your personality. All memories of you erased. Even those of your loved ones."

"I take it Mom, Dad, and William all make it out then?" Quincy asked. "I doubt we'd know who they were otherwise, let alone the fact that we'd not exist at all."

"THE SWANSONGS ARE THE ONLY PEOPLE WHO ARE KNOWN TO HAVE ESCAPED THE SUNDERING. AS FAR AS IS KNOWN, ALL BLISSFULLY IGNORANT. BUT THERE ARE RUMORS OF A FOURTH SURVIVOR, ONE WHO HAD SEEN AND REMEMBERED IT ALL—"

"That's not important right now," Lilly interrupted. "This might sound harsh, but outside of Mom and Dad, I don't care who or what makes it out with them. As far as I'm concerned, we find the third relic, and we'll have a shot at stopping…well, everything?"

"EVERYTHING," Tim echoed. "I BROUGHT YOU HERE FOR THAT EXACT PURPOSE. WITH THE EXPULSION OF MY FIERY SOUL FROM THE FLESHY HEAP OF THAT *IDIOT* HOPKINS, I FINALLY REACHED THE ZENITH OF MY TRUE POWERS. AND I OWE IT TO YOU, AGAIN, SWANSONGS."

"You're welcome?" Lilly said carefully.

"I HATE HUMANITY. I HATE EVERY LIVING THING IN THE COSMOS. EVERY. SINGLE. ONE."

"Oh—" Quincy tries to speak.

"BUT I DO NOT HATE YOU, SWANSONGS. YOU GAVE ME PURPOSE, TWICE. I GAVE YOU PURPOSE BACK ONCE, IN ANTARCTICA. NOW, I WILL AGAIN REPAY THE FAVOR. WE WILL RETRIEVE THE THIRD RELIC, THE TABLETS OF DISTANT QUASARS, FROM GLOOMY ARKHAM, AND WE WILL OPEN THE ARK OF THE COVENANT AT THE FLANDERS CHAPEL. WE WILL CALL THE ETERNAL GUARDIANS, THE ANCIENT ONES, THE ELDER RACE. AND WE WILL STOP THE APOCALYPSE."

JOSIE'S COFFEE AND CAKES, *Arkham, MA, United States – 1 day, 2 hours, and 45 minutes until the Sundering*

Quincy and Lilly followed their parents and great uncle outside. After their little discussion with Tim, they decided that the only way they were going to get anywhere was to play along, however awkward and hard it would be to be around the people they knew were dead and who they missed very much.

Stepping outside of the famous Arkham Witch-House, which had not lived up to its terrifying reputation in the short time they had been there, the weather and general feeling was drab. Arkham appeared exactly like the tales had described it.

The town felt ancient even amongst the oldest of New England settlements. It was as if a quiet and foreboding European village had just up and left the old world entirely and plopped down here long before anything else ever fully took root. The buildings were old and a lot of them broken down with chipping, rotting wood and rusty bent nails. Roofs were slanted and crooked with tiles that were broken or missing. Houses sported overgrown spiky fences, creaking black shutters all around, and ancient weathervanes. This was Arkham alright, and it was pretty much like Tim had described: doom and gloom. It really did feel like a place out of time, and this could not be more true for Lilly and Quincy who were lost in time and space.

In stark contrast to the rest of the town, not far from the Witch-House, was the brightly lit, neon-lettered coffeeshop known as Josie's Coffee and Cakes. A relative newcomer in town, Josie had supposedly made quite a name for herself by serving a variety of homemade cakes and other pastries inspired by tried-and-true recipes from all four corners of the United States and beyond. At the time, it was a novel concept, especially for a town such as Arkham where its inhabitants tended to stick to their ways. They would eventually cave due to the delicious mango-infused New York style cheesecake and the good coffee too. Josie's was the perfect place for the twins to settle into this peculiar area for the time being.

"Eh, Katniss and Marty, was it?" Tobias pulled the chair back for his wife, helped ease her into the seat, and sat down himself.

Quincy felt uncomfortable answering. He didn't want to lie or trick his parents into anything, and, like his sister, he'd much rather lay all of the cards on the table immediately. But he knew he couldn't. He could only play along for now while trying to ignore the brightly colored visage of Tim swirling around in his half empty cup of admittedly great coffee. "Yeah, that's right," he answered, much to his hidden dismay. "Potter," he added afterward with a slight cringe.

The three Swansongs in front of them nodded politely.

"And how on earth did you end up in a total state of exhaustion from your travel?" William asked coldly. "I mean no offense, but this isn't the 1950s anymore. Travel by bus, taxi, and even train is now totally normal here in Arkham and —" William took a good hard look at the twins. "Well, to be fair, you hardly look like the sort of drifters or vagabonds that you usually see coming up from the southwest."

"William! You have some nerve," Emily protested. "They are clearly running away from some hardship they may or may not want to share with us. You can see the pain and anguish written all over their faces. You have no right to talk to them like that." Emily's loving and caring personality was well known to the twins. Seeing their young mother speak up like that hit them with a pang of nostalgia and sadness.

"I agree with Emily, William," Tobias added. "Those questions are hardly important. What *is*, is that you are okay now. How do you feel?"

"We are…fine, I guess," Lilly answered. "We feel very thankful for you keeping an eye out on us here, but…" She swallowed hard. "I'm sure we'll manage our way back on our own soon."

"That's good to hear, Katniss." Tobias smiled. "You told us earlier that you were passing through? Where were you heading?"

This might be a way in, Quincy quickly thought. He had been fumbling for a chance to change up the conversation for a while. Even though he'd love to spend hours picking his parent's brains, figuratively speaking of course. "Eh, we were heading for… Nova Scotia, actually," he stammered. Unsure of whether he sounded wholly convincing or totally the opposite, he went on: "We have some family living along the coast in Vermont, past Maine, and well, Canada."

"Our grandparents live up there in this beautiful Victorian. Truly marvelous," Lilly added. "You know the type of house you can get lost in as a kid? They have this big attic that could be the basis for all kinds of fantastical stories." Lilly looked over to Emily, who could not help but conjure a big smile on her face. Lilly knew her mother loved these kinds of things, and it warmed her to see her mother happy. She only hoped it wasn't enough to cause some kind of paradox with all of this information she shouldn't technically know. A few seconds of anticipation later, Lilly concurred it should not be the case.

"Nova Scotia, *fantastical stories*." William said that last part with a slight bit of contempt. "You two sound like you are perhaps interested in the supernatural? You know, the paranormal, the afterlife, the great world beyond the veil and mysteries of the moon and stars beyond? If so, then I might have something very interesting to show you."

Yes! the twins thought simultaneously.

Emily dismissed the notion. "William, I really don't think this is the right time and place for—"

"Oh, but it's totally okay," Quincy reassured her. "We are very much into that kind of *stuff*." He smiled.

Lilly visibly agreed, a broad smile appearing on her face.

"Oh, that's nice." Tobias smiled at them and then to William. "Perhaps Katniss and Marty have some stories to tell themselves, hm?"

Quincy and Lilly smiled through gritted teeth. "Like you wouldn't believe," Lilly told them. "Lots of things going on down south."

Emily's ears pricked up. "Where are you from exactly?"

"New Orleans!" the twins answered simultaneously. They couldn't help but laugh at their 'inner twin sensors' still doing their job.

The twins noticed a wrinkle on Emily's brow. It was as if a tiny pang of familiarity crept up in her mind, not one that caused warmth, but rather a cold, strange feeling of confusion. It appeared to go away as fast as it came, and soon Emily had the same lovely smile she had sported the entire morning. "You are twins, aren't you?" She stared them down with a grin, as if having uncovered their darkest of secrets.

"Yeah, we are," Quincy answered. He and Lilly both looked down at Emily clutching her pregnant belly with love and care.

"Are you…expecting twins?" Lilly tried. She knew it could be construed as a very rude question to ask, but she could not help this beautiful feeling of reconnecting with her mom.

Emily's cheeks went red, and she looked away. "I certainly think so… Tobias isn't so sure, but I have asked my doctor to not let the cat out of the bag." She laughed. "I like my bets sometimes."

"It's *gone!*" William suddenly called out in anguish. "My bag, it's stolen! The tablets are gone." He turned to Tobias. "We've been robbed, Tobias! What could happen if the tablets fall into the wrong…ack!" With all the talk on birds, bees, and twins, William was getting a bit anxious that the topic of conversation might have steered away from his passion, so he took it upon himself to drop his *interesting* items right there on the table for the twins to see themselves. But now they were gone. William looked around in panic. The coffee shop was at its busiest this time of day, and the bustle of people did not help his mood in the slightest. William stormed off outside in a panic.

The realization quickly crept in for Quincy and Lilly that losing this relic was devastating for their ultimate quest. It did not take long for the seriousness of the situation to settle in. Quincy shot a panicked look toward Lilly that said, *Lil… We* don't *have time for this, what are we going to do?*

"William was robbed, that's horrible!" Lilly held back, trying for her best high school drama acting. "Who could have taken the bag?"

"AHUMCOLLEGESTUDENTAAHHUM" came a voice from Quincy's coffee cup.

Tobias and Emily turned around. Tobias raised an eyebrow "What? Was that you, Quincy?"

Quincy tightly clutched the coffee cup and tried to ignore the sweat forming on his forehead. "Eh, I—" he stammered. "Excuse the coughing, something in my throat," he lied. "I saw a college student who I think carried away William's bag."

"Are you sure? Did you get a good look at him?"

"YES!" the voice said again. The noise was enough for Emily and Tobias to look at each other in confusion.

"Yes!" Quincy mirrored, nearly squeezing the cup hard enough to tear it in half. "I'm pretty sure. I, eh, used to own the same type of satchel. I got a good look at it and can remember its design quite well."

"QUITE!" Tim bellowed.

Emily squinted. "Your voice is breaking up, are you okay?"

"Positively divine!" Quincy reassured her. He was sweating bullets and making plans to kill Tim if he dared to open his mouth again. Perhaps Tim felt or knew this because he kept quiet after. Quincy excused himself.

"Is Marty really alright?" Emily asked Lilly.

Lilly nervously blew away a curl from in front of her eyes. "Yeah, he's fine. He gets really worked up whenever these kinds of things happen. A mixture of genuine excitement for a good mystery plus anxiety. He'll be fine."

Tobias nodded. "I understand. I must admit, I think feel a little bit of the same jitters."

Lilly smiled. "How *peculiar*," she could not resist saying.

A young woman, perhaps a couple of years older than Lilly and Quincy, walked up to the counter. She held a bright pink pen with an equally pink feather attached to the top. She sported a big badge on her uniform that said 'Josie.' "Thanks for your patronage." She smiled widely. "Is there anything else I might do for you?"

"Hey" —Lilly read the badge— "Josie. Oh, *you're* Josie. Oh my god, I *loved* the cheesecake!"

"Thanks!" Josie replied.

"Nothing for now, I think," Lilly continued. She looked over at Tobias and Emily. They both shook their heads politely. "But, while you're here, have you seen a college student pass by with a brown messenger bag?"

"A student from Miskatonic University?"

"Yes!" Lilly replied. She wasn't even sure if it *was* a Miskatonic student, but it was the only university around for miles.

Josie looked around the coffee shop and shrugged. "Well, yes dear. Who are you looking for, exactly?"

Lilly, Tobias, and Emily took a good look around and noticed about ninety percent of the clientele for Josie's Coffee and Cakes during its busiest hour was comprised of college students wearing their titular Miskatonic University hoodies and nearly all of them were brandishing beautiful brown leather messenger bags. Outside, William was halting everyone in his path who carried a bag that was even remotely similar to the one he lost.

Chapter 13

Miskatonic University Campus, Arkham, MA, United States - 1 day, 1 hour, and 44 minutes until the Sundering

THE OLD WALLS of the Miskatonic University lecture hall stretched up high toward the plastered ceiling. A bell had rung and a group of about twenty-five college students stood up from their seats and started packing their books into their bags. The History of Religious Mysticism and the Occult lecture had come to an end. It was one of the more peculiar classes the university offered. Every year the university saw less students interested in the subject, but the class was still held as a symbol or tradition from days past when, in the 1920s and 1930s, it was one of the most popular subjects.

Eric Marsh was an average student. He was twenty-two, excelled in history and sociology but not much else, and ate mostly ramen noodles as his unwillingly chosen breakfast, lunch, and dinner. His pale, often sickly-looking skin regularly took people aback, but he was used to explaining that his unique looks merely ran in his family. He claimed it was a gene thing he, and other times he swore it had something to do with skin pigmentation. He'd reassure people there was nothing wrong with him and even with his sunken eyes, he had a certain charisma about him. The challenge of having to win people over lit a fire inside of him that continued to burn brighter with every single day. Eric Marsh certainly had ambitions, that much was clear.

When the lecture hall had emptied and only Eric and his professor remained, Eric stopped lingering around the back and paced up to his scholarly superior with confidence.

Without looking up, the professor spoke in a hastened whisper, as if he was paranoid that someone was listening around every corridor. "Did you manage?" he asked, still rifling through the papers in his briefcase.

Eric's eyes flashed from left to right and to the back of the hall. "Yeah," he whispered back. "They were too busy feeding and questioning two random strays they found on the streets to pay any attention to me," he told the professor in a mocking tone, a sneer appearing on his pallid face.

"Show them to me." The professor finally lifted his face out from behind the briefcase. His tiny beady eyes were wide with excitement. "Quickly, man! Quickly!" he hissed.

Eric plopped the brown messenger bag onto the desk and undid the clips. He opened the bag and without speaking, pushed it forward.

A groan of satisfaction escaped the professor's mouth as he pulled the ancient tablets from the bag and held the precious artifacts in his hands. "This is excellent, most excellent." The smirk on the professor's face was a type of nasty that was hard to describe, an uncomfortable display of ugly facial features and an inherent malevolent disposition. "The Organization will not forget what you have done for us this valuable day, Mr. Marsh. I am sure your continued dedication to the cause will result in your presence and skills being... indispensable in the long run."

"What do they...do, exactly? They just look like a few dusty rocks to me," Eric said carefully. He knew he might be stepping on a few toes with that remark.

The professor scoffed. "These dusty…rocks, as you call them, are but another key to the puzzle of finding the resting place of something extraordinary. Your mind could not fathom just how important this *dusty rock* is in the advancement of the human race into a new age of enlightenment." The professor's eyes narrowed. "Somewhere in Antarctica lies the answer to everything. Life, the Universe… I doubt I will live to see our grand plan unfold, but *you*, Marsh, if you are willing, you might have a very vital role to play in all of this."

Eric felt a rush of excitement run through him. His family always told him that he was bound for greater things and greater glory than the dirty rotten docks and gray coast of the fishing village he hailed from. Eric only needed one more thing to be convinced. "I do wish to *experience* something for myself really soon…" he told his superior, doubt lingering in his voice. "Many of my peers tell me it only takes a single experience, a quick flash beyond the veil, to truly be immersed and convinced of the cause," he said and gulped.

The professor looked down at the tablets in his hands. He felt them growing and pulsating ever so slightly in his palms. He grinned. "Oh, I am sure something will come up in the next few days." With a shiver of resentment, he pushed the valuable things back into Marsh's hands. "Keep them with you for now; your new employer will stop by to collect them soon. Or call with instructions."

Eric nodded in excitement. "I am sure something will happen. And rest assured, Professor Carter, *I* will lead Haven into Antarctica some day and *find* our answers."

TOWN SQUARE, *Arkham, MA, United States − 17 hours and 20 minutes until the Sundering*

The search for the uncovered artifacts had thus far, unfortunately, led nowhere. Tobias and Emily had done their best to support William in his wild claims that a Miskatonic student was to blame for the theft and surely the entire campus had to be on lockdown until the perpetrator, or perpetrators, were caught. It was something campus security and the local police force did not seem to agree with, and they proceeded to be escorted off campus under the threat of arrest if they resisted. Tobias and Emily were relieved to have William leave the area but were still taken aback by the total panic William had caused and how much he was shaken up. They were precious artifacts and valuable, but they would be recovered in no time at all, Tobias thought. He couldn't understand the rush behind it. The excitement of the tablets' supernatural properties had all but left his mind at that point. Tobias and Emily were ready to head back home. The only thing that kept them from doing so the need to protect William's and Tobias's reputation from faltering as a result of William's more eccentric antics. Another thing that stopped the young Swansong couple from leaving were the two youngsters, Katniss and Marty. Both Emily and Tobias felt a sort of connection with the two, and they didn't hesitate to invite them to dinner at their hotel after returning from their own search for the missing bag.

Katniss and Marty, or rather Lilly and Quincy, had taken a more subtle approach to uncovering where the missing tablets had gone off to. They knew time wasn't exactly on their side, but they were aware that asking too many questions too boldly would result in things going awry sooner rather than later. Due to their age, they blended in well enough on campus so that nobody questioned their presence. Using that to their advantage, they went door to door at the dorms, asking if anyone had seen the stone tablets from the Nova Scotia expedition that had been on display. There were some students that asked what the tablets looked like, which took the twins aback because they had no idea, only having heard a vague description from William. They were sand-colored stone about a foot long, half a foot in width, and there were two of them; that was about the gist of it. They conveniently left out that the things appeared to be growing considering that would only confuse people and open the twins up to ridicule.

Tobias and Emily sat waiting for their newfound young companions in a quiet bistro at the edge of Arkham's town square. The late afternoon sun shone down upon the roughly hewn stone blocks that filled the marketplace, glistening from the quick rain shower that had preceded it, a true smorgasbord of chaotic and beautiful autumn weather.

"I wonder, Tobias…" Emily began. "What do you think about Katniss and Marty? For real I mean, do you feel the same way I do?"

Tobias smiled softly as he took off his glasses to polish away the rain spatter residue. "I know what you mean. They have a certain flair about them, as if we have known each other for quite some time already. It's uncanny. As if we are family."

"Right." Emily softly hummed to herself and looked deep in thought. Her face revealed a mixture of happiness and some kind of faraway melancholy. "Their initial reaction to us was strange to say the least and the ease with which they seem to pluck away at our personalities… To them, even more than us I think, it feels as if they have known us for longer than we can possibly imagine."

A sense of déjà-vu flashed across Tobias's mind. "Do you remember the people in the fog, Emily?" He took a sip of his coffee and blinked. "My word, it was only this morning but somehow it feels like that was ages ago…"

"At the banks of the river?" Emily asked, to which her husband merely nodded. "I remember clearly. Those two lonesome figures, there and then gone in the blink of an eye. A product of our own imagination running rampant in the early morning from lack of sleep…or…"

"Or a passage, a gateway…a tiny microsecond view of a different time and place? A place we know not of and have no idea where it leads or what we might find there." The more Tobias started to theorize and connect the dots in his head, the more his speech slurred and the angle of his coffee cup tilted downward. Emily waited until the first drop was going to fall then she grabbed Tobias by the wrist which took him out of his train of thought. She did it despite the doubt in her mind that things might really have taken a supernatural turn and despite the fact that she secretly wanted to see him spill coffee all over himself.

"Don't overdo it, dear," she reassured him. "Let's not forget that science, and you are a *great* scientist, is based in uncovering the facts, right? We do tried-and-true tests to see if we can disprove anything beyond a shadow of a doubt. If the science doesn't succeed then, *only then*, are we—"

"—are we forced to accept the improbable and fantastical as a possible truth," he finished. "Yes, I know, dear." He sat for a moment in silence with Emily softly squeezing his hand. "Still," he continued as he watched Quincy and Lilly stand on the corner of Whateley Street in the distance. Lilly, whom he knew as Katniss, was waving. "Time travelers?" he whispered to Emily.

Emily swallowed hard as she felt her heart skip a beat seeing the two young people approach. She clutched her belly. "Perhaps more."

???

Quincy dashed down the flight of stairs with such incredible speed he had to restrain himself and think rationally before he decided not to jump out of a window for an even faster and more painful getaway.

"Stop right there, *fish for brains*!" The burly but very agile man dressed in the green and dark blue Miskatonic University colors ran after him. The man with the yellowed teeth was behind him, screeching into the hallway. They were fast, quick on their feet, and unrelenting, often trailing Quincy by mere inches. He grabbed and snatched at his collar with one hand and held a silver cross in the other. "Drop those tablets this instant!" the broad-shouldered cultist yelled. "You have no idea how valuable those are!"

Quincy, panting and sweating, looked behind him and threw a sly smile at the angry face beneath the dark robe. "Trust me, *shit* for brains. There's little to nothing that can faze me anymore. I have died and have experienced rebirth of my body and my soul. I have seen the black abyss yawning and churning beneath the wobbling thin thread that separates rational human thought and utter and complete madness. I have seen the world ending and I have traveled back in time to prevent it. I have overcome great odds and shall overcome your puny little resistance." *Wow!* Quincy thought. *Perhaps I should write a book about all of this when it's finally over. If there's something left to write for.* He ran out into the broader, open campus hallway that overlooked the inner garden. Again, he somehow knew exactly where to go and, despite the growing number of inconstancies now, he was well on his way in his escape. The weather was typical for New England—gray and drab. Quincy looked behind him to see the man with the yellowed teeth losing distance on him. The other one, the gorilla type, he wasn't anywhere to be seen at all. Quincy smirked. Perhaps being big and strong didn't mean you were automatically fit as a fiddle. Or rather, perhaps his words really did resonate with the guy? He always wondered how it would be to make the most terrible and cursed statements regarding to humanity's survival and the crisis of existentialism.

Quincy felt an overwhelming sense of déjà vu and panicked. He suddenly remembered things which he did not for certain were real, merely a passing thought, or something injected by a thing more sinister. *What is happening to me?* he thought. *It's happening again! Where am I really? Can I trust anything?* And then: *Never mind. I must bring these tablets to safety at all costs,* right before several more students appeared in front of him with shining silver letter openers they waved menacingly toward Quincy's face. "You do not belong here, traveler," one of them spat. "You should have stayed in your own doomed time," another one added.

"Ah shit!" Quincy exclaimed before jumping and diving through one of the open arches that lined the right side of the half-open hallway. He landed painfully on his shoulder but managed to roll through most of the impact, a maneuver Lilly once taught him to, in her words, *"You know, not die so quickly."* Before long, Quincy was back on his feet, adrenaline pumping through his veins. He was still on track, he convinced himself. Just a few more meters and he'd be out in the fresh air, into the getaway car and off across the horizon of the Eastern Sea, back to navigating the timelines toward the salvation of their own original time. He crossed the courtyard diagonally and was on the other side in a matter of seconds. The bright mass of green and dark blue-cloaked individuals scampered over the little knee-high wall with a lot more trouble than Quincy had anticipated. *Yes, I remember this*, Quincy thought, right before he instinctively ducked. At that very moment, he saw the glimmer of metal protectors on the corners of the huge biology tome heading toward his face. Quincy dashed right and pushed the somewhat clumsy book-wielding student back. Putting all of his weight into it, he managed to knock him on his butt. The heavy book landed right on the frail student's chest and a gust of strained breath released from his mouth as he looked at Quincy with pleading, tired eyes. "I must have them," the student grunted. Quincy noticed he had sickly pale skin amongst other peculiar features. The student tried in vain to reach out and grab one of the stone slabs resting in Quincy's arms to no avail before blacking out. *Now what?* Quincy thought as he waited a couple of seconds. His eyes darted from left to right. Nothing.

Good, he thought again, and brought the walkie-talkie speaker to his lips. "I– I found the guy," he panted, still dashing toward what he hoped was an exit. "I have the tablets. You were right, the student was working for Haven, although I'm not quite sure he was aware of what he got himself into."

He looked back again. Still nothing except for the figure lying on the floor breathing laboriously, but breathing nonetheless. Quincy was relieved. "He's…fine. But… No, I don't know how I know his name."

Moira said something incoherent through the walkie-talkie. The only thing Quincy heard was, "We're ready for you. Please save us. Save everyone." Moira's familiar voice was comforting and filled Quincy with warmth. He felt at ease even though the message did not make sense to him at all. "Everything is dark here, please help us," she pleaded.

"Sure, I…"

Quincy sped through an apparent teacher's lounge on campus and emerged outside on the north-facing side of the historic building. There stood a quiet gallery full of weathered and begging-to-be restored works of art. The stored artwork was surrounded by wooden panels and beautiful candelabras. Peculiar, but not as much as the feeling that Quincy had been reliving this strange sequence of events over and over again. He dismissed the idea because something else shut Quincy up. In the middle of the gallery stood a strange man. He was of average height, sported an impressive but finely kept beard, and wore peculiar seventeenth century nobleman's clothing; he was poking several students in the back and hitting them in the head with a ruler.

"Come out and fight, do not stand on ceremony in front of *me*, evildoers. You slick sickly green and blue lapdogs of Satan, you swine of Beelzebub, come forth and face the wrath of your Maker!" The man's face contorted for a moment before he spoke again. "BLOOD FOR THE GOD OF DEATH, FACE ME MORTALS AND TREMBLE IN FEAR, YOU KNOW NOTHING!" he yelled, shook his head in confusion, and closed his eyes for a second. "You cannot control me, demon! For the righteous will always prevail."

Quincy looked behind him. There was a distinct lack of any pursuers. In fact, he saw one of the doors at the other end of the hallway slam to a close and heard what sounded like boards being nailed over it from the other side.

"Quincy… I am so cold. Help us… Please, Quincy. We can't do anything without you and Lilly." The walkie-talkie crackled.

"Oh, no. Oh, crap. It's *you*. I forgot about all of this, forgot again. *Tim*. The familiar face." Quincy eyed the old timey gentleman up and down. "Why is this happening?"

The man's eyes flashed toward Quincy, who was sweating profusely now that his 'exercise' had come to a complete halt. "Who stands before me now? Another pawn of the Antichrist? Perhaps another shadowy denizen of Carcosa in disguise, flaunting itself like a scholarly individual, hmm?" His eyes grew wide. "MASTER SWANSONG, WE HAVE NO TIME FOR THIS NONSENSE!"

"Wh–what do you mean, Tim?" Quincy gasped. "We have to bring these tablets back in order to…to…"

"HMM?" Tim scoffed. The rotting gentleman in front of him, which Quincy somehow knew was once Matthew Hopkins, shook violently and the jaws clicked gruesomely.

Quincy looked down, defeated. "I cannot remember… There was something… I…"

The shape of Matthew Hopkins sped toward Quincy in an uncanny, unnatural motion. He grabbed Quincy by the shoulders and shook him wildly. "OUT OF THERE YOU COSMIC DEATH SLUG!" Tim screeched in Quincy's face, who was instantly terrified. "GET OUT!"

Quincy shielded his face by throwing his arms up. "What are you doing?" The tablets fell from his arms and shattered on the floor below. "No!" Quincy bellowed. "That was our only chance! What are we going to do now? We're doomed!"

"OUT, QUICK! MASTER SWANSONG, GET THEM OUT OF YOUR HEAD, THIS IS NOT REAL!"

Quincy looked up with tears in his eyes. "Is anything ever real? I don't know anymore. I don't know what to do."

The stinking corpse of Matthew Hopkins lifted Quincy up

and shook him again. "YES, YOU DO!" Tim grunted. "YOU KNOW WHAT IS REAL, YOU CALLED OUT HIS NAME. ERIC MARSH!"

"What…" Quincy struggled loose and dropped to the floor. "What do you…"

A decomposing finger pointed at him. "USE IT AGAINST THEM, MASTER SWANSONG. THEY GAVE YOU A NAME. CLAIM YOUR PRICE AND SAVE WHAT YOU KNOW IS *REALLY* REAL!"

THE WITCH-HOUSE, *Arkham, MA, United States − 4 hours and 58 minutes until the Sundering*

Quincy woke up in the rickety bed in the Witch-house's attic room. He was soaking from sweat and fever. Lilly, very concerned for her brother, hovered above him. She tried to open her mouth to say something, but Quincy interrupted her.

"Eric Marsh!" he yelled at her.

Lilly ignored it. "You were screaming in your sleep again!" she told him. "Are you okay, Quincy? Talk to me, please."

Quincy gritted his teeth as he tried sitting up; he was still dizzy. "Eric Marsh…" he said again. "That's the guy…the student who took the tablets."

Lilly grabbed the pillow and pushed it against the headboard for Quincy to rest his back on. "How? How can you possibly know? And why does Marsh sound so familiar?"

Quincy wiped the tears and beads of sweat from his eyes. He eyed his sister with concern. "Name's bad news, remember? Haven…Antarctica…everything." He swallowed.

"Wait, it's *him*?" Lilly was visibly shocked. "*That* guy?"

Quincy nodded frantically. "Yes, *that guy*."

"Well, I'll fucking kill him!" Lilly yelled. "He's the root of everything. Almost everything. I'm sure."

"No, you won't kill him." Quincy snorted. "I know you. But I do agree, he's the root of *almost* everything. We can't weed out the entire thing, but I'm pretty sure he's the *seed*, the apple that fell too far from the tree, if you know what I'm saying.

"No."

"That's fine. Eh, let's just make it a bit more subtle, okay? No killing the guy or spouting anything at him that may lead to us divulging more information than necessary, okay?" Quincy scratched his chin. He felt a surge of adrenaline pumping through him. It was time to go. "And as far as how I know…" he added as he ran a hand through his clammy hair and laughed at himself. "Call it… Deus ex machina?"

Chapter 14

The King's Port Bed and Breakfast, Arkham, MA, United States - 4 hours and 2 minutes until the Sundering

WILLIAM FRANTICALLY SHOVED a handful of papers from his hotel room's nightstand into a brand-new suitcase. As he spun around, the remaining strains of his thinning gray hair flung wildly around. He shook as he put his glasses onto his nose. "How can you possibly know that? Hm?" The question was directed at the twins who were standing in the door openly panting. They had just run three blocks from the Witch-house to the hotel where their parents and great uncle were staying. It was still early in the morning and more than one complaining tenant opened their door and sneered at the two young people who came barging up the second-floor stairs as if the place was on fire.

"There's no time to explain!" Lilly shouted at him. A bit too loud perhaps because the hallway filled with complaints and threats to call the manager and have *these ruffians* thrown out. "There's no time to explain," Lilly repeated, this time whispering. "You've just got to trust us that we figured this thing out."

"Eric Marsh is the student that stole the tablets from under your nose at Josie's," Quincy added. "You just said it yourself that you remember him as a gifted student who was hungry for knowledge."

William shook his head. "No, no. That's preposterous. The two years I taught the young lad he was eccentric, buzzing for knowledge yes, but that was because he was highly gifted. Immense IQ that one, and very on the nose considering the subject."

"That subject being History of Occult Symbolism, right?" Lilly asked.

Their uncle nodded.

The door clicked to a close and Quincy dropped his hand from the handle to point at William. "There's your motive," he announced. He almost felt like a police detective or prosecution lawyer. "When he found out what you uncovered in Nova Scotia, he could not resist getting his grubby hands all over them. He waited until the right moment and snatched them up from right under your nose in the perfect place. A busy crowded café where everyone is squished together and everybody is dressed in the same university attire."

"That's...very unlikely now, I—" The seeds of doubt were planted, Quincy could see his great uncle's expression change right in front of his eyes. "Does he– Does he even take classes anymore? I stopped teaching there last year, I—"

The bed creaked as Lilly plopped onto it next to the nightstand. She fingered the leatherbound Bible hidden inside its drawer as she spoke. "Yeah, we garnered as much from his classmates. He's majoring in it now, and everyone thinks he's an idiot." She laughed. "I can't imagine many viable career choices outside of joining—"

Quincy loudly cleared his throat.

Lilly stopped herself from oversharing. "Anyway, he's totally into it. So, we imagined that would give him enough incentive to at least want to check things out." Lilly tried to stay calm even though she felt like they didn't have much time to iron out every detail. Of course, they couldn't tell William that, which made the whole process even more annoying. Lilly also found it annoying that, given more time, they could've figured out the culprit all on their own without Quincy having some kind of weird premonition dream. She hadn't divulged that last bit to Quincy, but she was sure he would agree. Marsh was an easy target to spot. Perhaps even too easy. The future director of the entire Haven organization itself. Right here in Arkham. The *fourth survivor*. If it hadn't been for his name being associated with basically *everything* that went wrong in the past few years, they'd surely think he was set up by the real culprit.

"Who is teaching the course now? Do you know?" William started pacing around the room. He seemed impatient and defeated. Quincy thought he might have accepted that his former protégé might have instigated this betrayal.

"It's…Carter? I believe. Randolph Carter?" Quincy answered.

William's eyes grew wide at the name drop. "*Carter!*" he yelled aloud. "I should have *known*!"

"You know him?" Lilly asked.

"The man's bad news," William went on, not skipping a beat. "I once had the now displeasure of meeting with him and entertaining his, I admit fascinating, accounts of his so-called dream travels. This was way back in the '40s when I was still a struggling writer coming to terms with my wild ideas about the cosmos and writing them as fiction. Still not aware of the keen powers of the universe, I first dismissed Carter's claims as a form of shell shock the poor sap had acquired during his stint in Flanders during World War I. But, in the next few years, I would acquire the…right set of skills, you might say, to understand Carter might've been under the influence of something, or someone, very powerful that changed him forever."

"Who or what might that be?" Quincy decided to try his

luck and press William just a bit further to hopefully let out *something* that would tie this whole thing together.

"Bad people," William said grimly. "People… Organizations that lust for power and do not fear and do not understand the consequences their actions might lead…" William sighed and put his head down. Just a few moments later he looked up at the twins with newfound determination. "I don't know who you two are, but I get the feeling you have a bigger role to play in all of this… I hesitate to admit all of the ideas that run through my head that could possibly be *some* kind of origin story on why you are here at this very moment helping *me* instead of just going on your merry way… But no matter. All that matters now is getting those tablets back because I understand why you need them."

Lilly was taken aback. She had prepared a whole speech about once they got the tablets back why she and Quincy had to borrow them for a while, but it turned out to be for naught as William had apparently been thinking two steps ahead. Quincy stayed quiet.

"No need to explain right now." William tried to metaphorically raise the temperature in the room back from below zero. "Katniss, you go get Tobias and Emily, they're at 302 down the hall. Marty—" William threw Quincy a set of keys. "You know how to drive, right? Get my car from the lot outside and drive it around the building as fast as you can. We're heading down to the campus."

Quincy caught the keys but didn't move. He realized that, in their time, Arkham had disappeared. He figured there weren't many reasons to hurry *now* considering he had the knowledge that the tablets wouldn't leave town anytime soon. A strange gust of wind and the way the colors of the candle on the little desk in the corner flickered made Quincy come to his senses. *Master Swansong,* Quincy heard the strangely calm voice of Tim inside his head. *I AM HERE TO REMIND YOU THAT I MANAGED TO PULL SOME STRINGS AND DO SOME INVESTIGATING AND YOU'VE GOT TWO AND A*

HALF HOURS GET A MOVE ON YOU WORTHLESS SACK OF– I MEAN. BEST HURRY UP, MASTER. WE DO NOT WANT ALL OF THIS TO BE FOR NOTHING, NOW DO WE?

"Well?" William asked when Quincy did not move a single muscle.

A rub of the eyes and an involuntary yawn brought Quincy back to his senses. "Sorry, I'll get on it right away."

"Good," answered William. "We'll get Carter and stop their fickle attempts at messing with forces they do not understand."

And hopefully teach Marsh a lesson in humility, Quincy thought. *But first, I'm going to need to visit a library really quick.*

MISKATONIC UNIVERSITY CAMPUS, *Arkham, MA, United States – 2 hours and 55 minutes until the Sundering*

With unrelenting force and channeling the innate wrath of soccer moms from around the country, William Swansong's Chrysler minivan sped onto the Miskatonic University grounds on that dreary, rainy morning that would be Arkham's last. The iron gates that welcomed prospective students to campus from all over the world creaked as the sides of the car scraped by them. There was no reason for caution anymore, William Swansong thought to himself, although it left quite the mark on both Tobias and Emily who, at the moment, had little to no insight into the situation.

William threw the car into a parking space as close to the entrance of the main dorms as he could find. With a single swift movement, he shut off the engine, unbuckled his seatbelt, and leaped out of the car, shutting the door behind him. The twins followed.

"Stay in the car, we won't be long," William ordered Tobias and Emily. "It's better if this matter is solved efficiently and quickly. It's better if we don't have more people than necessary to avoid others questioning why we are on this campus."

"William, wouldn't it be better if *we* went instead of you?" Tobias rightfully asked. "You've already been kicked out once, haven't you?" He smiled slyly.

William scoffed. "Pah, Peterson has had a grudge ever since I started my work here all those years ago. He never works Thursdays, so I bet the one person who'd dare escort me out isn't even here." William turned around and started marching toward the entrance. "We'll be *right* back!"

As the twins started to follow, Emily rolled down the car window from the backseat.

"Hey, Katniss, Marty." She gestured toward them. They turned their heads simultaneously, somewhat confused but with the same mix of emotions that ran through them every time they engaged in conversation with their parents.

"Yeah?" Lilly answered.

Emily was alternating between two expressions, one of concern and one of cautious intrigue. "I have no idea what is going on," she admitted. "Whatever this revelation was that you brought to William has got him dead set on getting those rocks back no matter the cost, come hell or high water. Please tell me what is really going on."

"We…can't," Lilly admitted. "It's really hard to explain, and even if we could, it would be better not to."

Tobias frowned. "You two are tough nuts to crack alright. But is all of this really worth William's hassle? It's not like it's life or death here."

Lilly and Quincy remained quiet. Lilly visibly bit her tongue.

"Is it?" Emily asked.

Quincy sighed. "If we said, 'yeah, kind of, maybe,' could we leave it at that?"

"Yeah," Emily conceded.

A smile appeared on Tobias's face. "Kind of," he said.

"Maybe." Emily grinned.

Lilly and Quincy froze in place, their eyes wide. For a moment it felt as if they were looking in the mirror. It was an uncanny zap or sparkle of electricity that ran across their spines. An innate sense of connection. They wondered if the Swansong couple felt it too.

Quincy awkwardly scratched his back. "We better go get the things back, we'll be with you in a bit." He started backing up toward the big doors.

"Hey, wait a minute. We're parked in a handicapped spot, this will get us in trouble," Tobias exclaimed. "There's no room anywhere else."

"Your beautiful wife is pregnant." Lilly smiled awkwardly. "Tell them it's an emergency."

Emily laughed. "But we're standing on a *university* parking lot, the hospital isn't even close. And what if I really had the babies just now?"

"Wait…plural?" Tobias interjected.

"What day is it?" Lilly counted on her fingertips. "Nah, you'll be *fine*!"

"Emily…" Tobias tried again, but he did not appear to be able to get through to the two women.

Emily grabbed Lilly's hand out of desperation. "Wait, just a little longer." She looked desperate. Lily saw something change in her eyes. "Who are you, really? Please tell me."

She knows, Lilly thought panicked. "We've really got to go. I'm sorry." She pulled her hand back. "I'm really sorry. I– Quince, I'm coming, I—"

"Q-Quince? Quincy?" Emily stammered.

"Fuck," Lilly spat under her breath. She ran toward the doors where Quincy was impatiently waiting for her.

Emily watched the pair go inside. Tears stung the corners of her eyes.

"Em?" Tobias grabbed her hands. "Are we having…"

"Twins." She nodded. "A boy and a girl."

And right then, Tobias became suddenly and inexplicably light-headed.

. . .

THE ABSOLUTE BEGINNING *of the universe and its simultaneous chaotic end, impossible to place, immeasurable by space and time*

It is said that extraordinary events happen to extraordinary people. Yet when we ask ourselves whether or not it is these events or the people that make them extraordinary, that's anyone's guess. Thus, when Lilly and Quincy first arrived in Arkham, this distinct thought might've already sprung into your head, dear reader, that it wasn't to stop disastrous events from happening that led them here, but the possibility of them arriving at such a highly volatile place that might have been the catalyst. Lilly and Quincy caused the Apocalypse, the Awakening, everything.

Poppycock.

Sorry, I just like that word. But no, it's not like that at all. The essence is in the word. Catalyst. Cat. I am a cat. You will remember my ramblings from earlier acts, or the really observant among you might even remember me from earlier adventures. You might call me all kinds of different things. I am a watcher from the sky, a curator of events, a storyteller among you, I am *everything*. And yet, *not all*. Who am I really but a bystander that has watched worlds rise and fall. Eons of civilizations are to me but a blink of an eye, a small dot across millions of trillions of timelines. I can assure you that whatever line of thought you have or wild theories you conjured up about the twins accidentally setting up the events of the entire series will probably not be true. Poor twins otherwise, am I right?

But let us not get into all that mess. I am a curator, yes. But is everything under my control? No. Would I like to see our original timeline flourish and not become the intergalactic playground for a bunch of creepy, slimy, horrible monsters that have been so terrible to describe that they have had but fleeting roles in this gigantic hellscape of a real-life apocalypse? I would very much like that. So, you must understand, dear reader, that whatever which way you read the story, be it yours or someone else's, like our dear Lilly and Quincy Swansong, always remember this: whatever happens, good old Henry can only play with the long, endless strings of the universe but the outcome is never his to keep or control. *You* are in control, and you have the power to do anything.

When we follow Quincy and Lilly on their quest to acquire the relics they so desperately need to save their own doomed timelineand however many slight nudges in the right direction they receive, they still have the power to *move moun-tains*. Figuratively speaking, that is. I know a guy who used to do that. Complained about his back a lot, what an annoying little– Anyway, the catalyst. There's that word again. Even though I, Henry the cat, am a master of time and space, I cannot change a thing about what might already have been decided eons ago when almost everything you see around you is space dust left over from the heart of a dying star. What I can do is nudge someone in the right direction that *can* fix this mess. But not with all-seeing, all-knowing supernatural powers, but rather by just nudging good people.

The *catalyst*, my friends, is just a word. A scapegoat used to divert blame for the actions of other people. Actions that good folk like Lilly and Quincy might be able to divert.

But who, I hear you ask, is to blame for these horrible things known as the Gibbous Horde? Who brought them to us in the first place? What really happened and why?

I don't know. I'm just a cat.

Chapter 15

Miskatonic University Dormrooms, Arkham, MA, United States - 2 hours and 10 minutes until the Sundering

WILLIAM SWANSONG STOOD near the empty registry desk near the dorm's front entrance. He was casually loading 9mm rounds into a shiny new revolver that had been concealed in his belt. He also rummaged through a duffel bag he had taken from the car and produced an exquisite looking oil lamp. It appeared so shiny and immaculate the twins were certain it had never been used before.

Lilly closed the door behind her, and she and Quincy could only watch awestruck at the tableaux that started to unfold in front of them. The oil-lamp's wick started to pulsate with light ever so slightly before igniting in a purple flame with a glow that gradually turned a brighter and bigger red The flame, they noticed, had eyes and those eyes had a personality shining through that they were all too familiar. The twins felt it was kind of nice having Tim around during their adventures in the Arkham of days gone by. He was the one that brought them there in the first place and, even though they hadn't really started thinking about it yet, he must also be their ticket out of there when the time came. What they hadn't expected, save for Tim keeping an eye out like he did in Josie's diner, was for the Fire Vampire to appear suddenly in front of someone other than themselves. Additionally, what they *really* had not expected was for Tim to appear in front of W.A. Swansong and apparently feel very happy about it.

"GOOD OLD WILLIAM! I'D SAY IT IS A DELIGHT TO SEE YOU AGAIN BUT WE BOTH KNOW I ABSO-LUTELY DESPISE MORTALS MUHAHAHA!" the disembodied voice coming from the general direction of the strange flash of light in the oil lamp exclaimed.

"Timaxoatilaciluzipta, you old devil you," Swansong grunted with delight. "How's Crowley?"

"DEAD!" Tim cackled.

William visibly appreciated the morbid joke and laughed along merrily. "Are you aware of the issues we are facing?"

Quincy and Lilly, who had trouble speaking since their jaws had figuratively dropped to the floor at this cosmic display of madness, could swear they saw the oil lamp make a movement akin to nodding.

Without displaying any signs of explaining how, when, where, and why he knew Tim, or Crowley for that matter, William turned toward the twins and tucked the revolver back into his belt. "You two go and find Eric, get the tablets, and do what you have to do. Go home. I'll take care of Carter. He has been on my radar for a while now, he won't get away this time."

"Are— Are you going to kill him?" Lilly stammered. Out of everything that had happened over the past few minutes that didn't make sense, it was probably the most sensible thing to ask.

William looked grim. "I do not take pleasure in killing."

"I DO!" Tim yelped with glee.

"But I will if I must," William continued. "The likes of someone like Carter corrupting these young students and recruiting them into his doomsday organization… It makes me physically ill, and I will not have it. He must be stopped."

The hairs on the back of Quincy's neck stood straight up. "Did you say…doomsday organization? Do you mean Haven?" Quincy's mind felt like it was desperately gasping for air. His suspicions were all true. Haven was already here, their tendrils twisted in everything, corrupting the souls of all they touched. Every horrible thing they had faced up until now. Every death, every monstrous calamity, every inch of suffering. It was all Haven. Always Haven. And now, Eric Marsh, fourth survivor and future initiator of the Awakening, was but a stone's throw away from them.

William stared intently, his eyes piercing through Quincy as if he peered into his future nephew's very soul. "Go," he murmured.

"But—" Lilly hesitated. She was reaching the same train of thought as her brother.

"GO!" Tim echoed William. It was the fiercest Lilly and Quincy had ever heard him. At least, the fiercest he had ever addressed either of them.

Tears of anger and confusion stung the corners of Lilly's eyes as she and Quincy ran off into the opposite hallway.

MISKATONIC UNIVERSITY DORMROOMS, *Arkham, MA, United States – 1 hour and 39 minutes until the Sundering*

Without a single moment of hesitation, Lilly kicked down the dorm door that had the nametag *E. Marsh* hanging next to it and boldly walked in. "Hand it over *right now*, you *scum!*" Lilly yelled, loud enough for the entire floor to hear.

The yelp of surprise coming from the dark, dusty dorm room was to be expected, but Quincy had also expected to find a wholly different scene when he entered the little bedroom one filled with loose papers, blotches of ink, and old leather-bound tomes. Rather than coming face to face with the younger version of the disgusting Haven director they had come to know and loathe over the years, his only saving grace being he was devoured by a Mind Flayer before he had the chance to stink up their vibe some more, Quincy and Lilly were surprised to find a scrawny, extremely pale and scared to death individual on the ground. Marsh was shielding his eyes, having turned away from his attackers and dropped to the floor in a fetal position. He looked ready to pee his pants.

"Uh, hi," Lilly said in a much calmer, perhaps even rational voice in contrast to the dominating presence she had displayed just moments earlier.

"Wha— What do you want? Please don't hurt me. I haven't done anything wrong," Eric pleaded. He didn't move an inch from his spot on the floor. "I don't have anything valuable, nothing at all."

Quincy smirked. "As a matter of fact, Eric, you absolutely do." He told the heaping pile of misery, "You've stolen invaluable property belonging first and foremost to the Massachusetts Archeological Research Department which was graciously on loan for the Miskatonic University laboratory and by proxy W.A. Swansong so he could partake in scientific study of the objects for structural and historical analysis."

He's pulling this straight out of his ass! Lilly thought. *This must be that minor in Applied Criminal Law he took finally at work. This is amazing.*

Marsh stammered, "I— I have no idea what you are talking about." Finally, he lowered his arms and turned around, still prone on the uneven wooden floor that creaked with every motion. "Wait, you two?"

Quincy crossed his arms, his prepared lawyer-esque disposition at the ready. The glistening beads of sweat forming on Quincy's forehead could have been caused by the risk he took, or their general lack of time. But as far as Lilly could tell, Marsh didn't notice their farce so she played along best as she could, wondering what Quincy's ultimate plan was.

"You can't get away with this you know," she told Eric.

"We know you've got the tablets stashed away in that briefcase over there. So let's make this as easy as possible."

Quincy nodded. "Yes, let's." He looked at Lilly with bewildered eyes. If ever this uncanny connection twins were supposed to have would come back from retirement this was that exact moment. He could only hope Lilly felt the vibe enough to play along. Actually, he knew she would, there was no doubt about it. The question was, would Marsh take the bait?. "Here's the deal, Marsh. You give us the tablets, we'll tell the police you mistakenly took the wrong shoulder bag with you, no harm done." Quincy was bluffing. As he stared longer into Marsh's eyes, he started to see some of the ugly traits he had come to know and hate. This pale kid in front of him would never go for it, Quincy thought.

"I don't know what you're talking about."

Lilly sighed, walked straight up to a cluttered desk, and shoved a lamp onto the floor where it broke into tiny pieces. She opened the leather messenger bag and took out the two stone tablets. They were heavier and longer than William described, but they felt like just ordinary rocks to her. "Strange…" she murmured. "They're so…" But then she quickly turned and growled at Marsh. "There!" She gritted her teeth. "You know *exactly* what we're talking about. Oh, and thanks for not even putting up so much as a small fight. We'll be taking these now."

Phew. Leave it to Lilly to be intimidating as heck! Quincy thought. He swallowed hard.

A streak of panic appeared on Marsh's face. "You– You don't know who you're dealing with, man! These people… They're…"

"Dangerous? Crazy? Crazy, dangerous, and trigger happy?" Quincy squinted at Marsh. *Got you,* he thought. "Yes, yes they are, Eric. Trust me when I say that I believe *you* have no idea who you are talking about."

"Show him the evidence, Marty!" Lilly spouted. She saw Quincy's lips curl into a sleek smile for a brief moment. There was the twin connection they sought. Their setup was complete, the hook, line, and sinker deployed, and the fish was circling the bait.

Quincy plopped down a newspaper article from a couple of years ago on the desk under Marsh's nose. Satanic panic was rampant in the '80s, so it was easy enough to get their hands on some disgusting headlines after a quick visit to the library. The front-page article was about a cult whose base of operations had been ransacked after nearly fifty cult members had committed ritual suicide in the name of some old forgotten religion. They were convinced they had been chosen to bring forth its message into the twentieth century and beyond. Marsh's eyes began to widen as he read.

It was the first time Lilly laid eyes on the article that Quincy had been so suspiciously happy about finding. She was starting to put the puzzle pieces together now. She knew exactly the angle her brother was trying to take. "You think they're the only ones claiming fortune, fame and eternal life?" she told Marsh. She was worried about the immortality remark, not knowing if she overdid it. But when the gasp came out of Marsh's mouth, she knew she said the right thing. *Hooked.*

Quincy tried not to beam with pride at his sister's incredible performance. Now all that was left was to reel this guy in and spare his gross, miserable self an existence as a top dog in one of the worst organizations the world had ever seen. "There's nothing out there, Eric. We've been there. *We tried to see! To experience.* But there was nothing, just pain and misery."

"R—really?" Marsh looked defeated. His so-called charisma had been sucked away by the realization that his hopes and dreams might've been shattered forever before he even got a chance to experience *anything*. "How can I possibly know that's true?"

"You have to take our word for it. But realize *you* committed a crime here for someone who was too *cowardly* to do it himself. You were already becoming a pawn, just like these guys with their sheep." Lilly pointed at the newspaper article. "Get out now before it's too late."

"I don't know what to think anymore, I—"

A flurry of gunshots rang through the building, interrupting Eric and startling his fragile mental state to a point of near-frenzy.

Quincy tried to remain as calm as possible. "You see, Eric? Do you see? Did you hear that? Already this despicable group's recruits have started to take their own lives in the name of these horrid ideologies."

Eric was unable to say anything at all. He was pale as a ghost, even more so than usual. Quincy took the messenger bag from Lilly and flung the strap over his shoulder. "Don't fall for the trap, Eric."

"Yeah, stay in school," Lilly added right before she and Quincy calmly walked back out into the hallway, nervous sweat pouring from just about everywhere.

After a second or two of silence Quincy turned a sly eye toward his sister. "Those shots weren't part of—"

"No, I-wasn't-even-aware-of-a-plan-we-gotta-check-that-out-right-now!" Lilly exclaimed in a voice that was nearly too high-pitched for the average human to hear.

Among a bustling crowd of panicking and confused students, the twins headed in the opposite direction of everyone else—heading toward the direction where the shots had rung out from.

MISKATONIC UNIVERSITY DORM ROOMS, *Arkham, MA, United States – 59 minutes until the Sundering*

A few drops of blood turned quickly into an expanding pool underneath a heavily panting W.A. Swansong who was lying on the floor in the empty teachers' lounge. Lilly and Quincy arrived at the scene as quickly as they could with the local emergency responders flooding in mere seconds after.

"William! What ha—" was all Quincy could say before the

throng of police officers accompanied by medical staff pushed him to the side.

As the medical professionals started to do their magic, a detective knelt alongside Swansong. He looked like your run of the mill gritty cop. Short hair combed back, three or four-days worth of stubble, and he reeked of coffee and cheap gas station sandwiches. "Sir, are you still with us? This is really important, sir…" he said to William. "Who shot you? Where did they go?"

William couldn't keep his eyes off Lilly and Quincy. "Professor Carter…" he groaned. "Pulled a gun on me without remorse, without warning…no reason at all."

"Did he have a motive?" the detective questioned him.

William bit his tongue. It was apparent that the pain was nearly unbearable. "We were rivals…" he panted. "He just ran off… I– I don't know where…"

The detective turned toward the twins. "And these two? How did they get in here?" he asked his colleagues then looked at William, "Do you know these people, sir?"

"Students here…" William grunted. "I came to visit…" Through the pain, a sly smile appeared on his face. A first in many ways, Quincy and Lilly knew. "They're family," William ultimately told the detective, right before he drifted off into unconsciousness.

Quincy and Lilly saw one of the candles on a windowsill flare up when nobody but them was looking in that general direction.

"You two," the detective tried getting their attention. "Either of you see the suspect run away?"

The flame on the candle grew. It pulsated, as if with delight. It was a strange motion, like someone sinking in their chair with satisfaction after a good meal.

"Let them get some air first, Tony." Another lawman gestured at the detective. "They look positively mortified, man."

The twins could see two eyes squinting in the flames, as if the fire itself smirked. They were sure it did. Pretty damn sure.

THE BANKS *of the Miskatonic River, Arkham, MA, United States — 19 minutes until the Sundering*

There was no way to say goodbye. No quick hug and well wishes. It was impossible for the twins to come face to face with their parents in the state in which they found themselves. To be on the brink of traveling back to a doomed world in which everything that could go wrong had gone wrong, back from this time in which their parents were alive and well. It was a hard pill to swallow, and it wasn't one they could have possibly taken if they were face to face with Emily and Tobias Swansong, having to say goodbye again, this time forever. It was too much to take. So when the time came to go back, back to Earth, back to their original time, the time in which everything else was already dead and gone and only a single patch of old European woodland was left, they had to do so from quiet solitude a little ways outside of the bustling Arkham streets.

During the midday, the near ever-present fog of the Miskatonic had lifted somewhat and the twins could see the river trail from the rough-hewn stone bridge of town all the way inwards toward the countryside. Standing like silent sentinels along its path were cracked and crooked old willow trees interspersed with the mightiest of broad oaks. A true tree climber's paradise. There was no doubt in Lilly's mind that if things were different, they would have wanted to stay here for as long as they could, basking in the soft sunlight of the dying day, up in the treetop feeding nuts and trail rations to curious squirrels and other critters.

But this was not such a day.

The twins looked down to see the vivid colors on the water. It was ingrained in their memory just like Fire Vampire Time. The beautiful bright display of oranges, yellows, deep reds, and warm purples always reminded them of the end of summer, or at least the end of a bright summer day when the sun dips behind the horizon but its light still lingers across the vivid sky. At the end of summer came fall, they realized, and with fall, the death of the world followed by a cold slumber in winter. And next year when the ice melted and any surviving life emerged back from their hiding holes, only then would spring commence and the rebirth of life on Earth would continue until the universe sighed its last breath.

And even then, that would not have to be the end, Lilly had surmised.

With tears streaming down her cheeks, she realized the true beauty and wonder of the cosmos in all of its tiny intricate details. For what kind of existence would be able to end, she thought, if that same existence had allowed her to do the impossible on more than one occasion. The absolute cherry on top, the grand prize, the one thing everyone who misses someone could only dream of doing— hanging out with deceased loved ones in a more innocent time in their lives, seeing them happy. There was no way everything could simply end, she realized. For these precious and impossible moments live for an eternity not only in our hearts and souls but in the fabric of reality itself. Every tiny molecule brimming with the spark of life and memory would continue on and echo into eternity, not until some arbitrary end, but forever. And with that came hope, and hope was the tiniest sliver on which they could lean and have faith, faith that they would be able to finish their mission, do the right thing and save everything. Save everything so that, whenever the cold had passed and humanity awoke on that vivid spring day somewhere in the future, we could look at each other as a species and be thankful. It was what Lilly would fight for until her dying breath, and she only had to glimpse at her brother to know he too felt the same.

Quincy looked down at the sunlight reflected in the quiet churning of the river's surface next to them and saw the same dancing lights and familiar colors Lilly had already spotted. Between the flickering lights he could see the two strange slits of darkened red he recognized as Tim's eyes.

WE HAVE NO TIME LEFT, NEARLY A FEW MINUTES. THIS SPOT WILL SUFFICE, GET READY, Tim's voice rang in both of their heads.

The twins grabbed each other's hands and stood face to face, foreheads resting against each other's. A flurry of emotions flew through their minds as they felt the familiar pull of time and space bending around them. For any onlooker that would not understand the strange phenomenon that had manifested at the banks of the Miskatonic river on that day, the fog had risen to obscure this most unnatural of occurrences.

Right before the crackle and pop, the moment before everything would go black and it started to feel as if gravity itself was reversed and the sensation and weight of the ever-expanding cosmos was dropped on their heads telling them they were small and insignificant, Lilly looked away from Quincy for only a moment. What she saw made her feel like her soul was hit by a freight train.

Quincy turned his gaze southeast across the river where the first bridge stood like the last watchtower of a forgotten age lost to time immemorial. He saw two lone figures standing on the bridge, obscured by fog and the light drizzle of endless Arkham rain, watching them. Quincy felt his heart break and wondered if the guilt and pain that accumulated deep within him would ever fully heal.

Did they know?

It was all he could think before he felt his sister squeeze his hand and everything went black. The peaceful world, the satisfying happy world in which his parents were alive, happy, and brimming with hope was now gone, and Quincy knew it would never return.

• • •

EMILY STARED off into the fog for a few minutes after she and Tobias saw the two lone figures, which they knew were their newfound traveling friends, disappear. Emily had pressured her husband into leaving the car and heading back with her to the riverbank. She had known that the twins would not return. She wiped away a single tear and then turned toward her husband who stood there equally dumbfounded and awestruck as he stammered to form a sentence. Like Emily, he felt something deeply profound about the entire scene. He dared not express his full suspicions.

"I– I do not know what—" he tried to tell her.

Emily grabbed her husband's arm and gently squeezed it. "There's little I can add here, Tobias. There's so much we could discuss, wonder, philosophize about… But why not stay here for a while?"

Tobias turned to her, somewhat confused. "What do you mean?" He pulled the coat tighter around him as a gust of air blew the now steadfast falling rain into his face.

"Do not let the rain distract you from this moment, Tobias. Look at where we are, where *you* are. You are at the cusp of discovering the truth behind everything you have ever wondered about. You have just seen with your own eyes that which you have been pursuing your entire life. Isn't it wonderful, Tobias?" Emily moved closer and embraced him. "But I do think I feel what you might feel…"

Tobias sighed deeply. "There is a certain…melancholy about all of this, don't you think? I have no idea why…but…I feel like I would have very much liked to get to know them better. Think of the possibilities…to know where they really came from…what they really came to do…who they really are…"

With her right hand and arm, Emily cradled her belly gently and let her head drop onto Tobias' shoulder. "Time will only tell if we ever see them again." Tears started to fall. "But…I have a feeling we will…very soon."

PART IV

What Remains of Forever

Chapter 16

The Sonian Woods, Flanders, Belgium – 56 minutes until the end of the world

WITH A BRIGHT RED flash moments later, the twins were pulled back to their own time. A loud angry voice screamed in the air and there was a streak of red, orange, and indigo light phasing through and swirling around the treetops, drifting upward until it eventually disappeared.

A sinister voice rang out from the wood's edge. It was something that the twins had heard before, and it filled them with absolute dread to hear it repeated.

"Well done, well done. Swansongs and friends… You have found it, the Chalice of the Deep Wood, the embodiment of Paganism, the 'old' ways, the ancient gods…" The group heard mock applause coming from the edge. With each clap the voice came closer. "You have done it, my children. Now let me, Brother Azael, be your guide to the Apocalypse. For it all ends here…"

But at that very moment, unlike the first time this happened, there was no silence or panicked sighs and shouts but the roaring of four very distinct voices that cut through the air like knives.

"They have arrived! Lay down your weapons, Azael, or face our immediate wrath!" War cried out as he flew over the group with his trusty steed. The twins took advantage of the chaos and scurried toward their friends in the middle of the clearing while staring at the edge of the deep dark woods in fright. The pair of familiar yet sinister bright red eyes peered at them from the darkness just beyond, but they weren't the eyes of a fierce apex predator; these red eyes looked deathly afraid. Something was different, the sounds of weapons unsheathing were now audible in the clearing accompanied by what sounded like a wild beast growling as it got cornered.

Lilly flew into Liz's arms, who embraced her fully. "Hey, what happened there?" Liz asked. "You seemed kind of translucent and floaty for a few. You alright?"

"Yeah," Lilly reassured her. "We're fine, we——"

Sean crawled over to Quincy and with wide eyes started to laugh. He pointed at the two stone tablets cradled in Quincy's arms and then to the mossy gem-embedded chalice held by Lilly. Sean pulled out the cross he had been safekeeping and held it up, victorious. "You fucking did it. I don't know what the hell happened but you…you did it." He sighed with relief.

Behind them the terrible noise of monstrous wailing echoed loudly from the woods. The group looked up to see the other horsemen flying up above, on their way to take care of the little problem with Brother Azael and Deogen. For a moment, Moira pondered how it was possible for a human skull to wink when Morty flew over, but she decided there were more pressing matters at hand.

Lilly, Quincy, and Sean clutched the relics close to their chests with dazed expressions that betrayed their confusion. They had everything they needed to make all of this go away. With the exception for Brother Azael getting his dues just beyond the edges of the forest, the world still seemed like it was planning to end pretty soon. Within the hour soon.

"What now?" Liz asked, directing her question to nobody in particular. "You got the thing, and the other thing. So what do we do now?"

Then, from the tops of the trees, a familiar looking cat started dropping down to the forest floor. Gracefully it jumped from branch to branch until it safely landed between the group. It paced slowly alongside each of them, finally stopping near Moira and looked up at her.

"There is that cat again..." Moira said as she locked eyes with the critter. "Hey..." she said softly and squatted down. Without hesitation, the cat jumped up on her lap and kneaded, satisfied. Moira's eyes widened when the little beast turned its nose to her ear, and she heard the quiet whispers of the entity that was concealed within this body of one of the most beloved of animals. *South... To the chapel you must go*, it said.

"Uh... It's telling us to get back to the chapel at the edge of the woods. Like, ASAP."

"The *cat* told you this?" Sean was skeptical. "I don't know..."

Liz shook her head. "I don't care. We're rolling with it. I want to get the *hell* out of this place. Seems like our horsemen friends are still busy hacking up anything that would stand in our way."

"Agreed," Quincy said sternly. "We're ending this right now," he told Sean.

Sean blinked once or twice. "Alright, then let's...let's end it."

THE CHAPEL *at the end of the world, Flanders, Belgium — 10 minutes until the end of the world*

The chapel door swung open with enough force to knock an elephant off its feet, figuratively speaking that is, no one could possibly push an elephant. There was the slight discrepancy of how it was possible for them to return so quickly in contrast to how long they had actually been in the woods. But, like any lost traveler stuck in the wilderness, time had a way of stretching and working. They ultimately did not care how it all worked. The world was intact for now and that was all that mattered.

Sean held the door open as the party of five, together with the cat and a mysterious bulb of bright orange and purple light, streamed into the small space. "Okay, people, this is it," he yelled, taking the lead. He moved to push the cross into Quincy's empty hand and nodded. "I have no freakin' clue what's about to happen next, but I've got a feeling this is the only shot we got, is that right?" He held out his hand.

Before Quincy took the cross, in perhaps a peculiar for him move, he went in for the full hug, slapping his good friend on the back in a loving embrace. "It's good to see you, Sean. It's good you're here. All of you." Quincy took the cross from Sean who looked surprised but happy.

Hearing this, the way Quincy said it as if he had some glimpse of a terrible, alternative future, Moira was taken aback. She shuddered as she looked at the stone tablets that for all intents and purposes seemed to have just *appeared* in the twins' possession, not knowing what really happened. "We don't…want to know, do we?" she asked.

Lilly frowned. "No… You absolutely do not want to know." She sighed and took her brother by the arm, the mossy chalice with the beautiful emerald gem embedded clasped safely in her left hand. "Let's end this, Quince. Perhaps there's still a chance we've got a home to go back to after all of this is said and done."

Liz, Sean, and Moira stayed behind near the door together with the cat and the mysterious light which they were certain was Tim, detached from Matthew Hopkins's rotting corpse.

"You know, it's funny…" Liz could not help but grin at what ran through her mind. "I think *traveling the world in search of ancient artifacts to uncover age old secrets* has a fantastic ring to it.

Too bad *and almost always be nearly eaten by horrific monsters and dying that one time* has to be added. Otherwise, it would be a great career path, wouldn't you agree?"

Lilly turned around and laughed. She knew Liz was just trying to cheer her up, seeing she was so mortally afraid, and she also knew that it kind of worked. Not only for her, but for Quincy as well. Lilly blushed as Liz spoke, everything she heard Liz's lovely voice say filled her heart with warmth and familiarity; they simply couldn't fail.

"Don't forget the legendary Sean Cooper and Liz Borden that held these two together when they needed it most," Moira added, winking at Liz. "Truly the Sallah and Marion to their respective Indiana Jones's." She laughed.

Both Sean and Liz had to laugh. "Seriously, Moira…" Liz told her. "Don't sell yourself short. We could never have pulled this all off without your help. Now who else was in *Raiders*?"

Lilly and Quincy stood at the edge of the ancient stone altar at the other end of the chapel.

"Why does this all feel so typical?" Lilly wondered aloud. "We're standing here at the edge of the Apocalypse with three gizmos in hand that are supposedly the key to stopping it and our friends are back there discussing '80smovies again."

Quincy laughed. "It's like you say, typical. Like it shouldn't be any other way."

"I could do with *less* apocalypse, thanks," Lilly said as her eyes fell onto the slab of marble that was supposed to take them out of this nightmare.

It wasn't hard to see that the dais the altar stood on was made of an entirely different material than the rest of the chapel. It was much older, and its design seemed off, as if it did not belong here or anywhere else in the world. It was distinctly non-Euclidian and therefore enough to send shivers down their spines.

Lilly let go of her brother's arm and put the chalice down on the altar. "There," she said. "One down. I'll let you do the rest, Quince. After all the shit you've been through mentally, it only seems fitting you do us the honors."

Quincy stood in front of the altar as if he was in a trance. It was as if he was abandoned in a hostile, treacherous desert all by himself. He vaguely heard Lilly's words, but they gave him a glimmer of hope, like a streak of silk sliding gently across his face in an otherwise lethal environment. He felt his knees buckling and his hands shaking.

Lilly noticed immediately. Her first reaction was to take the relics from Quincy's hands and place them herself, hoping that whatever spell of trouble had manifested itself in him would not take root quickly enough in her for her to place them. "Quincy, what's wrong? Talk to me."

Quincy slapped her hands away. He immediately felt sorry. But something had taken him aback. "I can't do it…" he whispered through gritted teeth. "This isn't real. Everyone is dead already… So let us die with it…"

～

WAKE UP, *Quincy*.

The voice rang through Quincy's head with a familiar gnashing consistency that reminded him of a chainsaw. A chainsaw that felt as if it was digging its way into his inner ear canal to make sure everything was understood.

Quincy gasped.

He was lying on a wooden slab that was laid across an altar. He looked around and realized he was still in the chapel. Pews lined both sides of the walls and between each set was a window, any glass now long gone. There was nothing to see outside of the windows except for the familiar terrifying crimson glow that seemed so thick, impenetrable, and oppressive that it was like lava swallowing the world and turning everything to ash. It was hot as hell inside the chapel. It was so hot that the wood on which Quincy lay was soaked with his sweat. He could feel the dizziness and delirium of dehydration coming with any movement that was too quick or too sudden. Quincy knew he had been here before. But whether that was in a dream or another reality entirely he could not say for sure.

Why do you resist? You have lost, Quincy.

Quincy looked up to be greeted by the very thing he had feared seeing for a long time now. There were thousands of eyes opening from the roof of the chapel. They were all bloodshot with a red iris and an elongated pitch-black pupil. Worst of all they were all staring at him. "Why?" Quincy howled in defeat. "Why are you doing this? Why me?"

Because I am you, and you are me. For the same atoms that separated themselves from me eons past and drifted along the stars until they eventually settled on a barren rock dancing in space that would one day become known as Earth are the same atoms that make up your own biological and anatomical structure. We are all the same. You have been here before and perhaps you will come here again. In the end, it is all futile, as you know, as you have always known. And here we stand together, at the end.

"The end..." Quincy gritted his teeth. "Why Earth? What do you possibly have to gain from all this?"

You think you are the only one.

"You despise me."

As we should. You are too late. We are at the end of everything. The cosmos should not be seen as a grand ballet of beautiful chaos. Chaos, yes. But raw, primordial, savage. You are too late. You are all that's left. You know this, Quincy Swansong. You have been here before, haven't you? You have felt the loss, the crippling loss of losing everything. And why? Why would you ever want to go back to whatever hell on earth humanity created a long time ago? Why not end it all? Choose paradise over this doomed and dreaded existence. Because that's what you will face. You really are all that is left, you know. You are alone. All alone.

"No..." Quincy stammered. He tried crying out for his sister and friends. But like a real-life nightmare, no sound escaped his lips. "No, they were just here, I—"

You have been abandoned, Quincy Swansong.

"I– I do not believe you." Quincy felt as if his insides were turning to dust and his brain was tearing itself apart while still confined within the limited space of his mortal skull. "This cannot be…" he grunted. "They were just…here…"

They were never here nor there. You were already abandoned. Your sister ran off and left you alone to fend for a universe slated for sure erasure, choosing this hippie over her own flesh and blood. And then that Louisiana pond scum and Southern hick acting like they care for you, but you must have heard them talking behind your back. They wanted to leave you there in that bed, drowning in your own sweat as they ran off to the sunset trying to make something of their last few weeks on earth.

"You— lie!" Quincy screamed. "They were just *here*. They did not abandon me. They did *not*."

But of course, they did, Quincy.

Quincy screamed out in agony. "Your. Fucking. Hypnotic. Bullshit. Stops. *Now!*" Quincy pressed his eyes closed as he felt the proverbial slithering tendrils loosening their hold on his brain. It was as if something indescribably terrible finally left his body after having clasped onto it like a parasite for ages. It was as painful as it was liberating. Quincy reached out from the altar. What he felt was a hand.

Lilly's hand.

But that was not all. There was another hand—Sean's. And another—Moira's. And finally—Liz's.

Quincy opened his eyes, and he was back in the chapel. The *real* chapel this time. The one that he ran toward with the end of the world licking at their heels. He rolled off the wooden slab and plopped onto the ground. With Sean's help, he was back on his feet in no time. Whatever he tried to tell them, it would have to wait, for the pure adrenaline rushing through him had given him such a boost that it was hard to keep up with breathing. Quincy took a good few swigs of oxygen as he composed himself.

"That was some *Lord of the Rings* shit, man," Sean exclaimed. "Fully corrupted at the edge of Mount Doom."

Quincy smiled weakly. "I wouldn't recommend it," he told them through gasping breaths.

Place the relics on the altar, you wouldn't want to be late, the cat's soft murmuring voice rang through all of their heads. It was a welcoming, familiar sensation now, having a soft-spoken and gentle voice guiding your path during the most epic quest among epic quests, Lilly thought. Even Quincy would agree, although he had his fair share of disembodied voices now, enough to last him a lifetime and beyond.

Moira picked up the chalice that had rolled onto the floor during the previous endeavor and placed it on the cold marble.

The Chalice of the Deep Wood representing Paganism and the Old Ways, the cat's whisper floated into the air.

Sean took the cross and set it on the right side of the altar.

The Cross of Saint John, Christianity and the rise of the new faiths.

Then, Liz held one of the curious stone tablets while Quincy and Lilly held the other one, simultaneously placing the mysterious ancient texts onto the altar. A soft hum resonated from them, as if they had finally arrived where they were supposed to after so many years.

The Tablets of Distant Quasars… Cosmology and the great, endless Universe, the cat whispered. *Now… Together as one.*

A bright flash of light filled the room. It swallowed the entirety of the structure and whatever still laid beyond. To Lilly and Quincy in particular, but also their friends, a familiar pulling sensation indicated a shift through time and space. Did they succeed? Was it done?

The ark… Oh great kin of the Cosmos, it all ends here.

Chapter 17

???

THE WHITENESS, the pure nothingness of absolute none-existence, would not let up for quite some time. Quincy thought the sheer intensity of the flash of white-hot light had blinded him forever, but little by little with his watering eyes slightly obscuring his sight, he saw his sister in front of him. She looked as perplexed as he did, but not in any dire or panicked way; she seemed confused more than anything. The strange way she managed to communicate with Quincy even though her mouth did not move and the fact that the entire endless space in which they were present seemed to be a vacuum devoid of any sound was as weird as it was familiar.

Quincy! What the hell happened at— Hey, wow, I think we can talk without, uh, speaking again. Lilly's thoughts were directed at her brother. From the way his eyebrows twitched she knew he could understand her perfectly. *What is all this? Is this the after-life? Did we fail? Dammit we failed, didn't we? We were so close, this sucks!*

A low rumble near him, the first sign of anything happening at all, drove Quincy a bit closer to his sister. He did not know *how* he managed to get nearer. It felt like walking, he thought, but every instinct he had said they were floating. Or swimming? Were they supposed to hold their breaths? *Are we still breathing?* he finally thought.

What? Lilly answered in her own mind. *I dunno, Quince. Are we supposed to if we're* dead?

We're not dead, Lil, Quincy replied. A sharp burst of pain shot through his forehead. Migraines? *Ouch! No, we're definitely not. I— I think I recog...nize...this...*

Quincy fell silent as the endless void suddenly gave way and a gigantic being floated gently into view as if the colorless antimatter-like *something* that surrounded them had always been a part of this thing, rather than being actual... Well, nothingness. The scope of it was massive. Think of the largest life form you can imagine on earth, say a blue whale, multiply that by infinity and imagine yourself drifting past its incomprehensible form while it felt like you were somehow a part of it mere minutes ago if time was even relevant wherever you supposedly ended up. Like that. But then ten times more intense.

The twins were awestruck. The rumbling around them intensified before it let up, coming and going in waves. Gentle waves, but intriguing, nonetheless. Inside their heads, Quincy and Lilly heard something that could only be described as a gentle murmur, a soft, indistinguishable voice that was impossible to comprehend or understand. But rather than being intimidating or scary, it was the most soothing thing either of them had ever heard. It radiated kindness and it was like the voice was present all around them, like an aura of peace and safety. It might have been like hearing your mother's voice whispering tender lullabies to you while you were still unborn, nestled warmly in the safest place on earth while an energy of pure love cascaded over you at all times. Quincy could only wonder if he would ever feel such tranquility ever again in his lifetime, and one look at his sister told him she felt the same way. He nodded slightly as he stared into Lilly's eyes and tried his best to hold onto this perfect moment of blissful escape, a moment they both had been searching for for years on end ever since a piece of them died forever when their parents passed away.

It's one of them, Quincy thought, and nodded at Lilly again.

For Lilly, it was incredibly hard to keep up an expression that was not pure, unadulterated wonder. Taking a page from her brother's book, she tried to put the puzzle pieces together in her head, but the whole enigma was simply incomprehensible. The *why*, *how*, and *what* was something that could not, and should not, be explained for it was the mystery of it all that was so enticing and so enjoyable. For Lilly, it was a moment of pure ecstasy to drift along with this gentle giant. It reconfirmed everything she felt she had needed, and somehow, it had given her more strength than ever to cross the ultimate finish line, wherever that might end up being. *It's immaculate*, she finally whispered in her mind. *Beautiful, vast, endless…* Her eyes were open wide and filled with tears. *Quincy… What are we going to do? Is this our… Are you sure we're not…*

Holy crap *that thing is massive!* From one moment to the next, Sean was suddenly there, floating or whatever it was they were doing. *Hey, wow! I can talk without talking, can you—*

Lilly wildly shook her head. *Yes, yes perfectly*, she thought. *Cool, huh?*

This is simultaneously the most beautiful and the scariest thing I've ever seen in my life, Liz projected her thoughts into the space as she emerged into existence with her arms wrapped tightly around Lilly.

Woah, hey! Lilly thought, her surprise turning into sheer happiness in a nanosecond.

I have no words, I really don't. I literally don't, Liz thought, her smile fixed so tight it would take a bulldozer to rip it off her face.

Moira raised an eyebrow. *Have you all been here the entire time?* she asked without uttering a word. *Woah. Can you hear minds screaming? I think mine just screamed.*

Sean looked down at his dangling legs, whishing about as if they had been gently flowing in a non-existent ocean while simultaneously feeling as if his feet were planted firmly on the ground. The non-existent ground. *What's the meaning of all this?* he asked himself, but everyone could hear.

Is this how time travel feels? Did you…experience this before? Liz watched Lilly carefully.

Lilly looked away. *No… It feels more like…dying? This is all new to us, I mean there should be something more.*

Moira sniffed around as if there was anything to actually smell. The vastness of the entity alongside them had moved for hundreds of miles she thought, while all together appearing to have not moved an inch. How could it when the magnitude of the entire thing seemed to stretch out across, well, the entirety of everything.

YOU AREN'T DEAD, FOOLS! The voice of the Fire Vampire Tim burned in each of their minds while each of them immediately felt the great need to avert their eyes.

Oh my fuc– Aaaaah! Sean thought.

Holy crap on a stick… Oh my– No… Lilly could hardly form a sentence in her mind.

The other's minds simply screamed. Screamed aloud for finally the true form of Timaxoatilaciluzipta, Fire Vampire of legend, child of eternal Cthugha, came into being. This was, of course, impossible to describe without going insane in the process, but imagine heating up an icepick with a blowtorch to uncontrollable scorching hot levels and then jamming it into your eyes with the force of a thousand Formula One racecars. That's what staring at the true form of a Fire Vampire for longer than a few seconds feels like. Also, it's really gross.

Tim! Quincy yelled in his mind. *What the hell? You've been quietly following us for the last couple of, I don't know, and now you show up and…and…holy crap.*

I'VE ALWAYS SAID MY TRUE FORM COULD NOT BE COMPREHENDED BY YOUR MERE MORTAL BRAINS, MUAHAHAHA. Tim's horrific true voice boomed through their heads, latching onto their brains like friction burns. *But…* he continued, slightly less intense now. *Imagine this. You wouldn't feel any of this if you were dead. I am the wise old man in this story now and let me impart wisdom thus; now tell me Master Swansong, where have you felt this feeling before?*

You felt this before? Moira winced as she looked over toward Quincy.

Not this. Quincy waved toward the general direction of the Tim thing. *But I have–this feeling of exchanging…minds and thoughts and…*

A faint trace of a memory not forgotten but perhaps hidden away for safekeeping unfolded in Lilly's mind. *The tomb…* she thought, and the others could hear perfectly. *The tomb beneath New Mexico…the chairs…*

The dioramas and the history of… Where are we really? Tim?

You are exactly where you need to be… Now open your eyes.

SOMEWHERE BENEATH THE SONIAN WOODS – *15 days, 1 hour, and 59 minutes until the theoretical end of the world*

The room was filled with a dazzling display of lights in every color imaginable and beyond. It came through stained glass windows so expertly crafted they almost felt like they did not belong on Earth. The walls and ceiling were adorned with the most beautifully detailed finishes you'd ever see. Distinctly gothic in its façade, it had an air of otherworldliness that was difficult to describe and impossible to replicate. From the low rumblings of something stirring to the distinct smell of loose soil, there was no mistake that they had ended up somewhere far under the ground, but in what exactly? It was beautiful, gorgeous even. A tranquil chamber of absolute silence and beauty, only slightly less invigorating than the journey had been to get here. But there was a caveat—the one thing that was hard to ignore among this splendid display of European Gothic architecture. The room was, for all intents and purposes, the group instinctively knew, a tomb. Like the ruins beneath Three Rivers in New Mexico and the Celestian Sanctuary underneath Eldritch Island before it, this too was a place of the dead, not of the living. It was baffling to see how much the Celestians influenced, or perhaps shaped, the very Earth. Its architecture and perhaps its cultures, so varied, diverse, and terrific, were on full display whenever they had found one of their final resting places.

Still, the room they found themselves in felt different somehow. It wasn't so much a burial tomb, even though the great stone slabs of cyclopean concrete might betray them as otherwise. It was some sort of anti-chamber into a greater place beyond.

When they had shaken off the initial surprise and astonishment that came with temporal displacement, let alone an event of this magnitude, the first thing that Moira noticed when she took a step forward was that there was an unnatural light that shone through the windows. With every step she took, the light had a tendency to pulsate ever so slightly.

"What is this place..." she quietly whispered. The shock of *actual* sound escaping from her *mouth* rather than merely thinking it made her gasp. "Well, I guess we're back to... Seriously, what is this place... Did you check out the light refractions? It's beautiful."

"Hey, check your phones," Sean told them. "*Somehow* I have reception here, making wherever this is less cut off from the world than most of Missouri."

"Yow, did you check the date?" Liz yelped. She startled herself with how much noise she made and lowered her voice to respect the beings supposedly buried among them. "It's like two weeks ago!" she exclaimed in a furtive whisper. Holding the phone toward Lilly, the rings on her fingers ticked against the touchscreen's glass.

"That's amazing," Lilly gasped. "Does that mean it's before..."

Moira smiled slightly. "It's a day or so before the first disaster hits...but still well into the cult fuckery across the globe…" She sighed. "I guess time is on our side again… great. My initial question still stands, though. Where the *hell* are we?"

Quincy tried his best to remain calm while fishing for the flashlight in his coat pocket, clicking it on without hesitation once he found it. He shined the beam whenever the lights of the many-colored stained-glass windows didn't gleam making a bright ray of prismatic light appear that beamed all throughout the underground crypt. "I don't know how…or why we are apparently so very linked to these beings, but somehow, we always seem to end up in one of their sanctuaries. Except…" Quincy hesitated for a moment. "Except it's always…dark and abandoned. It's always tombs, crypts, barrows, abandoned underground cities. These beings. They have the power to travel among the stars and through the fissures of time and space and yet…"

"And yet they bury their dead here on Earth," Moira went on. "It's a very interesting idea. In some religions and ancient beliefs, the practice of burying the dead amongst the soil of their homelands was in some ways a ritual to fulfill the cycle of birth, life, and death. It would bring peace to the souls of the deceased and their family."

Lilly gasped. "Are you implying the Celestians did not actually come from the stars?"

"No," Quincy interjected. "Back in the tomb of Three Rivers a few years ago we saw the dioramas that clearly stated their origins and how they ended up here. We just don't know why they feel this planet is so important."

Liz laughed. "That's easy."

"Oh?"

"It's the same reason why *we* are doing our damn best to stop the world from ending as well… *Home.* It's why we feel like we belong, it's why they feel at ease here too."

Sean nodded along. "It's true. I mean—of course you can feel at home somewhere you're not actually from. It's logical, right?"

The rumbling beneath their feet became louder. Something was shifting the soil around them as if it was stirring in deep slumber, starting to wake up.

"The Celestians left when *we* arrived here," Lilly spoke softly. "They opened up the planet they had so fondly called home for eons for a new species to flourish and then proceeded to seek new knowledge among the endless stars…"

Quincy's mouth dropped open at the realization. "The Gibbous Horde…they're the invaders the Celestians tried to desperately fend off for so long… The ones that do not belong. Did they become lost trying to rid the planet of…?" Quincy struggled to form words. He looked over toward the faces of his companions who likewise appeared awestruck. It wasn't often that such a wealth of knowledge, knowledge on the great vastness of an endless and hostile universe, falls at your feet. "Whatever lies in the next room over there…" Quincy quivered. "Dammit, I can feel its hum. It's calling us, can't you feel it? The ark of the covenant… It's…"

"It's not there…" Sean spoke up first.

Lilly reeled, goosebumps crawling up her back. "The ark is a ship," she said sternly.

"What lies beyond is a beacon," Moira gasped. She clutched her hair in disbelief.

Liz sighed. "A beacon to call the Ancients home… And rid the world of its disgusting invaders…"

For a moment, each of them had to sit down for a second to grapple with the scope of what they were about to do. Lilly pulled on one of her curls. It was a tic she had displayed in times of stress. Liz had taught herself to automatically slap away Lilly's hand every time she started reaching.

"We really *were* in it over our heads, weren't we?" Lilly remarked.

Quincy could not help but laugh. "Oh sis, I have never been proven so wrong before in my life. The mere fact that I thought *we* could personally stop any of this from happening.

Turns out it took an entire army of undead willing servants, the Four horsemen—"

"And women."

"And women of the Apocalypse and, last but not least, an entire alien race that lost its way across the vast reaches of the infinite universe. How presumptuous of me to think that *we* had any say in what's to come."

"That's where you are wrong, though!" Sean told him. "Don't you realize none of this would have happened without you two?"

Moira nodded. "And with *all of this*, we're actually getting a fighting chance here to do some good. Sean's absolutely right. You two *somehow* got the last piece of the puzzle we needed to get here, right when we needed it most. Right when everything was slated to go to shit. And I *still* don't know where *here* actually is."

Liz stood up and walked a few steps ahead.

"I think we're at some kind of epicenter. A nexus," Quincy theorized. "I've been looking across the room at some of these stained-glass displays, and I can recognize some of them… The Seven Sister Cliffs in England, the poppy fields of Flanders… the Scottish Highlands and the green fields of Southern Italy. The great church spires looming in the distance and a…a dark sun I—"

Lilly poked her brother in the side. "*Hey* sunshine, let's not have another existential crisis here, okay?"

"Lilly, we've been *living* one ever since…you know. Anyway." Quincy turned toward the doorway leading away from the chamber and into the next room. "We don't even know what to expect beyond here. Do you really think there'll be some kind of computer with a big red reset button?"

Liz turned around from the doorway. "There's like literally a giant screen here with all kinds of red dots and a terminal with a huge button."

Chapter 18

Vaults of the Ancients

THE BIG CIRCULAR room was like a panopticon with hallways stretching out from it in all directions. The ceilings were very high with the novel Gothic architecture that adorned the resting places they had just been. High up was something that appeared to be a stained-glass sky light, although every indication the group could gather from their phones or general instincts pointed to it being night, and to them being incredibly deep underground. In the middle of the room sat a giant pillar filled with flickering lights, levers, buttons, and screens. Copper, green, and black tubes varying in size from giant to minuscule protruded from the metal pillar, which was made from some peculiarly unnatural smooth black metal and disappeared into the dark reaches of the room in every direction. The most striking thing was a huge screen flickering in the strange green glow of the darkened room. On the screen, the group could see the entire map of the world with red dots sprinkled throughout; they already knew exactly what they meant. Each of these dots represented a horror of unimaginable magnitude, indescribable and maddening to behold in all of its grotesque non-Euclidian terror. Lilly and Quincy had beheld such a monstrosity before in the deep swamps of Georgia, where they had first met their near death at the hands of Haven agents and the *thing* called Mother. Quincy, Moira, and Sean were unfortunate enough to see another, rising from the depths of the North Sea on the Brighton coast. Both beings were called forth by means of the excruciatingly vile task of human sacrifice. Blood for the hungry, unspeakable old ones.

Yet it was the Celestians who supposedly had the knowledge to fight the terrible things known collectively as the Gibbous Horde. Those same Celestians had left, or been driven off the Earth long ago, leaving the dormant evil behind. As to why they did not return, if there were actually even a substantial amount of them left, nobody knew. But they were here in this tomb underneath what for all intents and purposes would probably have been a giant city of the Ancients, which lay underneath the quiet flower fields and deep woods of Belgium. It was here that it could all end. Would it?

The red button had a strange tempting sheen in the eerie green light. Approaching the gigantic console gave each one of them a myriad of sensory stimulations. The hair on the back of Sean's neck stood up immediately. Goosebumps crawled over Moira's skin, and Liz felt gentle pressure applied to her temples. For Lilly, a very faint electrical current ran right through her body's very core. Quincy did not realize it at the moment, but for him, it was the most distinct. Approaching the big screen, he felt as if his soul was being pushed outside of his body. The sensation felt like being possessed, but rather than it being something malevolent, it was as if the driving force just wanted to take over to make sure he did the right thing. It felt as if he was a student driver who could control the car on his own, but who also had an instructor next to him ready to push on the brake if needed.

But there were no doubts in Quincy's mind. None at all.

And looking around him at the hopeful expression on Lilly's face, the concerned but stern demeanor of Liz, the excited ready-for-a-win look on Sean's, and the absolute awestruck and fascinated Moira, he knew there were no doubts. Not anymore. Everything had led up to this.

Quincy pressed the big red button.

It sounded like a low hum at first. Then came the low rumble from the ground underneath them. But then the giant black metal pillar started to shake and vibrate. A gigantic beam of silver and green light shot out of its top and up into the air high above. The electricity or whatever energy had attached itself to the space around them crackled and popped loudly but did not to do any harm. For a moment, it felt like the whole place was going to come down on them. Rubble and small debris fell from the ceiling, and Sean and Liz jumped dexterously forward and back to not get hit in the head. Luckily, it only *felt* like the place was coming down hard, for it weighed on Lilly and Quincy's conscience that they had already caused the mass collapse of one of these intricate tombs, or perhaps 'facilities' would be the better word, before, and they most certainly did not want to do it again. It reminded them of the inverted pyramid they had once uncovered beneath New Mexico. The one that had taught them about the true origins of the world and of mankind. The one that held the secret their family had tried to so hard to keep for over eighty years, but perhaps for far longer than that.

Familiar beams of yellow and green light shot out of the sides of the metal pillar. Their streaks fading in and out of each other. The lights slowly formed an image against one of the upper walls curving off into the sky light through which that magnificent beam of light now shone. The lights projected the image of several beings sporting cone-shaped bodies, with claw-like appendages and elongated heads. Next to the image of the Celestians, for they knew what they were supposed to represent, was projected what looked like a gigantic spaceship.

Preserve the timeline. This was our goal, for years, for eons, an otherworldly voice whispered. It sounded like pieces of metal scraping against each other interlaced with radio static and the howling of *something* rose through the halls. The voice was unnerving, but soothing. It felt gigantic, both in actual size, but also in terms of the scope of its place in the cosmos. *We tried, oh we tried to hold on. But the Horde proved too much for our efforts to be rid of them for eternity. So we sealed them away.*

The image changed to that of a bigger spaceship. Around it was flickering lights of what could only be the night sky. A million shining stars, a million worlds left to explore, a million worlds on which to plant a seed. But with this change of scene there was a feeling of remorse that flooded over all of the onlookers. Did the projections hold the power to convey emotion? One had to wonder.

There was no way we could muster enough strength on Earth to fight the Horde, so it was time to leave and gather the forces to destroy the unmakers for all time. To preserve the timeline. To prevent annihilation.

The image changed to that of an amalgamation of computers. More blinking lights, tubing, and flickering screens. There were two Celestians on either side, as if standing on guard.

We left the Deus device in capable hands, to make sure the planet was protected in our absence. And thus, we disappeared among the vaporous clouds of the endless stars. Back to Celeste, but ready to return.

Again, the projected image changed. Now it showed the ship flying *somewhere* but it was impossible to describe where. Everything surrounding the vessel was like a cloud of chaos, death, and destruction. There was an intense feeling of dread throughout the entire chamber. It was melancholy and horrible.

But we lost our way. Everything appeared futile when the connection was severed between us and the Deus device on Earth long ago. The few of us remaining were left to our own devices, and without our possible interference, or any way of reaching out, we feared the worse. Not only for us, but for the planet.

The diorama now showed, shockingly, a group of five humans, three females and two males. They were placing a cross, a cup and rectangular tablets on an altar. It was enough to send shivers down everyone's spines. They had no idea what was happening. How this all came to be. If they were but pawns on a galactic game board, puppets on a string, actors on a soundstage.

Salvation came from the Ones That Keep Secrets. For when the most dire of times presented itself, the well of endless knowledge would open and the way to create the beacon for us to come home was unveiled. Night will not fall forever on this timeline. Nor will Earth succumb to the most vile of beings.

The projection changed to show the giant spaceship hovering over planet Earth. The ground began rumbling as never before. Lilly nearly lost her footing but was held up by Liz and Quincy. Sean and Moira grabbed each other and held on tight, and it felt like the whole ground underneath them started to sink, and fast. There was a subtle shift in the way these projections presented themselves in contrast to how they were shown in the pyramid beneath the desert, Quincy thought.

You have guided us. Our Ark has found its way home, and thus the covenant from which it has gotten its name shall be honored in good measure.

"Remember when we said this was way over our heads?" Quincy asked Lilly in between all of the intensity.

"U-huh," was all she managed to say.

We have gathered the strength.

Quincy looked up at the beam of light shooting up into the windows above. The light that came through the windows was now gone. The room was dark, the light blocked out by something. "These aren't pre-recorded messages anymore."

We know where they are.

Liz's eyes went wide. Lilly, Sean, and Moira echoed the sentiment. "Are you…"

Your enemies are known to us. Your unlucky fate was foreseen by us. We will not sit idle and let this go by.

"I think— I think I am serious, yes." Quincy chuckled, sweat from fear pricking in the corner of his eyes.

You called us and we listened. We followed the sign, and we are stronger than ever. We will destroy them all. We will restore this doomed timeline. Restore the first timeline. Restore Celestial Equilibrium.

"They're here."

IN THE HEART *of the stars*

Whatever happened next, *how* it happened or even more importantly, *what* came after is, let's just say, quite the endeavor to describe. For Lilly, Quincy, Sean, Moira, and Liz it was hard to determine what came first; whether it was the weightlessness, the voices in the dark, that feeling of tremendous hope, the white light, or the glimpse of that endless entity they had seen once before, again so near yet so far away.

What they *were* eventually in agreement over is that the visions came *after* all of that. These visions, or images, glimpses into events all around the globe, were staggering. You see, there is not a right way of describing what they saw, for each of them saw, heard, and felt all manner of things, most of them separate and entirely different from one another and yet they all would come to the same conclusions on what had transpired, or, for the sake of storytelling, what was currently transpiring. Vague? Yes, sorry. In terms of cosmic horror and existentialism, it is very much the idea, rather than a detailed description of what exactly was going on, that so clearly underlines the magnitude of the events unfolding.

Call it giving the Earth a good sweep. The Ancients did. Long ago, they had pinpointed the location of each and every one of the dastardly Gibbous Horde entities that were still dormant on Earth. After all, they had sealed them away there in the hopes of returning before they would break out. With new force and vigor, the monstrosities were plucked away from their slumbers like parasites being dislodged from an unfortunate, defenseless animal and… crushed beneath the weight of countless eons of anger and resentment.

But some of them broke out. We know that without the mingling of the devious Haven organization and its terrifying off-shoot the Esoteric Order of the Final Dawn, things would look a whole lot different. So they too were *swept* clean off the planet. Think of it as a laser gun removing an ugly, horrible tattoo that's been adorning someone's arm for far too long. With the utmost care and pinpoint accuracy, you can zap that thing right off. Which is exactly how Lilly saw the obliteration and total destruction of the organizations and its members in her mind.

In Quincy's mind, it was like pressing the red glowing button on the console had the power of a literal reset.

The 'deletion' of the Gibbous Horde, Haven, and Final Dawn was like their throats were cut open and they were bleeding out on the floor, two pathetic entities that long overstayed their welcome on an Earth. Now the Ancients were ready to make amends, ready to move on from disaster and torment, ready to flourish instead of being led from one horrible thing into something even worse.

They all knew that not everything could be erased. However unfortunate that may sound. The years of torment Haven had subjected the planet to had left its mark and the countless lives that had been lost in the process were never to return, however unfortunate and dreary that revelation might have been. The Kraken Wars had still happened, Lafayette had still been nearly swallowed up by a Dimensional Shambler, and most of the Eastern seaboard was still gone.

There were still things hiding in the shadow, objects of strange and dangerous make, horrid entities that managed to hide in dark corners of the Earth, away from the prying eyes of the Ancient Race.

But there was no end of the world. No red sky or crimson

thunder. No undead army rising from underneath the ground to combat unspeakably wicked things with leathery wings and faces like octopi. No abominable giants rose from the oceans, no unholy thresher machines chopped up brainwashed innocents to sacrifice, and no evil cultists manned those non-existing machines. There were no longer the shadowy tendrils of the Haven organization that had inserted itself and its spies across all kinds of institutions and political circles around the globe.

the Apocalypse rebellion had never been formed, nor did it need to at this point. Every occultist, monster hunter, witch, white-warlock, or others in the know could keep carrying on with their own matters instead of risking their lives in a futile attempt to save time for an impossible task to be carried out at the edge of oblivion.

And the Ancients themselves? They were gone too. How did Quincy know all of this, you may wonder? He just did. Just like he felt the call to uncover the age-old secrets once before. He heeded the call to investigate the first signs of the primordial Gibbous Horde and ultimately answered that very same call again which led him here to Europe. That instinct he shared with his sister told him the Ancients had come and gone. They had made their mark, redeemed themselves, saved the planet and everyone on it, restored the precious first time-line, whatever that meant, and left again, even though he might have felt their watchful eye gazing down on him.

Quincy opened his own eyes. Together with Lilly, Liz, Sean, and Moira he was back where it all had started. The small chapel at the edge of the Sonian Woods. Outside, the sun shone, the birds were chirping, and a lovely early summer breeze greeted him from the opened window. It all felt like a dream, or rather nightmare, from which he had just woken. But now, more than ever, Quincy knew that it was the absolute truth. The reality in front of him was that they had won. For real this time.

. . .

THE CHAPEL OF THE ANCIENTS, *Flanders, Belgium — Two weeks before the end of the world that would never be*

"That was one *hell* of a display!" Marty had slammed open the doors to the chapel and strode in in absolute triumph. "You went out there and gave them the old one-two hook and punch didn't you, ha!"

Quincy, dazed and confused by the sensory overload he had been experiencing for the good part of however long it was that he had ping-ponged back and forth over the past couple of weeks, scratched his head. "Actually, we didn't punch anyone or anything."

Liz leaned against the wall. She had been rubbing her eyes as if she had been fast asleep but, a bit faster than the others, she had grounded herself back in reality after all that happened. "*We* didn't one-two punch anyone. But *you* certainly did." She nodded not only to Marty, but also to Mortimer, Aila, and Cookie who had just entered the chapel. "If it wasn't for you," Liz continued, "we would have never made it out of those woods alive in time to get the relics in their place."

"We *did?*" Cookie asked genuinely. She closed her pallid and sunken eyes for a second and sighed. "Ah, yeah, I see it know. About an hour beforehand."

The pale, ever-grinning skull of Mortimer shone eerily in the orange and purple light of the candelabra above them. "'Tis an hour that as of now will never take place," he told them. "Well, at least not in that way."

"But…?" Moira swallowed. "Guys, I feel a *but* coming."

Aila wagged her rotting finger. "No buts, we promise. You accomplished what you set out to do. In fact, we all did."

That's correct. The now familiar cat plopped from the open window onto the chapel floor. *After all this time, everything that has been set in motion ever since the dawn of life on this planet, even since before the Celestians ever touched down on the planet, everything has finally come to pass in the right way. The correct way. The way that leads to—* But the cat stopped mid-sentence. Instead of continuing, it just sat there. Purring.

"Lead to what, leads to *what?* Come on, you can't keep us in the dark like that." Lilly ducked down and scooped the cat up from the floor. In shock, perhaps even a bit mortified from the unexpected snatch and grab, the critter started thrashing wildly about. Eventually, Lilly had to let it go. As quick as it came, it flew back toward the window. It looked back a final time.

As much as we would all love to have the answers to what our true goals are in this world and what still lies in front of us, it is sometimes the process of not knowing *that keeps our hearts afloat, keeps our hopes up and our dreams alive. Not everything needs explaining. Life, like the grand cosmic ballet of the infinite stars, is full of mystery. It's what makes it fun and interesting. Farewell.* The cat disappeared through the window. All they heard was the soft rustle when it hit the shrubbery below and then there was nothing.

"He's right, you know," Aila told the group. "We all need a little mystery in our lives."

Marty laughed heartily. "A little bit of wonder, a little bit of the fantastical."

"It's what makes it worth living," Mortimer said before looking down at his skeletal torso and the white bones sticking out from underneath his black cloak. "So to speak," he added.

Sean rubbed the stubble on his cheeks and chin. "So," he said. "What's in store for you four?"

Cookie shrugged. "Maybe we'll take a bit of a break as well. But I'm sure there's still a lot more work to be done."

"Work?" Quincy asked. "What kind of work?"

Mortimer opened his jaws a little. A mouse plopped out, living and breathing. It crawled down the reaper's neck and sat firmly on his shoulder. "Remember when we told you the poppy fields were but *one* possible place associated with the end of the world?"

"We really don't want to know, do we?" Lilly sighed deeply.

Mortimer gently patted the little mouse on his shoulder. "Don't worry," he reassured the group. "I am pretty sure I do not own any Mr. Squeekums in *this particular timeline*. I guess we'll be off soon."

Quincy folded his arms. "So that's that? Just…on to the next?"

"On to the next," Marty echoed. He and the other horsemen and women were already fading from existence. "Thank you for giving us purpose," Marty told them as he waved goodbye.

Mortimer waved as well, Aila blew a kiss, and Cookie merely nodded.

"When you run into us in another time and space," Liz yelled after them. "Tell us that we've got absolutely nothing to do with saving anything or anyone!"

"Yeah, I've seen enough shit to cover a multitude of lifetimes and timelines," Sean scoffed.

Lilly waved. "Tell us not to put licorice on pizza because that's actually pretty disgusting and you won't be able to poo—"

Quincy loudly cleared his throat. "Well, okay. Ahem, that's all that taken care of. Now, before I sleep for a week straight to get to terms with all of this, there's just one more thing we've got to address."

"What's that?" Sean asked.

Lilly understood what her brother meant to say. "Hey Tim," she called out to the candelabra over their heads. "We know you're there, Tim."

"Yes, but please for the love of the cosmos don't come out and show your true form," Quincy added.

"I HAVE NO LOVE FOR THE COSMOS." The creepy voice of the Fire Vampire filled the chapel, and it was as if their surroundings immediately became somewhat darker.

"There he is." Sean grinned. "Where have you been?"

Quincy's eyes shot toward Sean, then back to the gorgeous candelabra on the ceiling. "Yeah, that's exactly what I wanted to ask. You've been tracking us for quite some time now, first in the corpse of an age-old witch hunter—"

Liz made a noise of disgust.

"Then you sent us– Well, you know what happened, and now? What's your goal?"

Lilly acknowledged everything her brother said and added, "You've helped us, on multiple occasions now, without anything to gain from it. You are not stuck in a dead body nor are you bound to a vessel that keeps you on this mortal plane. You've said before that you *liked* us, but I just can't imagine that's enough to keep a Fire Vampire around for this long. So, what's the catch?"

The lights flickered once or twice before the room retained its natural glow. "THE THING IS…" Tim started in a hushed whisper. "YOU REMEMBER MISTRESS SWAN-SONG…THE TALE OF HOW CTHUGHA, THE GREAT FIRE OUTER GOD FROM BEYOND, PERISHED?"

Lilly closed her eyes and let out a sigh. "I remember," she ultimately said. "You told me when we met. She clashed with another being, which resulted in millions of her particles being scattered across the universe, *one* of which is you."

"EXACTLY," Tim hummed. "THE ENTITY THAT DESTROYED US…DESTROYED CTHUGHA, WAS ONE OF *THEM*."

Liz gasped. "One of the Horde?"

"CORRECT."

"No wonder you were so adamant on helping us out. It wasn't just a *calling* for you, it was *revenge*, wasn't it?"

The lights flickered again. "THANKS TO YOU, I CAN REST EASILY KNOWING THAT THE INJUSTICE THAT WAS ONCE DONE TO ME AND MINE HAS FINALLY BEEN RETRIBUTED. I WOULD… THERE IS A REQUEST I WOULD LIKE YOU TO CONSIDER."

Quincy raised an eyebrow. "What's that?"

"I WOULD LIKE TO OCCUPY THE GOD-MACHINE."

If any of them had been taking a sip from a drink at that moment, there would surely have been some spitting along.

Quincy looked appalled. "Absolutely not!"

"WHY?"

"Do I even need to spell it out for you? You keep going on and on about how insignificant humanity is and how you hate each and every one of us."

"NOT YOU TWO. NOR THESE THREE, I SUPPOSE," Tim retorted.

"That's still like, incomparable to how many people are on Earth that you *would* actively hate."

"SO?"

"S– Are you hearing this?" Quincy turned to the others. "Surely this is preposterous?"

Lilly brushed a lock of hair behind her ear and took another approach. "Tim, can you at least tell us *why* you'd want this gig so much?"

"I PROMISE I WON'T." Tim cleared whatever thing that would count as a Fire Vampire's throat. "I PROMISE I WON'T DO ANYTHING BAD. I WOULD HOLD MYSELF UP TO THE STANDARDS FOR WHICH THE DEUS DEVICE WAS ONCE CREATED. PROTECT YOU, AND THE EARTH ITSELF."

Quincy rolled his eyes, but he felt his clenched fists loosening a little bit. "Then why…" He rubbed his temples in a vain attempt to understand. "What's the catch?"

"I WILL EXPLAIN," Tim started. "EVER SINCE I GOT A SMALL WHIFF OF WHAT THE TECHNOLOGY IS ACTUALLY CAPABLE OF BACK IN THE ARCTIC, I HAVE BEEN CRAVING TO TASTE MORE OF IT, BUT THERE WAS OF COURSE ALL OF THIS TO HANDLE FIRST. I BELIEVE I CAN USE THE MACHINE TO TRACK DOWN EVERY SINGLE ONE OF MY…CALL IT BROTHERS AND SISTERS…AND THUS EVENTUALLY I'D BE ABLE TO…"

"Reform. You want to get the gang back together, is that it?" Sean asked.

"QUITE SO, *FLESHB–*, I MEAN, CORRECT."

Quincy sighed. He couldn't believe he was actually considering this option. He started rubbing his temples again. "If… and this is a big *if*, Cthugha would return in all her…glorious form, would the Earth be safe from her?"

"YOU HAVE MY WORD. ABSOLUTELY NO ILL-FATE WILL BEFALL THIS EARTH BY THE HANDS OF ETERNAL CTHUGHA, NOR ANY OTHER KIND OF MALEVOLENCE WHILE I KEEP WATCH."

Lilly sprang up. "Hey, would you be able to destroy all of the B or C-tier hazards still roaming the Earth right now?"

"I ALREADY CHECKED YEARS AGO. UNFORTU-NATELY, I CANNOT."

She sat back down against the stone wall. "Ah… Well, it was worth a shot, right?"

Quincy looked around at his companions. "Well?" he asked. "What do you all think?"

Moira scoffed. "He can do what he pleases. He helped us enough to be granted a favor this big, even though I kind of shiver at the thought. But remember this, Tim, I have more than a few books on the bindings of lesser servitor races, so I'll *know* where to find you if you pull something." Moira waved a judging finger in front of him.

"I WOULDN'T DARE," Tim answered.

Liz folded her arms. "I can't say I think this is a very good idea. But you seem to know this thing a lot better than us, and Lilly told me all about how he came to your rescue against all odds, so…"

Quincy turned to Sean, who merely shrugged. "I mean, I kinda like the guy, what can I say?" He laughed. "It's a story for the ages. *Protector of humanity hates everyone.*"

"MUAHAHAHAHAAAAA," Tim cackled. "THIS IRONY AMUSES ME."

Quincy turned back from Lilly, who was whispering something in his ear that made him chuckle. "Okay, *okay*. Tim, you can have the gig, but you gotta keep in contact with us, okay?"

"RIGHT."

"And if we need you or any of your powers, you will at least listen to, and think about, any requests we might have, yes?"

"YES."

Quincy shook his head, still in disbelief at what he agreed to. "Hopefully, this won't come back to bite us in the ass," he wondered aloud.

"I HAVE NO TEETH," Tim answered. It was the last thing he said before they saw his vaporous body fly off into the ether and toward the destination of his desires.

It was kind of sweet of him to ask for permission, Lilly thought. Soon after, it was like he had never even been there. All was quiet, serene even.

"I'm curious. What next?" Sean asked. He was somewhat at a loss on what to do now that, well, they weren't really in a hurry to do anything. He felt the pressing weight of sleep on his brow and there was no doubt in his mind his companions felt the same.

Lilly rubbed her back all over the wall she was sitting against. She welcomed the embrace from Liz as Liz sat down with open arms and the two of them cozied up on the cold stone floor. Lilly yawned. "This place is as good as any, to be honest. I'm dead tired. I'm just going to close…my…eyes." Lilly was fast asleep, followed by Liz a few seconds later.

"Well," Sean grunted as he stretched out over one of the wooden pews. "Can't say I blame them. See you in an hour… or twenty." He chuckled softly but it trailed off quick. Knocked out cold.

Quincy looked over to Moira, but she was already slumped down against the altar, completely exhausted. "Well…" Quincy whispered to himself. "Didn't think after all of this *I'd* be the one that was the least tired but there you go. Eh, better get some shut eye too." He sat down at the edge of one of the benches, closed his eyes and tried his best to drift off. But right before he fell into a deep sleep, he opened his eyes wide. "Tim," he whispered. "Is this going to work?" he wondered aloud.

"Yes, Master Swansong? I am already in position. What do you require?"

"It *does* work." Quincy smiled. "Say, can you do me *one* little favor?"

Epilogue

TWO WEEKS *before the end of the world that would never be*

Quincy got behind the wheel and closed the car door. He looked to his right and smiled as he saw Lilly settling in and getting comfortable. It was something he had watched her do dozens of times, but this time gave him a pang of nostalgia for a time he didn't think he would ever want to think back on. The back doors of the Ford Fiesta opened, and Quincy saw Liz, Sean, and Moira trying to scoot themselves into the cramped backseats with glee. When the last of them stopped trying to reach the safety belts nestled warmly beneath their own butts or upper legs, Quincy started the car and drove into the upcoming sunrise.

It had been an extremely long road to get here, and, in a way, he never expected to be he at all. Quincy's vision of the future for his sister, his friends, and for himself, and the world had always been hopeful. Yet the past couple of months had weighed upon him so much, both physically and mentally, that right now he felt entirely out of place. The 'good ending' happened and, after all the heartache and terrifying things that had led up to this point, it was hard to embrace the silver lining and step back into the light while trying to forget all of the darkness that surrounded their group. The darkness would never fully go away. Quincy knew that, and his sister did too. Yet he realized it would take time to get used to a new world now, a world of actual possibilities and chances outside of trying to prevent the universe from collapsing. Would *actual* real-life scare Quincy more than what he was used to? The thought amused him; he had to figure that out when the time was right.

"Where did you get a Ford Fiesta so quickly?" Sean asked, trying to get comfortable while being pressed up against the glass.

Quincy laughed and vacantly stared outside for a few seconds. "Turns out there's a lot of positives if you've got friends that can bend time and space a little bit. Call it Tim's parting gift. It's the one we left behind in Lafayette a couple of years back when we first met. Think of it as the O.G. Swan-song mobile, I guess."

"This thing, however much sentimental value it has, had better be spurting out gold coins from the exhaust based on how freakin' uncomfortable it is to sit in," Moira complained. She jerked out her hand from behind her and put it in an even more annoying position in front of her, twisting her shoulder. She sighed. "Couldn't you have wished for a minivan or something? I mean, I *know* it's kind of a legendary car, but I don't know about this..."

At the brink of the twins' first major adventure, it had outrun one of Haven's most dangerous agents. In the process, the Fiesta made sure that the world still stood where it did today. Legendary was right.

"What's wrong with the Fiesta?" Lilly asked. She would have been genuinely insulted if not for the fact that she was so dead tired.

Just like her brother, Lilly had felt a certain emptiness creep up inside of her. When against all odds the sun *had* actually risen that morning over the fields of Flanders, it came with an overwhelming sense of exhaustion and the question, what now? Still, in Liz, Lilly had found her purpose for moving on earlier. There was already a seed planted in her brain for the inevitable aftermath of their grand adventures, but like her brother and their friends too, Lilly had to come to terms with everything first. It was only now that there truly seemed to be hope that the weight of the past couple of years, looming over their heads like a giant mountain, would begin to subside. It would only take a single avalanche to make all of it come crashing down and suffocate them with sorrow, pain, and dark thoughts. Lilly tried her best not to think about it. They would need time. They all would. But time to put things into place would come, Lilly realized. The mountain would eventually crumble. All there would be left was new fertile land to settle on. Life had to go on.

Liz, perhaps sensing something in Lilly or just recognizing the somber expression on her face, reached around the seat and gently patted Lilly on the head. "Hun, I love you, but this car? *Everything* is wrong with this car. I just don't think it was made for a party of five. I seem to recall from some of your stories that it barely supported a party of two." Liz tried her best for a whimsical smile.

Quincy adjusted the rearview mirror and smirked at his three best friends lumped together in the backseat. "Hey now, stop hating on the Fiesta. Who knows how long this ol' buddy is going to have to take us to get where we need to go. We've got an ocean between us, for starters."

"That's an astute observation." Liz remarked. "There *is* an ocean between us. Where *are* we going, anyway? We're still stuck in Europe, and also, we have no idea what the outside world looks like. Who knows what's out there now?"

Quincy hesitated for a moment. "Well," he started. "I figured now that we're here, we might as well, you know, check out everything together. Take a little break, have a road trip."

A *break*, Quincy thought to himself. Who would have ever thought they had time for a break, let alone a permanent one. Thinking about it was strange. He had to get used to it.

"No chases, no monsters hopefully, no bad guys, no apocalypses or strange aliens or any of that stuff." Lilly nodded. "I've got to admit that sounds pretty darn good. Although, I think I'd rather sleep for a whole month, but something tells me my brain will need to adjust more."

"It does sound good. Very much so," Sean replied. "As long as we know that any and all traces of Haven have been destroyed… I'm skeptical to say the least. What if they're already reforming and up to their old tricks?"

Throughout his life, Sean had faced hardships headfirst and was always able to because of his military background. He had always believed in the fight between good versus evil and, with the fight now over, it was as if a void inside of him had replaced it. It wasn't as if Sean *loved* warg, or the fighting and the chaos that surrounded it. But he felt like it was the only thing he was good at. He had wondered what he would do if there was ever a chance at true peace of mind. He didn't have an answer. And the thought scared him.

"Oh, lighten up!" Moira shoved her elbow into Sean's side. It was unclear whether she meant it as a silly jab or if it was accidental due to their pile-up. "Sean, I'm pretty sure a hyper intelligent race of alien beings who had the knowhow to build an interplanetary beacon device consisting of a wooden cup, an iron cross, and some algae-eaten slabs of rock know how to rid a planet-wide hazard if they see one," Moira jokingly ranted. She had always been more in tune with the darker sides of life, even before the Awakening. Her family history had made sure of that, for better or for worse. It wasn't strange for Moira to feel the same kind of dissonance the rest of them felt. But, like Sean, it was different for her. She felt out of balance. It was as if, on a cosmic level, the scales of harmony were totally out of whack. Perhaps mentally, Moira fared the best out of all of them after all that happened. But like them, she had to take her time adjusting.

"Let's, you know, live a little," she continued. "We can finally say that. We can finally *do* that. And I say we *do* take a little European tour and visit all of those dark places we heard all of the scary stories about that might not be so dark anymore. What do you say?"

Liz looked out of the window toward the clear skies, and she felt as if a breath of fresh air washed over her, revitalizing her spirits after such a long dark time. She had never been one for fighting. In fact, she had a habit of always trying her best to see the good in people, to try and bring out the best in them. It was a trait Lilly shared and it was one of the things that gave them such a deep connection. But in the past couple of years, Liz had found that pinch of goodness in people was increasingly harder to find. The actions of organizations like Haven had sucked the life out of her so much that she was out of tune with herself. She finally had the chance to start believing in the good of people again, but she'd have to take time for the healing process. Not everything would resolve itself within a few days. She knew this, just like the others did. It would take small steps. "You know," she started, "after having *just* come back from all of these dark places, I'd suggest we try something a bit more *mild* first. I'd like just a little bit of a pick-me-up and I'm sure all of you do too."

"I heard they got great fries here in Belgium," Moira suggested. Food connected people, everyone knew that. Things looked brighter when something tasty was involved.

Lilly's eyes grew wide. "Oh my. What a great idea. Don't they have amazing chocolate too? Here's a suggestion, let's have a European food tour. Spain, France, Italy... Greece! I can't wait." For a moment, the darkness that everyone said hung over this poor young woman seemed to be lifted completely away. What was revealed under that throw of bad thoughts and guilt was someone who was ready for a new shot at life. It was still a strange, very strange, world out there with all kinds of ghastly things set loose. But after today, Lilly knew, things were at least a little bit brighter. The healing could truly begin. They had a new shot at life.

"Well okay, that settles it." Quincy gripped the steering

wheel with confidence. "First, we'll figure out where to get the best fries in all of Belgium, then the chocolate…and then we're going to *have* to visit the Netherlands for their cheese…"

"Oh my, I *love* cheese!" Liz grunted while halfway falling asleep.

Quincy smiled at the sight. "Right? I'm looking forward to it. Especially with all of you with me…" Like his sister, the guilt that had once been nestled deep within Quincy's conscience had lifted. The heavy burden he had been carrying ever since they had lost everything coming back from the realm of the Nearly Departed was less of a weight now. Quincy realized his friends would always be at his side to carry this burden with him. He was not alone, and he never would be. He knew that now. That darkness would come now and again. But with these people at his side, it would never win. He wouldn't let it.

"Hey. I have a question. What are all of you going to do when we get back?" Lilly asked awkwardly. "Because Liz and I kind of had this idea."

Quincy turned to her. "Let's hear it."

Lilly twisted one of her curls around her finger. "We talked before about starting up a museum based on witch-trials and the like. All of that pointless sacrifice and superstitions that ended horribly. We could collect accounts from all around the world. That way we'd try to get a message across about how to understand things you might not know so much about. Getting to know people… Proceeds could go to good causes and non-profit foundations around the country… We'll fight oppression, stand up for the eco-conservation, all kinds of awesome causes."

Quincy felt all warm inside. This was exactly Lilly's thing, and he loved every detail of it. "Go for it," he said proudly. "That's an awesome idea, you two will rock the hell out of it, I'm sure."

Liz laughed. "We know!" She cocked her head toward Moira. "What about you?"

Moira bit her lip. She had wanted to keep this a secret, but she figured it wasn't *that* shocking. "I'm going back to New Orleans and finally starting up that restaurant chain I told you guys about a couple times. With that book I found back in Darkness Falls, a lot of new culinary doors opened up and I can't wait to try them out back home."

"Wow, so you're going to use that ancient occult recipe book filled with long lost delights to start a whole new sort of food experience?" Lilly laughed.

Moira shrugged. "Eh…kind of like that. The truth is I bought an updated e-book copy. It turns out the book isn't quite as rare or forgotten as I'd wish it was. But on the flipside, it being a first edition should help when I need my start-up capital."

"Wild." Sean laughed.

Moira smirked. "How about you, man?" She turned to Sean. "You didn't draw the short end of the stick for once—"

Lilly and Quincy exchanged nervous glances. No short ends of sticks that they weren't able to reverse.

"You got off relatively scot-free," Moira continued. "What are *you* going to do once we're out of this horrible tin can and are back on mainland U.S.?"

Sean looked a tad melancholic. "I'm eh… I think I'm gonna go right back to it. Monster hunting and mystery solving." Sean chuckled nervously. "Hey, I think it's great you all got these ideas, and I'm supporting that one hundred percent. But this is kind of all I know, ya know?"

"We say the words *you know* a lot," Liz remarked.

"I know," Lilly answered.

Sean sighed. "There's still a lot of people that need help."

Quincy pondered that for a moment. "Sean, I'm sure you won't ever be alone in the fight, man. Hell, I've got plans of my own, but if I *can* help, I'll get out there as well now and again."

"Us too." Lilly smiled.

"Hell yeah," Moira confirmed.

Sean seemed relieved. At first, he felt a bit alone thinking everyone had moved on from the grim realities of the supernatural into a blissful state of ignoring everything that happened. But he knew that couldn't be true. And it wasn't. And that knowledge made him glad. "Shit man, that's a comfort to hear," he exclaimed. "But hey, Quincy. You said you got plans?"

Quincy nodded calmly, keeping a close eye on the road ahead. "Yeah, I finally figured out my major." He couldn't help but laugh at his own stupid joke, especially after the snort of laughter that came from his sister. "Nah, I think I'm done with traditional college, in a sense. I'm still aiming at education, but as a teacher instead of a student. I'm going to try my best to get a new, well old actually, curriculum reinstated in colleges around the U.S."

"What's it going to be?" Moira asked him.

"Simple, I'm going to teach Occult History and Symbolism and, like Lilly and Liz, try to get at least a few people to open their minds and think about how actions can have serious consequences."

"That's an awesome idea, man," Sean exclaimed. "I don't think I could imagine something else for you."

"I'm so proud of you, Quince," Lilly told her brother. It was a long time ago when she last felt all this warmth and happiness bubbling up inside her; she almost didn't know what to do with all of it.

A glow of pride appeared on Quincy's face. "Thanks," he told all of them. "But first, I'm going back home. Home to Eldritch Island I mean, and I'm going to rebuild the mansion and make it as breathtaking as it once was."

"Amazing." Moira nodded. "That place must've looked positively gorgeous back in the day."

Lilly nodded. "Oh, it absolutely did. But I'm sure Quincy will do a bang-up job of restoring it to its former glory! But he won't be able to without my help. Obviously."

"Nor mine," Moira told them. "I want in on this."

Liz laughed. "Speaks for itself. I'm in too. I am a mean, lean, home decorating machine."

"Without a doubt in my mind, I'm in on this as well." Sean plopped his hands on Quincy's shoulder. "We're gonna make that place look like a million bucks."

Quincy tried holding back his tears. Tears of happiness. Happiness that flowed through him, finally, after such a long time. "Thank you…everyone. I don't know what to say. Truly."

The car was quiet for a few minutes. Everyone felt they had their chance to release some of their enthusiasm they had for the future, and they had now sunk back into a quiet moment of mental solitude. Eventually Lilly spoke.

"We did it," she said quietly. It was a faint whisper, but everyone heard it clear as day.

"Yes, we did," Quincy answered and fell back into silence. It was still a very strange thing to say. Those three simple words had such weight behind them, such unspeakably heavy connotations.

The three on the backseat exchanged a few uncertain glances for the first time in a good while.

Liz tapped Lilly on the shoulder while smiling awkwardly. "Hey, about that. I think us *three* might be out of the loop a *little* bit on what exactly happened with all of these aliens and whatnot. And you like, haven't really told us *how* you got the tablets and stuff so…if you could go ahead and explain, that would be great."

Lilly chuckled. "Yeah, yeah, we will. But later, okay? It's kind of a long story."

"Long, long story," Quincy echoed. He felt the tiredness descend over him like a very soft blanket. He wouldn't be able to drive for long, but at least now they finally had time on *their* side.

Sean scratched his head. "I don't understand. How is it a long story? We were with you the entire time, remember?"

Sweat started forming on Quincy's forehead. "Eh, the important thing for now is, we made it. All of us."

"Can you imagine what would have happened if we weren't there on time? We could have died!" Liz gasped. "Remember what the cat told us about the infinite branching timelines?"

"Yeah." Lilly looked back. "Yeah, we remember."

"It's strange stuff. Thinking about it makes my head hurt. Still, you've got to wonder what the world would look like if things had gone differently…well, whenever really. What would *we* do, how would *we* feel?"

Quincy kept his eyes on the road. "Well, we can never know for sure. But I hope we would have been okay."

"Yeah," Lilly added, "and happy."

"LET ME, LET ME!" Lilly exclaimed, and she pushed Quincy's hand away right before he pressed the doorbell.

Quincy smirked. "You're so immature sometimes."

"She's just excited," Liz said, and she tilted her head upward to take a good look at the beautiful seaside mansion. "Wow, this place looks amazing."

Around the imposing building grew a beautiful garden with all manners of flowers in every color imaginable. There was an intricately crafted gazebo with exquisite detail in every inch of its structure. Next to it and a little bit further off were quaint benches crafted in the same motifs. A row of old timey lanterns, tall and square at the top, stood along a neatly kept cobblestone path that trailed into the yard beyond the house. The lanterns would light the way for anyone who felt like wandering the gardens at night and would shed enough light to make sure the edges of the cliffs overlooking the sea beyond were always visible. In the quiet early evening of fall, with the sky clear as day but the breeze firm, the whole scene was positively serene. It was something else. A tranquil haven for the lost and weary. A place for solitude and contemplation. For writers and poets.

"You could get lost in here," Moira said to her friends. "It's like something out of a movie or a book."

Sean whistled. "That's absolutely true. This is nothing like we're used to back home, I can tell you that. Very nice."

The old oak door of the house opened, and in the doorway stood the beautiful sight of Emily Swansong. Next to her, smiling contentedly, was Tobias Swansong. Emily threw her arms wide, and without falter the twins flew into their mother's arms.

"Mom, I've missed you so much," Lilly told her.

"Your mother doesn't want to admit how worried she gets,

especially with your chosen career path, honey. We didn't exactly envision you in the military of all things, we've got to admit. But you know we support you all the way," Tobias told his daughter.

Emily laughed. "That doesn't mean we can't miss you. Oh Quincy, how are you?" She turned her loving gaze toward her son.

"Fine, Mom." Quincy smiled. "I'm glad we could both come down here on short notice. And, like we said, we've even brought some company," he told her nervously.

"Oh, I'm so sorry!" Emily exclaimed. She was slightly embarrassed. "You must be Elisabeth?" She took Liz's outstretched hand but quickly pulled her in for a hug.

"Yeah, this is Liz, my girlfriend," Lilly told her parents, she twirled her curl nervously between her fingers.

Tobias smiled. "We know, honey. Welcome, Liz. Or wait, is it Liz or Elisabeth? What do you prefer?"

Lilly's heart filled with warmth. She felt a load fall off her shoulders. She asked herself why she was so nervous about her parents meeting Liz. She knew they were the most accepting people around.

"Thanks! But please," Liz told Emily and Tobias. "No Elisabeth, I'm hardly royalty," she joked and smiled wide. "Liz or Lizzie is fine. Or if you really want one step fancier, go for Lizbeth, ha ha!"

"And this is my best friend all the way from boot camp: Sean!" Lilly went on. She flew around Sean's neck and hugged him tightly, which made him laugh. "He's been keeping me sane while we're abroad!"

Slowly easing out of Lilly's firm grasp, Sean stepped up and gave both of the Swansongs a hearty handshake. "Thanks so much for inviting us, Mr. and Mrs. Swansong. I kind of don't have any family of my own. It really means a lot."

"The pleasure is all ours, Sean," Tobias told him. "Lilly told us so much about you that we feel like we know a great deal about you already. Being there as a friend to her when she's gone on these possible dangerous assignments means a lot to both of us.

Sean was grateful. For the first time in a while, he felt like he really had something resembling a tried-and-true family.

Quincy stepped up. "Mom, Dad, this is my college roommate, Moira."

"Hi!" Moira stepped up and shook both of the elder Swansongs' hands. "Like Sean and Liz said, thanks so much for having me. Your house is absolutely beautiful."

Emily radiated beauty and warmth. "Thank you so very much," she told Moira. "Are you making sure Quincy does his part of the chores around your dorm?"

"Oh definitely," Moira told her. "Quincy knows our deal and…he loves my Cajun cooking too much to even think about breaking it." She winked at Emily and even Tobias got a hearty chuckle out of that one.

Emily turned her gaze toward the entire group standing before her in the doorway. She looked at each one of them, Lilly and Quincy especially. At that very moment, she had the strangest of feelings creep up on her without warning. In her heart she felt a pang, a small twitch of something greater that was lodged somewhere deep within her. She had seen their faces before. Well of course she had, but this feeling was different. It felt like a sense of déjà vu, as if she remembered something that felt like a lifetime ago. Something she had blocked out of her memory, or perhaps had dismissed as a dream. She turned to her husband and could read from his expression that he was experiencing the same thing. "Okay," she suddenly spoke as if awoken from a dream. "Let's get you all out of these eerie winds and into the dining room where the fire is blazing."

"It's just a breeze, mom." Lilly chuckled.

"Your mother and I were just reminiscing about something special that happened right before you were born when we were in Arkham together. We can tell you over dinner. It's a story involving your great uncle William," Tobias suddenly blurted out.

It caught Emily off guard, but she couldn't help but laugh it away. "Let's do that," she confirmed.

"Sounds like a lot of fun, Dad," Quincy told him. "You know, I read one of William's compilations the other day. Compelling and fantastical stuff, very well written."

"And it's a lot less *problematic* than, say, Lovecraft." Lilly nodded. "Yeah, I read some stuff too. Lots of time to kill while on duty."

Emily stopped the twins in their tracks as Tobias led the rest of the gang into the house. She hugged her children, all grown up into wonderful human beings, and looked them deep in their eyes. "I'm so very proud of you, and Dad is too," she told them. "You know that, right?"

"Of course we do," Lilly answered.

Quincy kissed their mother on her cheek. "You and Dad are everything to us."

Then, as Emily led them inside, the sturdy oak door closed, and the only eerie thing left in the world was the cold breeze from the Eastern Sea right outside.

Acknowledgments

As of the time of writing it is nearly twelve years ago that I packed up my bags and moved away all by myself, away from friends and family. I had started my journey into media- and culture studies at the University of Utrecht and, as a quiet and reserved person, I was terrified. Unbeknownst to me at the time it would become a period in my life in which I really found out who I was and how I belonged. For I had always been an outsider.

I never quite liked the same things as my peers in high school, never quite the same music, games or what have you. Even though a lack of friends was never an issue it was as if from the outside looking in I felt I was the weird one out, the one with peculiar interests. But when I was at university I found others like me, and for the first time in a very long while I could share my interests with people who had those very same niche likes. It was those very same wonderful people who had taught me to embrace what made me unique. It was them who eventually, whether they are now aware of it or not, inspired me to start writing in the first place. It was the first seeds sewn of what would eventually become The Eldritch Twins. A book series about outsiders, desperate to find their place in the world. Full circle.

Nevertheless we are now here, at the end. The end of the series and, for the foreseeable future, the end of the story of Quincy and Lilly Swansong. The Apocalypse Rebellion was an extremely hard book to write. Not because of lack of inspiration but because there was a kind of finality around the whole project. Coincidentally this was not just due to the book's themes but also due to the fact that the story would actually come to a close, and that scared me. I had to come to terms with myself and realize that for now, it would be the end of a long tale that had been brewing in my head for years. Not only that, but if there's one thing that studying film, television, games and more for years in Utrecht taught me it's that there are few things more sour than bad endings. The pressure was on.

And now we are indeed here. I made it. I accomplished one of my life goals that I never taught I would succeed in or be able to do in the first place. I often think back on my time arriving all alone at university but eventually leaving with experiences I would never trade in the world, the good times and the bad. This book is dedicated to all the outsiders. Like you and me, this book series is peculiar, niche and weird. But frankly, we wouldn't have it any other way, right?

Thank you to the amazing folks at The Parliament House for giving the adventures of Quincy and Lilly a home. My super special thanks goes out to Malorie for your kindness, support and patience.

About the Author

Nick Vossen was raised on blockbuster films from the 80s and 90s as well as fantasy and sci-fi novels, comics and games. No matter the medium, his love for storytelling grew ever larger. Having always had a fascination with the fantastical and weird, he quickly grew fond of authors such as Terry Pratchett, H.P. Lovecraft, Neil Gaiman and many more. During the winter of 2017 Nick released an anthology of short, weird fiction entitled The Fissures Between Worlds, which delves into the strange places on Earth where time does not flow as it should. It was received quite favourably, and so Nick's desire to tell more stories grew. He has since been privileged to appear in several other anthologies, magazines and short story compilations and has quite a few projects still in the works. His biggest fascinations and inspirations are old forgotten woodlands, the deepest depths of the oceans and the unsettling, uncanniness of retro futurism.

Nick graduated in Media- and Culture studies at Utrecht University in The Netherlands. He is currently working as a freelance creative writer and author. He also frequently works on projects in the Dutch indie-film industry, putting his talents to use in art-direction, set-dressing and of course screen-writing.

Nick has been working on and off on The Swansong Conspiracy since the tail-end of 2017. The idea first came when Nick wanted to give Lovecraftian Horror a much lighter and charming edge. But what started as a 'Monty Python-esque' parody eventually turned into a tale of equal suspense and horror but also humor and personality. Nick likes to write fluently and to the point, resulting in fast-paced action and quick & witty dialogue. It is also no secret that The Swansong Conspiracy is dripping in pop culture references and easter eggs, all done in loving tribute. Nick is extremely proud of the little strange world he created, and is ecstatic to be able to work on its two sequels for The Parliament House, as well.

www.nickcronomicon.wordpress.com

APPENDIX

The Eldritch Twins — Original Earth Timeline

Primordial Earth — The ancient alien race known as the Celestians descend upon Earth and build their peaceful civilization. A seed is planted that will one day turn into humanity

Primordial Earth — The four horsemen and women of the Apocalypse and Henry the cat materialize from the ether

Primordial Earth — The Gibbous Horde arrives on Earth. Approximately half of their population perishes in a war with the Celestians, who lost approximately two-thirds of their entire population

Primordial Earth / After Third Ice Age — The Celestians create the God-Machine and flee Earth in search of a permanent solution to rid it from the Horde. They leave only a few of their own behind. The first signs of humankind appear

Somewhere in the 1000s A.D. — Several occult groups and pagan religions band together and form what would someday become Haven

1893 — W.A. Swansong is born

1916 — Aleister Crowley conjures and binds a Fire Vampire in his Louisiana estate

1956 — Tobias Swansong is born

1961 – Emily Sullivan is born

1985 – Tobias Swansong and Emily Sullivan marry

1987 – As part of an archaeological expedition, W.A. Swansong uncovers a set of mysterious tablets filled with an unknown language in Nova Scotia

1988 – Arkham, Massachusetts mysteriously vanishes from reality as well as from the human conscience. Emily and Tobias Swansong, W.A. Swansong and a student named Eric Marsh witness the event and are the only known survivors

1989 – W.A. Swansong dies

1989 – Quincy and Lilly Swansong are born

1997 – Tobias Swansong finds the tomb of a Celestian under his ancestral Swansong home on Eldritch Island

2005 – Tobias and Emily Swansong perish in an airplane crash on their way to England; Quincy and Lilly are temporarily moved into foster care after which they move south to Louisiana

2006 – Haven uncovers the hidden Ancient city in Antarctica; The God-Machine is broken

2007 – The God-Obelisk appears in Egypt. The Earth 'Awakens' and 'Kraken Wars' commence

2008 – The Global Defence Force is formed. Haven partially emerges from secrecy selling themselves as an 'expertise organisation'

2008 – Lilly Swansong enrolls in the Global Defence Force. Quincy Swansong starts college in New Orleans

2008-2010 – Civilization adapts to the constant threat of supernatural and extradimensional events

2010 – Events of *The Swansong Conspiracy* unfold; Haven Director Marsh perishes in Antarctica

2010-2012 – Quincy and Lilly Swansong encounter and fight against several supernatural occurrences while they flee from the clutches of Haven; Sean Cooper lays low in a remote location in the Chihuahuan Desert.

2011 – Haven finds the Mother creature in remote Georgia; The Order of the Final Dawn is formed in secret as a religious offshoot of Haven in honor of the Gibbous Horde.

2011-2012 – Humankind begins to forget its supernatural history. Anomalous occurrences happen with lesser frequency and out of the public eye. However, they remain severe.

2012 – Most of the North-eastern seaboard is swallowed by the 'Daemonic Depths'

2012 – Events of *The Nearly Departed* unfold

2012 – Lilly Swansong and Liz Borden move to Tenebrae, WA; Sean Cooper, Moira LaGrande and Quincy Swansong keep investigating Haven, The Final Dawn and their connection to the Gibbous Horde

2013 – The Final Dawn comes out of the shadows and continues its devastating influence on humankind with three-fold efficiency

2013 – Events of *The Apocalypse Rebellion* unfold